AF267878

PANDORA
THE BOOK OF HOPE

by

Eleanor & Russell Hopwood

PANDORA

THE BOOK OF HOPE

Published by: DARTON Publishing

Cover Design: Russell Hopwood

ISBN-13: 978-1-9993033-1-0

For my husband -

the man with a story, who gave me Hope

Chapters

Prologue

Pandora drew her hand gracefully across the fire. Her fingers danced as the flames licked at her skin. I was mesmerised by the beauty of her indifference, her lack of reaction to the heat. She'd changed since the last time we had met - her eyes had a hollow weight to them that made me feel unbearable pity for her. We'd been here for hours and I had listened intently as she shared her story.

"So much has happened," I said, reflecting on her words, a solemn smile etched across my face. She nodded weakly, pulling her hand from the fire and running it through her hair, her fingers catching in the matted knots. Unsure what to say, we sat in silence for some time.

After a while, Pandora shifted her weight awkwardly. "What do I do now?" she asked.

"I don't think I'm the right person to ask, my dear. This isn't exactly my area of expertise."

"No, it's not," she said, a dry laugh forcing its way past her lips.

A thought flashed through my mind. "Maybe there is something I can do."

"What?"

"I can write down your story, take it far and wide," I said, my voice raising with excitement. "The whole world would know of your bravery and maybe it would help bring people to—"

"That won't work," she said quietly.

"Why not?"

"It just won't, Aesop."

"Well then, my dear, I am at a loss."

"I think we all are."

Sunrise

Pandora awoke to the soft, delicate song of the larks. A sound so gentle and sweet it danced across the air like a gossamer thread. Opening her eyes, she saw ribbons of sunlight stealing their way under the wooden door and into her room, an unwelcome guest. Not willing to accept the intrusion of the morning, she longed for just a few more lingering moments before the real world made its full intrusion. As her eyes adjusted, the ribbons of light became deep, opulent pools of amber on the floor. The smell of warm wood and hay filled her nostrils and she could hear her father's voice outside the room; the coarse, comforting sound was unmistakable and Pandora couldn't help but smile at the sound of it. A humble man, Pandora's father believed in maintaining a pastoral life and had raised his daughter to uphold these values. She was all he had, and he was all she had ever known.

Sitting up in bed, her limbs stiff from sleep, Pandora rubbed her eyes and sighed. Just as she did every morning, she took a few moments to stretch her arms and legs before standing, a habit built upon necessity. As human as she appeared and felt, it was clay, not blood, that coursed through her veins and, if she was still for too long, she found herself feeling somewhat brittle. Though painful, it was something she had grown accustomed to and had learned to accept. The fact she existed at all was a miracle.

As she ran her fingers through her matted, fiery curls, a sudden wave of panic swept across her: it was late, much later than she had thought. She really should have been up hours ago to help her father with the morning errands.

Anxiety swept over her. Swinging her legs abruptly over the edge of her bed in haste, she felt a deep ache as her limbs adjusted but she didn't care. Her father was not a young man anymore and she was afraid of how much time they had left together, not that she would ever voice it to him. He was a stubborn man and having failed to convince him to ease his workload, Pandora found the easiest way to help him was by doing as much of the work as she could without him noticing. No amount of pain would stop her from doing her duty. She moved swiftly to the door and upon opening it was consumed by the friendly warmth of the mid-morning sun. It was a feeling that never got old.

As her eyes adjusted to the light, she lunged out of the house, her stance panicked, only to find her father sitting on the porch, calmly dipping his morning bread into a small cup of wine by his side. Her panic evaporated and left behind a combination of relief, shame, and mild confusion.

Miltiades, humble in his ways, was a broad man with dark, tanned skin, the result of a lifetime of hard work. Turning from his breakfast, his weathered face softened into a brilliant smile. He took Pandora's hand in his and held it to his cheek.

"Good morning, my girl."

He was a man of few words but those he spoke were thoughtful and sincere. Pandora kneeled next to her father's chair and met his kind gaze with exasperation.

"Father," she said as calmly as possible, "why didn't you wake me up to help with the work this morning?"

"Darling girl don't worry yourself. If I had needed you, I would have woken you."

"But, Father—"

"Come," he said, "sit and eat." He waved vaguely to the store at the side of their home. "You can deliver the order of vases to the port when you are ready if that will appease you." There was no point arguing. When it came to her father, he was kind but he was firm.

"Of course, Father." Pandora nodded, collapsing heavily onto the bench next to him, resting her head on his broad shoulder as she picked at her bread. She wasn't particularly hungry but she knew better than to refuse food. Like all those living a pastoral life, Pandora and her father had experienced their share of poverty. She remembered all too well the burning taste of hunger during times of hardship. It had taught her resilience and strength but most of all, it had taught her gratitude. She turned her gaze towards the store shed. "Are the vases going to Karpos?"

"Yes, he's sailing to Delphi in the morning and has requested ten amphoras to store the wine he will be taking. *Ten, I say!*" He paused to snort at the man's audacity. "Gods forbid he give me any notice. I tell you, if he didn't always bring me back a pot of those delicious Delphinian olives, I might not be so accommodating." Miltiades rose from his chair with a groan and slowly shuffled over to the small store shed that leaned lazily against his pottery.

"These should do nicely, fit for the Oracle herself." He strained as he opened the rickety doors to reveal ten beautifully engraved vases lined up like soldiers.

Behind the vases were shelves stacked to the brim: large jugs for keeping preserved meats, hardy bowls and cups for everyday use, and delicate plates used to carry offerings to the local temple by way of supplication to their chosen goddess, Athena. They all shared the same beautiful russet colour that was the result of the iron in the local clay. Although his pottery was small, Miltiades always made sure he had plenty of items saved away for the use of the village. A broken bowl would always be replaced, an unexpected guest would always have a cup for water, and a friend would never go wanting. His kind nature was well known throughout the town and as a result, he was never out of business and never without a friend.

Leaving the doors open, Pandora's father turned and smiled at his beloved daughter. He cupped her head in his hands and gently kissed the tip of her nose. "You finish your breakfast. If you need me, I'll be at the kiln." He exhaled deeply, stretched his arms and ambled his way back to his work room, muttering to himself as he walked, "*Ten!* By the gods, that man and his frivolous demands will be the death of me, I tell you, my girl."

While Pandora sat and ate, she took in the surroundings she had become so used to. Kyparissi was a quiet port, predominantly known as a stop-off for weary sailors. It was the kind of place where everybody knew everybody. Pandora watched the children playing in the street, groups of neighbours gossiping loudly and weary traders walking their carts steadily to market; the entire scene was framed by the sprawling hillside that surrounded the peaceful village. As a young girl, she had spent many an afternoon alone exploring the lush banks of the hills. She was comfortable in her own company. She knew people looked at her differently and she had quickly grown tired of the inquisitive looks, the whispers and giggles, the intrusive nature of their curiosity. Finding the company of people difficult, Pandora gained her strength from the solitude of the mountains and forests that surrounded the village. Over the years she had explored every path, climbed every tree and had found true comfort in the chaotic diversity of the wilderness. She understood the land, how it breathed, and how it moved and changed through the year. A place where the gentle streams of the forest meandered down to a turbulent mouth that collided with the vast expanse of the Aegean Sea.

Years of exploration had given Pandora a unique education. Her body had grown strong and nimble from traversing the uneven terrain. She had taken time to observe the environment and was confident in her ability to identify the tracks and habitats of nearly all the forest animals. The few times her father had been able to explore with her, he had taught her which berries and mushrooms were good to eat and which to avoid at all costs. He had often spent time in the same woods as a boy and relished the opportunity to pass on his knowledge to his beloved little girl. Although every moment with her father was a joy, there were times when Pandora wondered what her life would be like if she had a mother. It was not something that crossed her mind often, though in those quiet moments of longing, the hills were always where Pandora would find herself. As if hypnotised, she would seek out the embrace of Mother Gaia and find comfort in the woods. It was the perfect escape, the perfect place to be alone.

~

She sighed as she turned her gaze reluctantly away from her haven for there would be no time to venture out today. Finishing her breakfast, she rose and gathered her things ready to join the others in the never-ending cycle of pilgrimage to market. She looked at the sky; the sun was close to its pinnacle for the day. A sudden realisation stole the breath from her lungs. She would have to get moving soon before – *oh no,* she thought, dread washing over her.

Like the tell-tale smoke that warns of an impending fire, an impossibly delicate yet piercing laugh cut through the background noise. Pandora had heard it many times before. It was a sound that she loathed and a sound that often, if not always, meant trouble.

Letting out a long sigh, she turned with lowered eyes to see a woman walking towards her, followed by three others. *Breathe, just breathe,* Pandora thought, *maybe she won't come over, maybe today she won't.* The woman's soft leather sandals were the first thing that came into focus. She glided towards Pandora like an ethereal siren, her feet barely touching the ground. Soft pink robes of silk cascaded over the curves of her body, accentuating both her beauty and crippling vanity. As Pandora lifted her gaze, she gritted her teeth before letting out a low mumble of greeting, "Hello, Eugeneia."

It didn't matter that they had known each other all their lives- Pandora never got used to Eugeneia's terrifying presence. She had a soft heart-shaped face, pale skin and her emerald eyes pierced Pandora's carefully perfected guard with ease. Eugeneia lifted a hand gracefully to her forehead and ran her fingers through the waterfall of golden curls that framed her face. By now, an unnervingly inviting smile had spread across her face. To Pandora, it felt like staring at the deadly grin of a wolf tasting the copper scent of blood in the air, and she was the rabbit with a broken leg.

"Honestly, Dora," Eugeneia said, her voice dripping with amusement, "no wonder you haven't found a husband yet. You spend so much time with those hideous pots you're actually starting to look like one."

The gaggle of girls accompanying her laughed unkindly behind their hands. Eugeneia just loved having an audience.

Of course all the girls knew Pandora was different. It was not the sort of thing that stayed quiet in a village like theirs but it was also not the sort of thing that was spoken about openly. Unfortunately for Pandora, Eugeneia was the type of girl who found entertainment in the degradation of others and currently, she was her favourite target.

"How was your lesson with Euterpe today?" Pandora quickly changed the subject, knowing that Eugeneia wouldn't be able to resist talking about herself.

The girl pulled a face in disgust. "Ugh, tiresome old crone. I am bored of the lyre," she said in a nasal tone, "it is infuriating and that woman – she practically works me like a slave."

One of the clique, a slender, limp-haired girl called Medea, moved forwards and put a sympathetic hand on Eugeneia's shoulder only to be shrugged away with a scoff. The girl had a sharp, stony face and she moved silently back in line, pursing her lips at the humiliation.

The other two girls were less imposing. Two sisters: the older, Petra, had a permanent expression of boredom on her face while the younger, Letha, had a sweet look to her and was now staring at the clouds in quiet ignorance.

Eugeneia sniffed, wiping an imaginary tear from her eye. "I don't know why Father is forcing me to learn. I've already *got* a husband. Why I have to waste my time with that tedious old woman I'll never know."

Pandora's jaw tightened, and she clenched her teeth. Euterpe was well respected within the village. She had been a remarkable musician in her youth and had settled in Kyparissi to live out the rest of her years passing on her knowledge to aspiring young women. Pandora had never really had an interest in music and did not begrudge her father for being unable to afford lessons. However, she always offered to deliver orders to Euterpe as she found her a kind and gentle woman, one she did not believe deserved to be spoken about so spitefully. She could only imagine how exhausting teaching an entitled girl like Eugeneia must be. Unfortunately it was Eugeneia's tuition that meant the girls' paths crossed all too frequently, Euterpe's villa being one of the only places farther away from the town than Pandora's home.

"This horrid walk does make my feet ache so. I don't know how you can live out here, Dora. It's just awful." Eugeneia grimaced as she looked at her surroundings in obvious revulsion.

"Just awful."

"The worst."

"I don't know how you do it, Eugeneia," the other girls echoed.

They all spoke over each other, eager to appear sensitive to their leader. Eugeneia rolled her eyes and waved a delicate hand in acknowledgement. "I'm going to speak with Father and *demand* that she teach me at home. It's just not fair that *I* have to travel all this way. It's such an imposition, don't you think?" she asked, her eyes glinting. Pandora could see that she was deliberately goading her.

Don't say anything, Pandora thought to herself. Don't bite, you know it won't end well; just nod and smile.

"Well, I—"

But before she had time to speak, Eugeneia went on, "Anyway, what was I saying? Oh yes, Dora, why aren't you trying to find a husband? It's almost as if you *want* to be alone forever." A cruel snicker left her lips and Pandora could see the fire in Eugeneia's eyes; she knew she was trying to start an argument. She must have had a really bad lesson today because she was being even more intolerable than normal, and that was really saying something.

"I'm quite happy alone, thank you, Eugeneia. Besides, my father—"

"Oh, please, your *father*." The word dripped with judgement. She walked closer towards Pandora's house before turning back to face the poor girl she was berating. "Dora, this – well, this *shack* is no place for an eligible young woman." Her voice drawled with palpable disdain as she looked the house up and down.

"Just awful."

"The worst."

"I don't know how she does it, Eugeneia."

Pandora let out a snort of amusement at the army of parrots Eugeneia had recruited.

"If you'd only let me introduce you to some suitors," the mean girl continued relentlessly, "Karpos has many friends all of a good position, few particularly choosy." A shrill torrent of laughter escaped her lips and was met with wicked cackles from her underlings.

Of course, as the most desired young woman of the village, Eugeneia had been betrothed to Karpos at a very young age. He was a hugely influential man and their union increased her position within the village greatly. The vast age difference – for Karpos was nearly as old as Miltiades – was neither here nor there. To him, she was a valuable asset and to her, he was life-long security. To show his complete devotion to his young bride, Karpos constantly showered her with gifts: gold from Lydia, jewels from Athens, and delicate garments of silk from the East. Unfortunately, as generous as this was, these things changed Eugeneia. The innocence of her youth turned into hardened expectation that left her overly spoiled and unnecessarily cruel. Once an equal among the women of the village, she now saw herself as superior in every way and relished every second of it.

Eugeneia reached out a hand and took a lock of Pandora's hair in her fingers, gently pushing it behind her ear. Pandora winced at the contact.

"Look, I know you aren't exactly a *conventional* beauty," she cooed, the words dripping with disdain, "but that doesn't mean you won't find a husband. If you were to look for an older man, they're far less picky when it comes to choosing a second wife."

"But I don't want—"

"Oh stop it, Pandora. You can't seriously tell me that you want to be a burden to your father for the rest of his life."

"Well, I—"

"Because once he's gone, I don't know what on earth you'll do."

"Eugeneia, please, I—"

"It's just so sad. I don't understand why you won't let me help. That's all I'm trying to do, you know."

Tired of the unkindness, Pandora turned her back on Eugeneia and went about her work. One of the benefits of being made of clay was that Pandora couldn't cry. In this kind of situation, this proved to be a strength that she was grateful for. As she began to load her cart, Pandora spoke calmly, "I'm sorry, *Geenie*, but I have to deliver these to your husband before he leaves for Delphi.

It has been lovely to see you, but I must get on." She used the nickname that had been given to Eugeneia in her youth as a subtle reminder that they had grown up equal. Her words were met with quiet whispers of amusement from the girls.

Eugeneia pursed her lips and scowled, her narrowed eyes dark with fury. "Well, have fun, Dora. Wouldn't want to disappoint *daddy*, would we?" With an exasperated sigh, she turned on her heel and beckoned sharply to her friends to follow. As she walked away, she screeched, "Oh and tell Karpos to bring me back something decent this time. The olives he brought back last time were so cheap I had to give them to the poor."

Pandora knew it would be pointless to rise to the last remark – clearly a shot at her father – so she turned back to her work. She tolerated the stares, she tolerated the curiosity, but she wished more than anything that she didn't have to tolerate *her*.

~

Once her cart was loaded and tied to the ox, Pandora began her journey down the path through town towards the docks. The load was heavy but the ox her father had reared from birth was strong, well weathered, and had done the journey with her many times before. Having been brought up around animals, she had found comfort in their company. As they walked, she admired the stalwart nature of the creature striding gently beside her. His coat was a soft, warm brown and as Pandora ran her hand along his flank, he lifted and shook his head, letting out a snort of satisfied approval at the affection. The walk into town was always the same. People of the village went about their daily lives, moving trade between the town and the small port. Pandora waded through the sea of activity with little bother. Kyparissi was relatively small in the scheme of things and there was rarely any trouble or excitement. The streets always conveyed an air of tranquillity. This all changed once you got into the town centre; with it being located so near the coast, the marketplace itself was always a buzz with traders and a myriad of travelling merchants selling all sorts of exotic wares. Nearly all roads led to the sea and as Pandora walked, the smell of salt in the air became stronger, the stiff breeze that travelled in from open waters sweeping her hair into a blazing veil around her face. She had never been particularly fond of the water, preferring to spend her time exploring the sprawling hills in the other direction. This being said, she appreciated the cerulean expanse and occasionally sat to watch the boats vanish over the edge of the horizon.

Looking ahead, she noticed a small crowd of people by the edge of the road. Curiosity getting the better of her, Pandora tied her ox to a nearby post and made her way over to see what the fuss was about. As she drew closer, she saw men arguing light-heartedly and shouting at each other over the throng of people. Peering around the bodies, Pandora saw a small, lithe man standing behind a table. He had long dark hair the colour of oil, thin and limp, and it fell lifelessly to his shoulders. He was slight but didn't look malnourished; in fact, he looked sharp and nimble, not a man to be crossed. His features were pointed and harsh and his eyes were dark. Very dark. Pandora had never seen eyes like his: they seemed endlessly black. His clothes were ragged, as if from travelling a long distance. He fit all the trademarks of a beggar; however, something told Pandora that there was more to this man than met the eye. On his table lay three beautiful cream shells, the likes of which she had only seen on the most expensive stalls at the market. Examining the situation, Pandora saw the man hold out his hands, beckoning to the crowd for silence. He said no words – he didn't seem to need to – and instead, his long fingers reached into his robe and pulled out an exquisite pearl. It was the size of a pea and glistened in the sunlight. Pandora had never seen anything so beautiful. Scanning the crowd, he held it up and then pointed to the shells. With two delicate fingers, he lifted one of the shells and placed the pearl underneath. Then, as the crowd watched in intense silence, he began to move the shells, switching their positions on the table with a swift pace that was intensely difficult to follow. After a few moments he stopped, stood straight, looked at the crowd and gestured towards the table.

"The middle one," someone shouted from the back.

"No, you fool, it's under the one on the left."

"Middle."

"Right, it's the right one."

Soon the people in the crowd were throwing their coins on the table to place their bets. Once everyone had determined their choice, the man smiled and lifted the shell on the left to reveal the shining pearl. This was met with cheers and shouts from the crowd as the winners collected their rewards and the losers shouted in dismay. Pandora rolled her eyes. She had never understood how people could be so eager to part with money for something so frivolous and unpredictable. The man went through the process another couple of times, each time resulting in a roar from the crowd as the pearl was revealed and the winners named victorious. Pandora was about to turn back to her errand when she saw the man hold up the pearl again, ready to begin another round. As he moved to put the pearl underneath the shell, Pandora saw him flick his little finger, causing the pearl to roll up into his sleeve. *Cheat!* she screamed in her head. Apparently nobody else had seen this transpire as the bets were flooding in and people were shouting and cheering in excitement. By this time, the crowd had become so enormous that the pile of coins people had bet were falling off the table into a heap on the floor. *This isn't right,* Pandora thought, panicked, *what should I do? Should I say something?* She watched him move the shells around on the table and saw a hint of a smirk on his face as he looked up at the crowd in anticipation.

"It's the one on the end."

"Which end?"

"No, it's in the middle."

"Oh, I don't know."

"I can't tell. I lost where it went."

"It's on the right, you idiots."

"IT'S A FIX!"

The turbulent crowd went silent at once. People began to look round to see who had said it; they couldn't tell where the sound had come from. The beady-eyed man behind the table snapped his head up and scanned the crowd, a look of fury on his face. One of the men at the front flipped the shells to reveal that the pearl was indeed missing.

"A fix?"

"Go on then, where is it?"

"You cheat!"

"I want my money back."

"Where's the pearl?"

"Scum!"

Instantly the crowd was in uproar. Arguing among themselves, they scrambled to retrieve their money, falling over each other and pushing the table over in the process. The man didn't move; he stood like a statue among the chaos, studying the people in front of him. As the angry townspeople swarmed around him, something caught his eye: a small girl, frantically untying a cart from a nearby post. Pandora looked back at the scene for a moment and as her eyes met those of the con man, time itself seemed to come to a halt. Slowly he raised a bony, barbed finger and pointed right at her, his dark eyes now burrowing into hers. Her heart started to race, her stomach knotted and her face grew pale. The man was now smiling. A cold, terrifying smile was etched from ear to ear. He twisted the pointed finger towards her and mouthed a single, terrifying word: "*You.*"

He closed his fist tightly around the air in front of him and drew it back with harsh force, as if snatching something from her.

As soon as he pulled his fist in, time corrected itself and Pandora saw the crowd of people tear him down. Within seconds he was lost among a swarm of angry men. Shaken to her core, Pandora grabbed the reins of her ox and pulled with encouragement, willing it to flee the scene. Moving as swiftly as she could, she gripped the bridle of the ox so tight her knuckles shook. *Just move, don't look back*, she thought, *get to the docks. Get away. Don't look back. DON'T.*

A Home in Ashes

Pandora had never felt so relieved to see the bustling market in the town centre. She had always considered herself a brave, headstrong girl but something in that man's eyes had shaken her. Now a safe distance away, she looked back down the road to find that the crowd had dispersed, the table had gone and there was no sign of the man anywhere. It was as if it had never taken place. Curiosity swept across her face and Pandora moved as if to investigate but much to her relief, the part of her brain governed by better judgement decided that her delivery was more important. She turned to her ox and patted him gently on his nose. "Come on, you, we better get these vases to Karpos."

By the time she arrived at the docks, the golden sun had begun to fall back down towards the horizon, sending glittering reflections across the waters of the bay. Looking around the harbour, Pandora found Karpos' ship but it was unmanned. She was unsure what to do and decided to walk along the dock to try and find someone to help. Coming to a nearby trade ship, Pandora watched as a throng of sailors carried stacks of boxes on board. The boat was one she did not recognise. Two broad men, both sporting thick, dark beards, were fixing the rigging while a small boy climbed the mast with the delicate ease and speed of a monkey, positioning himself atop the sail and sitting on the uppermost beam with impressive agility. Pandora tied her ox to a hitching post under the shade of the trees where it drank eagerly from a trough. She marched over to the ship, intending to find someone to speak to, but before she got the chance, a tall man with cropped silver hair called out to her.

"Need help with that, girl?" he said, pointing to her cart as he strode towards her.

"Oh no, I'm fine, thank you. I just need to find Karpos. His ship is empty and I have these vases—"

"Going to Delphi?" His tone was commanding but kind.

"Uh?"

"The vases, are they going to Delphi?"

Pandora nodded and watched as the man strode boldly towards her cart. He looked the same as the men around him, but something about the way he carried himself made Pandora feel he was of some importance.

"Well, you're in the right place, girl. Let me help you with this."

"Sorry, you're very kind but Karpos—"

"Is already on board," the man finished her sentence and her anxiety subsided a little.

He picked up three of the vases with surprising ease and began to walk up the boarding plank. Despite being older, he moved like a young man, muscular and athletic. His skin was tanned and taut, with only a scattering of wrinkles around his eyes and mouth. Pandora felt awkward as she watched him work.

"Thank you, but you really don't need to do that. I can manage," she called out to him with cautious exasperation. Seeing how easily he had carried the vases, she was particularly mindful of her tone.

"Oh, I have no doubt." The man nodded in amusement as he turned back to face her. "Call me a fool, but my mother always taught me to give my assistance when I could offer it."

"Well I—"

With a light jump, the man landed on the deck and began to walk off. Taking a vase in each hand, Pandora scurried off after him.

"Sir, really I—"

The man carried on talking to her as if she hadn't spoken, "Besides, considering you're bringing them onto my ship, it's a good chance for me to inspect the inventory."

"*Your* ship? Oh, I didn't realise, I…"

Pandora had been right to think he was different from those around them. The captain of the ship let out a warm laugh at her confusion, smiling kindly as he set the vases down.

"Don't worry yourself, girl, no harm done. Besides, nothing you say could irritate me more than the fool I'm transporting." He turned and nodded in the direction of the bow. There stood Karpos, an enormous beast of a man, twice as wide as he was tall. Swathed in colourful robes, he stomped across the deck, overseeing the sailors preparing for departure.

Pandora looked back at the sailor, her eyebrow raised. "I thought you said this was your boat?"

The sailor gritted his teeth. "Huh, it *is* my boat. Karpos decided that he wanted to get to Delphi swiftly and unfortunately his boat goes at a rather leisurely pace." He slapped a hand down appreciatively on the side of the boat and ran his palm along the grain of the wood. "With my girl being the fastest trader for miles, he offered me a sum of coin I thought I couldn't refuse. Now, gods know I wish I had." Leaning his forearms on the side of the vessel, the man looked wistfully out to sea and sighed. "This is going to be an interesting journey," he said, shaking his head. He turned back to Pandora before waving towards Karpos. "You should probably make your introductions. It was nice to meet you, girl. Don't worry, I'll see to your delivery. Rest assured, your amphoras will be handled with care."

"Thank you. I… my name is Pandora," she stammered, feeling embarrassed that she hadn't already introduced herself.

The man stood still for a moment and looked at her with a curious expression. He smiled to himself and stepped towards her. "Well greetings, Pandora, I am Pelagios, and this" – he gestured to the boat they were standing on – "is the *Eirene*."

The captain's expression made her uneasy, but Pandora had no time to question him. It looked like the ship was due to leave any moment and she didn't want to keep Karpos waiting. Turning away from Pelagios, she hurried over to the ongoing commotion at the other end of the boat.

Pandora could hear Karpos shouting at the crew; a knot grew in her stomach. *Don't say anything stupid*, she thought, *you know what he's like; just get it over with.*

"Not there, you fool. Those are the finest figs this side of the mainland. They can't stay out in the sun. Put them in the store before I throw you off the ship."

A young sailor carrying a basket of fruit ran past her, head bowed, trying not to attract any more attention. In as bold a voice as she could muster, Pandora addressed the mountain of a man who stood with his back to her.

"Greetings, Karpos, I have delivered the vases you requested from my father."

"Ahh, Pandora" – Karpos turned to face her – "welcome, welcome."

Karpos was a paragon of gluttony. His round belly strained under his lavish clothes, his fingers swelled around his many bejewelled golden rings, and his thick, dark beard, woven with turquoise beads, was so saturated with perfume that it was all Pandora could do not to take a step back in revulsion. He raised one of his colossal hands and placed it on her shoulder. Karpos' attitude towards Pandora had always been one more of curiosity than anything. She was unique, special, and as a trader of uncommon goods, he found her fascinating.

Pandora, on the other hand, found him pompous and greedy. She hated the way he looked at her, not like a person but like an object. She clenched her jaw and smiled through gritted teeth. "Everything is in order. Father, as always, sends his regards."

Karpos clapped his hands together. "Gratitude. Your father is a good man, Pandora, please send him my thanks. I know I don't make his life easy." He chuckled to himself as he turned away from her and began to walk back across the deck, his gait so very similar to her ox: wide and slow in order to accommodate his enormous frame.

"Of course, he will receive payment as soon as I am back from my trip," Karpos said over his shoulder as he plucked a grape from a nearby basket and popped it into his mouth.

"Of course," Pandora echoed with a disappointed sigh. As their biggest source of income, Karpos' business was invaluable. However, getting him to part with his money in a timely fashion was always somewhat of a struggle.

"Well if there's nothing else…" Pandora began to step backwards as she spoke, desperate to get off the ship.

Karpos turned his attention back to the girl and sauntered slowly back over to her. "Unless you feel like accompanying me on my journey?" He moved his body close to her, putting an uninvited arm around her waist. She could feel his hot breath on her neck and his beard scratched coarsely at the skin on her shoulder. The desire in his body language enveloped Pandora in a wave of darkness and made her feel queasy. He smelled like stale wine and perfume. It repulsed her but she didn't flinch; she refused to show him weakness.

Karpos took a lock of her hair between his fingers, drew it to his nose and sniffed deeply, a low rumble of desire escaping from his throat. Pandora couldn't breathe, she couldn't move, not a single sound left her mouth as she stood frozen, a statue of hostility.

"I know a lot of people in Delphi who would be very interested in meeting someone of your… origin.”

The knot in Pandora's stomach tightened even more. This was not the first time Karpos had made such an offer. Knowing how people spoke about her, Pandora wanted nothing more than to hide away from the world. To be paraded round like a trophy, a thing – she couldn't stand the idea.

"Thank you for your generous offer," she said, the words hoarse and staggered, "b-but I can't leave my father, he needs me." She prayed for him to move on.

"Mmm, well, you're a good daughter. Go then" – he dismissed her with a wave of his hand as he stepped back – "go back to your father. You'll join me next time."

I'd rather swim the river Styx, you wretched man, she thought bitterly before calling out in a sickly-sweet tone, "Yes, Karpos, next time, maybe." The words came out so shrill she was sure he would notice but he had already grown bored of her presence. Moving out of her path, Karpos turned and began shouting at a boy stacking crates nearby.

"What on earth are you doing? Don't stack those there, boy."

~

Pandora took this as her opportunity and swiftly moved to leave the ship. Before she could go ten paces, her path was blocked once again, this time by Pelagios. The sudden movement caused her to jump.

"Apologies, I didn't mean to scare you, girl." His face was full of concern and he looked at her with a sympathetic smile. "Are you alright? He can be quite imposing, even for a fool." Pelagios turned, looking back in frustration and disapproval at the man in control of his ship.

"Yes, I'm… I'm fine." The shake in her voice surprised her as she spoke. She hadn't really processed how the conversation had made her feel and now the residual emotion felt overwhelming.

The captain could see that she was clearly shaken up by the brute. "Come," he said, more as an order than a request, "let me help you with your cart." Pelagios strode boldly onto the dock and made his way over to the ox that had been patiently waiting in the shade. Pandora followed willingly, eager to get away from the ship. As she began to untie the ox, she could feel the man looking at her with the same expression that had made her uneasy when she had introduced herself.

"You said your name was Pandora?" His voice was much quieter than it had been, as if he didn't want them to be overheard.

She shut her eyes and sighed. *Have people been gossiping so much I'm now a village attraction?* she thought, feeling disappointed that this man was no different from all the others.

"Yes," she replied through gritted teeth.

"So, *you're* the girl with the box."

Frozen in place, her eyes widened in horror. She had heard a thousand questions: *Are you like us? What are you made of? Why are you here? Are you human?* But nobody had ever asked her about the box. *How does he know?* she thought in panic. *Run, run now!*

She could barely get the words to leave her lips, "How do you—"

"How do I know?" Pelagios murmured, his face now lifeless. Looking at his expression, Pandora saw a sadness in his eyes that confused her; she felt numb. Unsure what to do, she watched as he turned to look back out to sea.

"Don't people know about—"

"Nobody," Pandora whispered in panic, "please, what do you want?"

"Do not fear, child. I wish you no harm." He turned to face her, clearly surprised by her fear. "I have spent so many years waiting to hear that name that it took me a moment to remember its significance."

"I don't understand—"

"Well, calm yourself and let me explain," Pelagios began. "I have had a profitable career. My ship is known for its speed and my crew are loyal to the death." He looked to his ship with pride before the sadness crept back into his eyes. "I come from a town further down the coast," he said, gesturing to the south. "It's where I started my business. Of course, I was only young then." Pelagios looked around at the market square. "It's a port much like this, though a little bigger I'd say, much more competition there. Getting any sort of reputation was hard work. I feel I was lucky." A hint of bitterness coloured his words and he picked nervously at his fingernails. "I do not believe myself to have been any better than the men around me, and unfortunately, others did not take kindly to my success. There was one man in particular who was convinced I was taking more than my share of the work." Pandora watched as Pelagios walked back towards the edge of the dock, desperate to understand how this story was relevant to his knowledge of who she was.

"Agathon had been a friend in my youth." the man continued. "We were of similar minds. We'd known each other since our childhood and were both set for a life at sea, determined to find our fortunes. When his business failed, instead of accepting it, he blamed my success. No matter what I said, he was convinced that I had orchestrated his failure. Mad with jealousy after a night of drinking, Agathon made his way to my home with a few of his crew and thinking that I was inside, burned it to the ground. What he didn't know was that I was still on board my ship, tending to repairs. It wasn't until I saw the smoke from the town that I knew what had happened." Pelagios crouched down and slowly lowered his weight onto his knees.

"So what happened?" Pandora asked, captivated by the man's tale.

"Well, he didn't kill me, which I presume was his intention." The man stood with a sniff, trying to hide the tears in his eyes. "He killed my family. My beautiful wife, my son, they had been asleep when the attack happened. By the time I got there, there was nothing I could do."

Pandora watched the man struggle to control his emotions. His lip quivered and his hands shook but he refused to let the grief out. With a loud cough, Pelagios shuffled from one foot to another before clapping his hands together. "I'm sorry, my dear," he apologised with a gruff laugh, "I don't talk about it often. I made my peace a long time ago but it never gets easier."

"I'm so sorry, it's, well it's…" Pandora stumbled over her words, unsure how to comfort the man she barely knew.

He held his hands up in embarrassment. "Oh please, young lady, don't worry about me – I do have a tendency to ramble. I suppose you must be wondering how this relates to you?"

Pandora looked sheepishly at her feet. "Well I—"

"Come," he said, gesturing towards the ox, who, despite having been untied, remained dozing in the shade. "Good creature you've got there," Pelagios said, then chuckled to himself as he stroked the animal's flank.

Pandora smiled briefly but her anxiety remained evident in her expression. The sailor smiled reassuringly. "When I lost my family, I lost myself. I'm ashamed to admit it but I was weak. I turned to drink and gambling." His expression turned sullen as he relived what was clearly a dark time in his past. "I needed something to numb the pain, but unfortunately nothing even came close. After a particularly rowdy game of cards, I got into a fight that left me broken and bruised in the street. As I lay there, begging for death to take me to my family, a woman appeared to me. Even if I had an eternity to find the words, I would still be unable to do her beauty justice. She wore sky-blue robes that complimented her beautiful dark skin perfectly and her raven hair was adorned with golden leaves. She introduced herself as Tyche."

Pandora looked at the sailor sceptically and raised an eyebrow. "The goddess of luck?"

"I hardly believed it myself," he said, laughing at her obvious doubt. "I didn't understand what she could want with me. She told me she had been watching me for some time and was touched by my story. She explained that there was little she could do to heal my pain but she could give me a prophecy. The prophecy was that I would meet a young girl by the name of Pandora. A girl with a box that contained secrets that could change the world." Pelagios waved a hand in Pandora's direction and smiled. "She said that it would be you, Pandora, that would change my luck. However, given my state at the time, I dismissed it. I never thought I would meet you."

With a startled expression, Pandora stared back at the man. *Me?* she thought, stunned, *A prophecy about me?* "But I don't understand, what can I do to help you?"

"Don't worry, girl, I don't expect you to know. The gods work in mysterious ways. I should think neither of us will know until it happens."

"So, y-you don't want the box?" Pandora stuttered tentatively.

"No, Pandora, a box that powerful is no possession for a lowly sailor such as I," Pelagios said with reassuring kindness.

"It's no possession for me either," she muttered. "It was given to my father along with me when I was a baby. I… I don't know why it was given to him but I know that no one can ever find it. Even I don't know where it is. I've never even seen it." The words tasted bitter in her mouth. She hated that box, hated that something so dangerous was a part of her life, a constant shadow hovering over her. She had never expected to speak to anybody about it; in fact, a part of her had always hoped it wasn't real. Now, speaking to this man, she felt both relief and fear that such a thing was present in her life.

Pelagios could see the torment in Pandora's expression. "Don't worry, child, you have come this far. Don't fear what you cannot change." Pelagios took Pandora's hand in both of his. "May the gods bless you, sweet girl. I am so happy to have met you. I hope our paths cross again someday." And with that, he walked back to his ship, leaving Pandora alone.

~

Feeling an overwhelming mix of emotions, Pandora drew in a long measured breath. The captain's story was indeed tragic, but she didn't understand how she could alter his path. *I'm not special*, she thought, *I'm just different. Gods know they aren't the same thing.*

Noticing that the light was beginning to fade, Pandora turned from the docks and, with her beloved ox, began the walk home. She hoped to get back before sunset to help her father with any remaining work. The whole walk home, all she could think about was the box. Knowing now that it was indeed real, she didn't understand why the gods would have given such a thing to a mortal. A knot formed in her stomach as she thought about how it had been hidden from her for all this time. She tried her best not to dwell on it, but she couldn't shake the feeling that there must have been a reason why she wasn't allowed to know its location.

As days in a sleepy seaside town go, it had certainly been an eventful one. Pandora watched as traders packed up their stalls, mothers called their children in for the evening meal and weary sailors made their way to one of the many local tavernas for an evening of respite away from the dangers of the sea. The air was filled with the sounds of laughter and song. It was arguably a pleasant evening. With her ox marching steadily at her side, Pandora began to feel at ease again. Even having met Pelagios and learning of his prophecy, she couldn't help but feel deflated. Nothing had really changed: she was still a potter's daughter, still an outcast stranded in a sea of people that simply didn't understand her. *Maybe it's not about me*, she thought. *Maybe he mistook me for someone else.* She didn't understand how her boring life could affect the path of such a man. For as unusual as she was, nothing of note had really ever happened to her.

As she walked, pondering the events of the afternoon, she felt the air change. The harsh salt winds of the sea mellowed and the fresh earthen smells of the forest consumed the air once again. It comforted her and, for the most part, put her troubles to rest; she was glad to be going home to her father. "Nearly there, boy," she said, then reassured her weary companion with a scratch behind his ear. Her father's house lay just on the outskirts of the town, at the end of the dirt track that led away from the port, towards the hills.

Turning a corner, Pandora looked down the street only to find it empty. No people walking by, no children playing, not even a stray dog picking up the scraps from a neighbour's evening meal. A gust of wind blew her way and in that moment the ox stopped its pace. "Come on, boy, what's wrong?" Pandora asked, concerned at the sudden change as the animal snorted in panic. No matter how much she encouraged it, the ox would not move. Pandora looked around her in confusion. She had never seen the street so quiet. Anxiously, she ran back to the corner only to find that the road behind her was equally as deserted. She couldn't understand where all the people had gone – they had been there seconds ago; it didn't make sense. The merriment in the air had gone; there was no more singing, no laughing or shouting. There was nothing, not even the sounds of evening birdsong – it was completely silent.

Fear catching in her throat, Pandora walked quickly back to her cart and tried desperately to get the ox to move. "Come on, boy, MOVE." She could hear the panic in her voice, but all she wanted was to get off the streets and back to her father. As she pulled on the animal's reins, she noticed something strange about him. Looking at his coat, she saw that he was now flecked with tiny black spots. She ran her hand along his flank and then raised it to her face and stared in confusion at her palm. "Ash?" she whispered. Snapping her head towards her home, she inhaled a deep breath of panic. "Smoke… Is that *smoke*!"

Dropping the reins, she ran – the smoke burned her lungs and the ash stung her eyes and stuck in her hair but she didn't stop. She tore through the street and before long was confronted by her worst nightmare. Her home was intact but she could see the glow of flames under the door, could hear the roar of the blaze through the windows and could see thick black smoke billowing from the roof. "Oh gods, no, please, NO." Her scream echoed down the deserted street.

Pandora tried desperately to open the door but it was jammed. She called out hysterically, "Father?! Father, please, where are you?" Looking around her wildly, she screamed, "Help! Someone, please help! Fire! There's a fire!" Nobody came; there was no one to help. As she paced frantically in front of her home, she heard a weak cough come from inside.

"P-Pandora?"

Her eyes widened as she heard the familiar sound of her father's voice, coming from inside the house.

"Father! Oh gods, hold on, I'm coming."

"No, Pandora, don't. Stay away, it's not safe."

"Father, I can't leave you, I can't."

She screamed in agony and frustration as she tried the door one more time. The power of her desperation gave her new strength and this time, the door flew open.

Pandora stared in horror at the sight of her home. Flames had engulfed everything in sight. All of her belongings were already burned beyond saving. The only thing she couldn't see was her father.

Being made of clay, Pandora had learned at an early age that fire didn't affect her the same as it did others. She knew she could withstand intense heat without pain. The same could not be said for her father.

She took one more look behind her, covered her face with her sleeve and stepped into the room. As soon as she had crossed the threshold, the door swung shut with a loud BOOM. The noise rang in Pandora's ears; it was like the entire world had gone silent. She called out desperately for her father, the sound of her voice muffled. "Father, can you hear me?"

The ringing in her ears continued as she stepped further forwards into the room. A beam behind her fell with a crash and as she turned and crouched in defence, she saw it had fallen and blocked the door, too heavy for her to lift. There was no way she would be able to get her father out that way. Coughing into her hand, Pandora narrowed her eyes and moved steadily forwards, calling out for her father. A weak voice replied, "I'm here, my girl, help me. I'm here."

His voice was in the room with her but she could not see him. Looking round, Pandora saw only fire. "I can hear you, Father, where are you?"

"I'm in here, Dora. Help, I'm in here."

As Pandora walked slowly forwards, she realised the sound was coming from underneath a pile of debris. Crouching on the ground, Pandora pulled the burning rubble aside, anxious that her father had been trapped under it. Seeing nothing but more debris, Pandora stuck her arm into the pile and scrabbled desperately for her father. As she searched, she felt her hand touch something smooth and cold, unnaturally cold despite the fire. Cautiously she pulled the object from the flames. It was barely the size of an apple. Octagonal in shape and made of dark, almost black, polished oak. Though she had never seen it before, Pandora knew instantly what she had found.

She wasn't sure what made her do it, but she drew the small box close to her face, turned her ear towards it and whispered, "F-Father?"

To her sorrow, the voice of her father echoed back. "I'm in here, Pandora. Help me, I'm in here."

"But how?"

"I don't know, I don't know. Help me, oh gods help me."

"But you said—"

"I know what I said, but it doesn't matter now. If you don't save me, I'll die, we'll all die. Pandora, please, let me out. You have to help me."

Confusion and pain filling her heart, Pandora sank to the floor. "Father, I can't," she said, her voice hoarse.

"Dora, please. I need you. I love you… my darling girl. Listen to me, I need you to open the box or we are all going to die."

She looked at the devastation around her. Her home was gone. She had nothing left. She couldn't lose her father, she just couldn't.

Breathing slowly, eyes screwed shut, Pandora raised a tentative hand towards the clasp of the box. She exhaled deeply and opened her eyes. "Please don't leave me, Father."

Her fingers shaking, she flicked the clasp open with a snap and cautiously lifted the lid. Nothing happened. The box was empty, its black interior so dark, it appeared not to end.

She called out desperately, "Father, Father, where are you?"

"I'm here, my girl, I'm here. Thank you, thank you, thank you."

The sound didn't come from the box – it was coming from behind her. Pandora lifted her head and turned slowly to look behind her.

"Thank you, thank you, *thank you*."

The door behind her swung open with such almighty force that it broke free of its hinges and shattered, the sheer force of the motion causing the debris blocking it to disperse and the box to fly from Pandora's hands. The bright light from outside blinded Pandora and as she held a shaking hand up to her face, she saw the silhouette of a man standing in the doorway. The voice she heard slowly changed from the warm comforting sound of her beloved father to a low, stinging rasp. As her eyes adjusted to the light, she looked in horror as she began to identify the pale thin frame, the long, dark, limp hair and the piercing eyes of the con man she had revealed earlier in the day.

"No, NO! Where's my father? What have you done?"

He said nothing. The man just stared at her, smiling wickedly, and laughed.

Pandora staggered forwards, covering her ears. "Please, please stop, why have you done this?" she begged.

The man stopped laughing, narrowed his eyes at her and pointed a bony talon towards the box. Eyes wide in terror, Pandora stumbled in the debris, dragging herself back through the flames, and flung herself at the box. Picking it up off the floor, she looked at the man in fear and confusion. He smiled eerily and raised one skeletal hand up to his ear in cruel encouragement. Reluctantly Pandora lifted the box to her ear once more. Hardly noticeable at first, she heard a low rumble coming from inside it. As she listened, the sound got louder and louder until she could distinguish individual voices: screams, screeches, cries, shouts, a retching cacophony of horrific noises enough to terrify even the gods themselves. The sound became so unbearable that Pandora dropped the box and fell to the ground. As she writhed in pain on the floor, she saw the man watch her, a haunting smile on his face, until eventually she could take no more. Her head dropped, her eyes rolled back and finally, as she lost consciousness, the world went silent.

THE BROKEN OFFERING

The first thing Pandora became aware of was the smell of smoke. The acrid, bitter taste of ash coated her throat and tongue with a putrid film. She became aware that she was lying on the floor; the cold stone beneath her once soothing to the touch now felt gritty and rough, and her aching limbs were sore and stiff. Pandora was afraid; she was desperately afraid of moving. A part of her wanted nothing more than to lie in this moment for an eternity, for she knew as soon as she moved, she would return to a reality that she wasn't ready to face. She whispered a prayer under her breath, her lips barely moving, and opened her eyes. The darkness was surprising. She realised she must have been lying there for some time. With a groan, Pandora raised her head up gingerly and pushed herself upright.

As her eyes adjusted to the lack of light, her surroundings came slowly into focus and the grim realisation of what had happened became all too clear. She stared solemnly at the charred corpse of her home, devastated by the fire. There was nothing left. The home she had loved had been turned into a funeral pyre and now the cremated remains were slowly, unceremoniously drifting away with the northern wind. She had been given no time to mourn, no chance to say goodbye. It was all gone. All was lost.

Silently she pushed herself up from the floor and staggered forwards a little. Even in the darkness, she could see the fallen beams, the broken tiles, the furniture burned to cinders. Nothing had escaped – her entire world had been destroyed. Everything and everyone she loved was gone. As she staggered through the ruins of her life, she became aware of her breathing. It grew faster and faster and as it did, her chest began to feel tighter, her lungs felt heavier; she clutched her hand to her heart and with a deep breath in, she let out a dreadful howl of pain. It echoed around the ruins, cutting through the excruciating silence mercilessly.

Pandora spun around, fixated on finding the cause of the horror she had witnessed. Fuelled by her anger, she scanned the floor for the box. Unable to see it, she began to tear desperately through the debris, scrabbling through piles of ash and rubble. Her fingers turned black and her nails became broken and torn with the savagery of her determination. It didn't matter how hard she looked – the box wasn't there; it had vanished. She didn't understand where it could have gone but she didn't have the energy to care. Collapsing in a heap, she covered her face in her hands and wished more than anything that she could cry. Exhaustion and mourning fuelled her as she sobbed, willing the tears that she knew would never come.

~

Paralysed by grief, Pandora sat there in the ruins of her life until the darkness began to wane. The early morning sun felt harsh and intrusive muted only by the haze of ash and smoke that had not yet left the air. It wasn't until this moment that Pandora thought of her neighbours. Nobody had come to her aid, no cries for help… nothing. It took all of her strength but eventually, Pandora peeled herself up off the floor and stumbled towards the hole that had once been her front door. Peeking tentatively out into the street, her heart dropped at what she saw. The destruction had flooded out of her home and towards the town. She looked down the road at the crumbled houses, the ruined homes, horrified at the sight. Lurching out into the street, she looked around, desperate to find someone, but there was nobody there. Fearful and cautious, she walked to the nearest house. It had belonged to an elderly couple and they had lived there since

Pandora could remember; they had always been kind to her. She would have knocked at the door but there was no longer one there. Scanning the room, her heart sank. It had been abandoned. Bowls had smashed on the floor, belongings had been discarded and the back wall had disintegrated entirely. Panicked, Pandora rushed to the next house, and the next, only to find similar scenes. Homes that had housed families for years, generations, had been destroyed, deserted… There was no sign of anybody.

Walking back out into the street, Pandora looked around her with pained confusion. Images of the box, the fire, the man, flashed through her mind at a terrible speed and she clutched her head in pain. Her whole body felt numb. She couldn't believe that such a small thing had caused all this destruction. Denial swept through her thoughts, and she couldn't bring herself to accept what had happened. Her stomach knotted as images of her father ran through her head. She wondered if it was possible he was still alive. She could see no bodies in the streets so whatever had happened here, it seemed that people had escaped it. There was a possibility that her father had been one of them. *But he'd never leave me*, she thought, *would he?* Turning back to her home, she saw the only place she hadn't looked.

~

Despite the devastation of her home, the small kiln and store behind the house lay relatively unharmed. Pandora raced hopefully towards the shed and threw the tattered doors open with abandon. Her heart sank instantly. The pots and bowls, the urns and plates that made up the vast collection of her father's work lay shattered and broken on the floor. She looked bitterly at the mess, feeling foolish for having hoped for more. Bending down she picked at the debris, hoping to find something still intact. Running her hands over the shards, she picked up a piece of vase. As she stared at it, she could feel the anger build up inside her until, unable to hold it in any longer, she threw it at the wall with all the force she could muster. What she had not anticipated was that the piece of vase she had thrown would not fly into the wall where she aimed, but would instead arc straight into a large vase on the top shelf causing it to shatter, blasting shards of clay in every direction. Flinching at the backlash, Pandora turned her head away in defence, though was unable to avoid a large, razor-edged shard flying straight in her direction. The sharp edge caught her arm with a decent amount of force before it hit the floor, continuing on its new trajectory out of the door. To her frustration, Pandora noticed that it had taken a small piece out of her left arm. As traumatising as this might sound, she looked upon her arm in frustration and rolled her eyes. Unfortunately for Pandora, one of the hazards of being made of clay meant that rather than being prone to cuts and bruises, she would chip or crack if wounded. To anyone else, this would of course be rather a shock, but to her it was simply something she had to deal with. Wounds to the skin didn't hurt her and she had always been grateful for this. Lifting her right hand up to her arm to inspect the damage, she blew lightly on the small chip in her skin and watched a tiny cloud of dust fly up into the air. She ran her fingers over the coarse edge of the wound. It was a minor injury, easily fixable.

Pandora strode out of the store towards her father's kiln, muttering to herself in frustration. She lifted her hand to the rusted handle of the door and gently stroked the weathered metal. So many times she had opened this door to see her father working. A flicker of a smile danced across her face for a moment at the thought of him before the reality of the situation extinguished it. Pushing the door lightly, Pandora stared bleakly at the pottery. Everything was as it had always been. The kiln lay dormant in the corner, her father's tools sprawled carelessly over the worktop as if waiting to be picked up again. The room felt so empty without him. It took all of her strength to cross the threshold.

She moved swiftly over to the mound of raw clay that sat by the counter. As she pinched a small piece of it between her fingers, she found comfort in the familiar texture. Delicately, with practised execution, Pandora pushed the clay into the chip on her arm and smoothed the surface with her thumb. She dipped her hand into a cup of water on the table and ran her fingers over her skin. The water blended out the clay and erased all trace of the wound. Unlike her father's work, she wouldn't have to fire the clay in order for it to harden. Once it bonded with her body, it became a part of her. The russet colour of the clay faded and as it did, the appearance of skin formed on the top. As she stroked the newly healed skin, Pandora came to the realisation that she had lost the only person in the world with whom she had truly shared who she was. Her father was the only one who understood *what* she was. So many times during her childhood, he had smoothed out dents and chips in her skin. He had cared for her lovingly as any father would and, now that he was gone, she knew she would never have that connection again.

~

Her mind drifted back to a time when, as a young girl, she had taken a nasty fall out of a tree and had chipped a large part of her leg, a landing that for most people would have resulted in a nasty break. These sorts of injuries did not cause her much pain; it was more of a discomfort. Her father had found her and carried her – despite much protest – back to his workshop. He sat her down on a stool and she folded her arms with a sigh and scowled at him. Unfortunately for her, this only made him laugh.

"Oh, my dear child," he cooed affectionately, stroking a coarse hand across her cheek, "why so sad, my love?"

"I fell." The young Pandora glowered as she spoke.

Miltiades let out a low chortle. "Yes, I suppose you did, little one," he said. "Now tell me, what did you do after you fell?"

"I don't know."

"Oh, I think you do, my surly child. Come on, tell me, what did you do?"

"Well, I got up and—"

"You got up," her father echoed, bending down so that his kind eyes met hers. "My darling, you are going to fall sometimes. That is life." He stroked her hair and she saw his eyes filled with both concern and pride for his little stubborn daughter. "Darling girl, it doesn't matter how hard or how many times you fall, what matters is that you always get back up."

Pandora's embarrassment faded as she looked into her father's loving eyes. Her face melted and with a cheeky smirk she threw herself into his arms. Slightly taken by surprise, Miltiades lost his balance and the two of them fell to the floor in a giggling heap.

"There's my girl. I knew that smile was hidden there somewhere."

Lying on the floor, Pandora cuddled herself close under her father's arm. "I'm sorry, Father, I love you."

"I love you too, my child. I just want you to be strong for me, my darling, so that when you are grown and I am no longer with you, you will be able to look after yourself."

Pandora paused a moment, saddened by the thought that he wouldn't be with her forever, then shook her head and held her tiny hand out to him. "Come on, Father, you need to get up."

Miltiades roared a ferocious laugh and pulled his daughter back into his arms despite her squeals and giggles of protest. "Alright then, you, let's fix that leg."

~

She could still hear his voice. The warm, low tones of his words had always been so comforting to her and the ghost of his laugh still echoed in the room. Pandora knew she couldn't stay there. If she was to survive this, she needed to leave to find somewhere safe to rest. Without her father, it wasn't a home – it was a tomb. Unsure where to go, Pandora left the pottery and assessed her surroundings. She could go into town but judging from her street and the silence in the air, she suspected that it was also destroyed and consequently abandoned too. She had no money, no food, nothing but the clothes on her back; even her beloved ox had gone for there was no sign of him or the cart in the road. Pandora looked out into the distance and saw the thick band of wilderness that surrounded the town. She knew it well and was confident she would be able to make an adequate shelter, even just for a night or two.

Resolved in her decision, Pandora strode with determination back to the road. Feeling something jagged under her feet, she looked down and saw the piece of vase that had chipped her arm and flown into the yard. Picking it up, she realised it was one of the items that would have been taken to the temple as an offering. The outside was beautifully adorned with ornate carvings, one of the finest examples of her father's craftsmanship. Tracing the details with her finger, Pandora looked closer at the work. There was a small carving near the bottom, different from the rest: "Miltiades made me." Pandora read the words out in a whisper. She sighed deeply at the sight of her father's name and drew the piece of vase to her chest, holding it close to her heart. "I think I should take you to where you belong. You were made for Athena, so that's where we'll go. Maybe she has the answers I'm looking for," Pandora said aloud, as if to solidify her decision. Turning one last time to look longingly at her home, Pandora began walking out of the village, towards the hills and the temple of Athena.

~

The warmth of the morning sun had begun to colour the air. The wind was low and fresh and although the road was long, it was easy to walk. It was a well travelled road for there were always supplicants walking in pilgrimage to pray to their beloved goddess, Athena. She was the goddess of war, wisdom and craft, and Pandora's village worshipped her above all others because she was benevolent and just. Miltiades had always said she was a wise and honourable deity and he was a devout believer. Pandora hadn't spent much time at the temple, having never really found reason to travel there. She often heard the villagers speaking of their encounters with the goddess, her father included, though Pandora was sceptical. She did not understand how a village of such little importance could attract the attention of such a beloved goddess. As she walked the well-trodden road, she thought of a time her father had returned from supplication.

He had come home much later than Pandora had expected and she had grown restless with worry. When he finally appeared at the door, she ran to him and he embraced her warmly.

"Oh, my darling girl, I am sorry I'm so late."

Pandora heard a sadness in his voice that she had not expected. "Father, what's wrong?"

He held her face in his hands as he had done so often before, only this time she could see the anguish in his eyes. His lips tapered down in a worrisome frown and he stroked his fingers across her cheek. "Nothing is wrong, my darling, the goddess came to me with news. It was not what I had hoped, but there is nothing I can do. It is as it must be."

Pandora wanted to question him. She wanted to know what he had meant but something stopped her. She feared that whatever it was, she would not want to hear it. Looking back now, she wished she had pushed him to explain. Maybe it might have changed how things were now. *Don't dwell on it*, she thought to herself, *you can't change anything now*.

Pandora felt uneasy travelling such a busy road alone. She had never felt as small or insignificant as she did in that moment. Walking up the hill, she turned back to look upon her home. In the morning light the destruction was bleak. The smoke from the ruins was being whipped up and dragged out to sea by the wind. There were no ships in the harbour, even the water looked grey. It was as if she was walking away from some long-forgotten ancient ruin, not a bustling trade town. Her heart ached at the sight.

The journey up to the temple took most of the day. The further away from home Pandora walked, the emptier she felt. Thirst burned her throat and her limbs shook from fatigue but she never stopped walking. Sometime in the mid-afternoon, Pandora came across the two cypress trees that marked the final ascent to the temple. They stood tall and proud, either side of the path, like ancient soldiers, followed by another pair a few feet further down, and another pair beyond that. These trees ran parallel to the road all the way until its end, marking the final ascent to the temple. So many times Pandora had reached these trees then veered off to the left to journey into the woods on her own. She paused for a moment and considered stepping off the road to follow the path she knew better. It was comfortable and familiar and she felt safe in the forest. Something about the temple made her feel uneasy. She was respectful of the gods, but she had always been fearful of their power. Exhaling with definitive resolve, she stroked the broken shard of vase, marched past the cypress trees with determination and proceeded on the road to the temple.

~

There was now a considerable chill in the air. Pandora could feel the day slipping away. She knew the light would only last for a while longer. Anxious to get to the temple before dark she quickened her pace, despite her limbs protesting. Looking up the road, Pandora saw beautifully ornate braziers in between each set of cypress trees. They had been lit in preparation for the evening. The welcoming glow not only lit the path but also assured her that there would be somebody at the temple. Her father once told her that the priestess who looked after the temple would throw grape vines into the fires to make the smoke smell sweet. The pleasant smell hit Pandora with comforting familiarity. She could see the temple now and was relieved that it had been untouched by the carnage.

Surrounded by the forest, it was a modest spectacle, organic in its habitat.

The four columns of the portico were laced with ivy and clematis vines, purple flowers dripping down like precious jewels. The stone was worn and looked impossibly old, as if the vines that wrapped around it were now holding the structure together. Moss and lichen covered the edges of the steps in a thick blanket. It was as if this place had been born of nature. Three enormous, low-seated braziers stood in between the columns. The glow from the fire bathed the walls in a beautiful amber haze. The steps that connected the temple to the road were shallow and wide and Pandora walked up them cautiously. The temple was tended by a single priestess along with her two handmaidens, none of which Pandora had ever encountered; the only people she had ever seen there were other supplicants. Now, with the devastation of her village, she was unsure who or what she might meet within these walls.

As she walked up the steps, Pandora gazed up at the pediment that crowned the imposing columns. It had been carved with the story of Athena's birth. The scene depicted Zeus, her father, on his knees as the Titan Prometheus cleaved his head in two with a tremendous axe to reveal the fully formed Athena in all her glory. Pandora was so fixated on the scene that she didn't notice the small hooded figure, swathed in robes, slowly appear at the top of the steps.

"An interesting story, don't you think?"

The sound of the soft, shaking voice made Pandora jump out of her skin. "Oh! I'm sorry, I was just—"

"Please, my child, do not fear."

The figure stepped forwards, arms outstretched in welcome. Pandora could tell that the voice belonged to a woman. Something in the softness of her words put Pandora at ease.

Clutching the piece of pottery close to her chest, Pandora spoke with determination, "I have come with offerings for the goddess. I wish to speak with her."

The old woman laughed softly, though to Pandora it did not seem unkind. "Oh, sweet girl, of course you have. You are not the first, and I am certain you will not be the last."

With a wave of her hand, the woman encouraged her forwards. "Come, come, child, I am old and my sight is not what it used to be. I wish you no harm, please, come closer so I can see you."

Gingerly, Pandora walked up the steps, her offering still held tightly in her hands. "I'm sorry, I didn't know if anyone would be here," she called out as she walked.

"I am always here, child. I have offered my life in devotion and servitude to our beloved Athena, so here is where I stay."

"So, you must be the priestess?"

"A strong deduction, girl," the woman said with a slight laugh in her tone.

Pandora reached the top of the steps and as she did, the priestess's features became clear. She was incredibly old, older than any man or woman Pandora had ever seen before. Her aged face was carved with lines that travelled in every direction; she had kind eyes that sparkled in the light and a gentle smile that filled her cheeks with warmth. The robes she wore were grey and faded, their edges fraying. She was quite unlike anyone Pandora had ever seen before. The woman lowered the hood from her head to reveal a flowing river of long silver hair. Her movements were slow and each one seemed to cost her much energy to perform.

Smiling at Pandora, she raised her weathered hands and clasped them around the young girl's face. "Such youth, such beauty. Though" – concern filled her eyes as she spoke – "I see much sorrow in you girl, oh so much sadness."

Pandora pulled her hands away as she looked back out towards her home. She didn't know how to explain what had happened. "My home, my father, it's—"

"Ah yes, Kyparissi. A terrible tragedy."

"You know? You saw it?" Pandora asked with surprise, turning towards the woman who was now walking into the temple. Pandora followed her, eager to hear what she had to say.

The temple was a simple room. It was usually lit only by natural light; however, in the evenings and especially in the winter months, braziers in each corner were used as an alternative. There was no altar, no carvings on the walls; it was beautiful in its simplicity. All that filled the room was a magnificent statue of the goddess which stood proudly in the centre.

"I'm afraid not, girl," the woman said over her shoulder as she walked. "I have not left the temple for many moons. I only know what the goddess had foreshadowed." The priestess picked up a lighting stick and began to ignite the braziers in the corners. "She told me a terrible thing would happen here, the repercussions of which would alter everything to come. I did not think it would happen in my lifetime but when I saw you appear, it was clear that the worst of predictions had come true."

The old woman blew out the stick. "Tell me, Pandora, what happened?"

Pandora walked over to one of the braziers and stared into the fire. She watched as the flames danced and licked at the sides of the bowl. "They're all gone. Everyone is gone," she mumbled. "I've lost everything."

"How, child?"

"I don't know," she said with exasperation. "There was a man. He… he burned my home. My father, I think he did something to my father. I… I think it's all my fault. It *is* all my fault." She hid her face in her hands as she spoke.

The priestess shuffled towards her and put a comforting hand on her shoulder. "You have witnessed a terrible thing, girl. A burden no child should have to bear and it is with great sorrow that this is how we should meet. Unfortunately, your part in this was unavoidable. Your path has always been written.”

“My path? Wait. How… how do you know my name?”

“I’ve been waiting to meet you.” The priestess smiled, a gleam in her eye. She turned and walked towards the statue; Pandora followed but kept her distance, now fearful of what the woman had to say. “I have observed you since your birth or, rather, since your creation,” the old woman explained. “It was always going to be this way.”

Pandora stared up at the statue in front of them. The carved curls of Athena’s hair tumbled down over her armour, spear in one hand, helmet in the other; she stood the champion of the village.

The priestess walked up to the statue, put one hand out towards it and sighed. “They never do get my hair right.”

In one fluid motion, the old woman threw off her robes and turned on her heels to face Pandora. The girl fell to her knees in disbelief. The figure that stood before her was no longer the old woman but the goddess herself. She was breathtakingly beautiful yet fearsome to behold. Her perfectly straight hair was the colour of cinnamon, the sides pulled back from her face in a striking plumage that mimicked the horsehair crest of her helmet which she held loosely at her side. Her robes of brilliant, dazzling white clung to her body as if a second skin, pulled tight under her bust with a thick gold band. She held a gigantic winged spear with a shining leaf-shaped blade. The goddess was surrounded by a soft, divine glow. There was absolutely no question of her identity.

Pandora was awestruck. She couldn’t believe what she was seeing. As she kneeled on the floor in terrified supplication, she lowered her eyes to the ground. Athena moved with ethereal grace, as if walking on water, and stopped in front of her.

"Come on, child. I'm not that scary, am I?"

"I-I-I…"

"Oh dear, I probably should have given you some warning. It's alright, girl, like I said, I wish you no harm."

Athena laid her spear and helmet down beside her and reached out her arms as a gesture of kindness to the now petrified Pandora. With shaking limbs, the young girl placed her hands in Athena's and the goddess gently pulled her to her feet. Pandora concluded that Athena was at least a good foot taller than she was, and all in all, was thoroughly intimidating.

Athena patted Pandora sympathetically on the back, rolled her eyes in mock frustration and chuckled to herself. "Come on, little one, we have much to discuss."

REMEMBRANCE

"I don't understand," Pandora spluttered, "are you really… I mean, how did you… I mean… but…"

The goddess raised her hand to silence the now hysterical girl, causing Pandora to trail off until she stood, petrified, in awed silence. Satisfied that Pandora had recovered from the initial shock, Athena moved closer to the girl as if approaching a skittish wild animal.

"Whenever I have needed to visit your town to offer my assistance, I have always come in the guise of the old priestess," she said in a calm, reassuring tone. "I found it became an easy way to offer my advice to those who sought it. Most of the time my handmaidens tend to the temple, but I always know when I am truly needed, and that is why I am here now."

"How do you know who I am?" Pandora asked in bewilderment.

"Pfft, please," the goddess said, feigning insult. "Who do you think you're talking to?"

Pandora lowered her head in shame. "I'm sorry, I don't doubt you, I just don't understand why you'd care about me."

Athena looked at the young girl with both compassion and exasperation. "The fact you are still asking that question after today is truly amazing, Pandora. Do you mean to tell me you don't know who you are?"

"Who I am?"

"Yes, child, who you are. How you came to be? Why you're here?"

Pandora shrugged. "Well, my father and I have lived here since I can remember. I was made for my father because he was lonely. He told me he prayed every night for a daughter and then one day, the gods answered his prayers and brought me to him."

"Hmm, well, that would be the abridged version, yes. Though there is much more to it than that." Athena sighed and pinched the bridge of her nose with her fingers. "I suppose he was just trying to protect you. Well, it doesn't matter now. It's done. The box has been opened."

The goddess beckoned for Pandora to come closer and tentatively she stepped forwards.

"Pandora, you were made of clay, true, but you were not intended for Miltiades." Athena began, taking the girl's hand and walking her back to the steps of the temple. She sat down on the top step with serene elegance and gestured gracefully for Pandora to do the same. The girl collapsed willingly in a heap next to the beautiful woman. The goddess looked out at the little town she had grown so fond of over the years. "What do you know of the Titans, Pandora?"

A look of surprise crossed the young girl's face. "My father spoke of them sometimes. He said they were divine beings that preceded the gods and goddesses that we worship. They came before you, the children of Mother Gaia."

"Your father taught you well," Athena said, nodding appreciatively. "What do you know of Epimetheus?"

Pandora furrowed her brow, thinking for a moment before she shook her head. "I'm sorry, I don't—"

"No, I suppose you wouldn't know, dear girl," the goddess said, patting her hand kindly. "Epimetheus was a good-natured Titan, the brother of Prometheus. He was integral to the creation of nature within the mortal world, helping with the characterisation of the animals. Unfortunately, Epimetheus was so generous with the animals that when it came to man, he had no gifts left to bestow upon them. Prometheus stepped in and gave man the secret of fire to secure their place in the world."

"He was punished, wasn't he?" Pandora said. "I remember my father speaking of him."

Athena nodded. "He made his choice and accepted the punishment for it. The gods were sceptical at first but we have found man's progress to be satisfactory. We don't begrudge you humans for the decisions Prometheus made."

"So what happened to Epimetheus?"

"Well, Zeus was… let's say, a little disappointed with his lack of forethought. Rather than punish him for his foolishness, he decided to try to teach him."

"Teach him?"

"Yes, he gave him a gift to help him understand the importance of responsibility and obligation."

"A gift?"

"Yes," Athena said, "you, Pandora."

It took a moment for the words to register; they swam around in Pandora's head for a few moments before she could make sense of them. She shook her head in disbelief. "I'm sorry, what?"

The goddess looked into Pandora's innocent eyes and saw the doubt in them, the confusion and denial. Though obviously a young woman, so much of her was still just a child. Athena took hold of Pandora's hands in a comforting grasp.

"My father wanted to help Epimetheus. He commanded my brother Hephaestus to mould a human, a life from the very earth itself. A human that would help him learn, help him understand his responsibilities as a divine being."

Pandora stared at the goddess with wide eyes; she couldn't believe what she was hearing. "Me?" she whispered. "That was me?"

"Yes, child." Athena did her best to remain calm so as not to spook her. "My brother was eager to help. Hephaestus is a gentle soul, much like yourself. He's a kind and honourable god but he is often teased by my other brothers and sisters for his… less than divine appearance." The tone of her voice lowered and Pandora could see a sadness in her eyes. "I have always stood by him. He is my closest friend."

Pandora had only heard stories of Hephaestus, of how he looked unlike any other god. She had never understood why such a thing would be reason for him to be treated so wretchedly but she knew it best not to ask, at least not now.

"I always wanted a brother," she said with a shrug that didn't mask the emotion in her words.

Athena smiled and patted her hand sympathetically. "My brother decided that the best way for Epimetheus to learn from a human would be when it's at its most innocent." She chuckled under her breath. "I believe my father had intended for him to create a woman as a bride for the Titan. My brother, however, had other ideas and created a baby. He created you, darling girl, and a delightful baby you were."

The look of utter scepticism on Pandora's face was so honest that Athena couldn't help but laugh.

As Pandora tried to process the information, she looked down at her hands wrapped tightly by those of the goddess. "So, how did I come to be with my father?" she said, her voice strained as she struggled to speak of him. "Why… why was he given the box?"

"Well, the actions of the Titan brothers required both praise and punishment. Prometheus was allowed to keep his immortality but was also condemned to a sentence of near eternal suffering for his crimes. Epimetheus, on the other hand, who was not completely to blame but who was also not entirely innocent, was given a punishment that mirrored the sentiments of his gift: responsibility. He was given the box or, rather, the contents of the box." Athena's voice became low and pensive. "When it was given to him, it was a vase that contained horrors that could destroy the world he had helped create. He was to ensure for all eternity that this vase was never to be opened or he would have to witness all the nature he loved be destroyed."

"But, I don't understand," Pandora said with mild exasperation, having not received the answer she had wanted. "How did my father end up with it? How did *he* end up with me?"

Athena stroked Pandora's head affectionately. "Epimetheus was a kind soul but he was a fool. He didn't know how to care for a child – or indeed his punishment. Time at Olympus does not run as it does in the mortal realm. You remained a baby for a long time, far longer than you could imagine, and Epimetheus simply just wasn't up to the challenge. As your creator, Hephaestus loved you dearly and couldn't stand to see you harmed. He realised quickly that the Titan was not able to keep you safe. He believed that Mount Olympus, our home, was no place for a human child, for there you would have never grown old."

As Athena spoke, Pandora tried her best to keep up with the story but she couldn't believe that it was her Athena was speaking about. She couldn't comprehend how her life had been so very different from what she had believed.

"My brother went to Zeus in supplication," Athena continued. "He begged for you to be given to someone more worthy, more caring. My father didn't want to allow you to live among the humans. When you were born, he had bound your life to the evils within the vase. Wherever you went, they must follow. Hephaestus pleaded that he would watch over you, that he would keep you safe. All he wanted was for you to have a real life. A life full of love."

"So you found my father?"

"We did," Athena said, smiling. "It was I that suggested we search for a human family for you. Zeus agreed to allow you to leave Olympus as long as we found someone suitable to protect both you and the vase. Hephaestus created the box to contain the evil – for he believed it would be much more practical in the mortal realm than a vase – and Zeus agreed to let you go. We decided to begin looking here." She moved her arm out, gesturing across the lands that stretched out in front of them, the lands Pandora had called home. "It was here that we met Miltiades."

Athena became silent for a minute. She lowered her head and appeared deep in thought. Pandora looked at her in frustration. She was desperate to know more, to understand her place in this world. She couldn't believe she had gone her whole life not knowing the truth of her existence.

Finally the goddess raised her head and looked at Pandora with a smile. "I understand that this is difficult to comprehend. I think it might be easier to just show you."

~

Athena raised both her hands and placed them gently on either side of Pandora's head. "Close your eyes, Pandora."

Raising one eyebrow sceptically, Pandora shut her eyes tight. After a few moments, she felt the goddess let go of her head. Opening her eyes at the movement, Pandora was shocked to find herself standing outside the front of her house, Athena beside her.

"How did we—"

"This isn't real, Pandora," Athena said quickly, "think of it as a waking dream. What you are seeing is the past – living memories. This isn't your home."

Pandora soaked in the scene. It was just like so many mornings she had seen before. The bustle of everyday life was vibrant, but with a graininess to it, a haze-like cover across her vision, the edges of the scene not quite coming into focus. She could hear children near them playing and laughing but they sounded distant. She could even feel the wind in her hair. Taking in the moment, she drew a deep breath in. It even smelled the same but somehow the air seemed thinner and the breeze felt softer than it should be. It was both wonderful and agonising all at once. It was so beautiful, but the pain of knowing none of it was real weighed heavy on her heart.

"Come with me." Athena beckoned as she strode boldly past the house, towards the workshop. Pandora was hesitant. The curiosity was overwhelming, but she knew there could only be one person in that room, a person whose fate she was still unsure of.

Reluctantly she followed the goddess, her footsteps slowing as she reached the open door of the pottery. Athena stood by the door frame and waved gently for Pandora to move closer. Pandora closed her eyes and stepped forwards, using her arms to feel for the door. She could smell the wet, earthy tang of the clay and it caused knots to twist and tighten in her stomach. When her fingers found the rough wood of the door, Pandora took a deep breath and opened her eyes. Her father stood a few paces in front of her. His back facing her, he was working at his bench, tidying away his equipment, whistling gently as he worked. The sound sent a shiver through Pandora, straight to her heart. The halo of hair on his head was darker, fuller. He looked strong and full of youth. Without thinking, Pandora walked forwards, her arm outstretched towards the figure. In that moment, her breath seized as her father turned round and marched towards her. Her face lit up in a brilliant smile at the sight of him, though he did not see her. In fact, he passed right through her and walked out into the yard.

"What… I don't…" Her voice became choked with emotion.

"He can't see us. We aren't really here, remember," Athena explained gently.

Pandora's face fell. She looked under her lashes at her father, now walking towards their house. "He looks so young."

"Go, follow him, child. I will wait here."

Pandora darted towards the house, eager to see him again. She hovered by the side of the porch and watched as he went inside. She breathed in deep; it was all so surreal, she didn't know what to do with herself. It was so strange to see her father like this, so young, so full of life. She had often imagined his life before her but had never thought she would have the chance to see it. As she stood, wrapped in her own thoughts, Miltiades strode back out onto the porch with a cup of wine in his hand, cracked his neck, sat in his favourite chair, and let out a relaxed sigh. Their house was exactly the same. Pandora had never thought about what it might have been like before she lived there. It warmed her heart to see everything as it should be.

"Miltiades!" a coarse voice shrieked in a rather startling manner, and Pandora turned on her heel to see where it had come from.

"Now, now, dear, he's ten feet away, not ten miles," a soft, low voice scolded gently in response.

Pandora saw two people walk away from the road, towards her father's house. She recognised them as the elderly couple that had lived next door. Though much younger, they were unmistakable. The woman was a formidable character, stern but kind, her features angular and her posture immaculate. She walked with purpose and had a stare that could bring even the bravest men to their knees. Her husband was almost the polar opposite: he was a good head shorter than she was, a portly man with a comfortably round face and cheerful personality. Most of the woman's time was spent bossing people around, and for this reason she was often avoided by those who didn't want to find themselves doing a task they had otherwise intended to not be doing. In comparison, her husband's friendly disposition was one that people naturally gravitated towards.

Miltiades laughed gently and waved to the pair to join him. "Alexander, Zina, greetings. Come and join me. Would you care for a cup?" He held up the wine in his hand.

"No thank you, Miltiades," Zina said with curt politeness. "Don't encourage him." She waved vaguely towards her husband who was clearly about to take Miltiades up on the offer. "He doesn't have the stomach for it."

"Now we both know that's not true, dear," Alexander said with a laugh, patting his rather large belly.

Miltiades laughed and raised his cup to the man. "What can I help you with today, Zina?" Miltiades enquired.

"My foolish husband managed to knock over two of my bowls this morning. I was wondering if I may purchase replacements?" She shot a look of derision at Alexander.

Miltiades stood up and pointed towards his shed. "I would be honoured, my lady. Allow me to get you some to choose from."

"No need. I can manage perfectly fine by myself. You stay here and entertain the oaf," she ordered. Alexander blew her a kiss as she marched purposefully towards the shed. He chortled deeply and sat himself next to Miltiades.

Pandora stepped closer towards the porch and watched the two men enthusiastically.

"Honestly, if I didn't aggravate her so, you know she'd get bored," Alexander jested.

Miltiades laughed heartily and clapped the man on the back. "Are you well, Alexander?"

"Quite well, thank you. Zina is just all worked up because our son is coming to visit. It has been at least eight seasons since we last saw him so she's determined to make sure everything is perfect. Unfortunately as anyone could tell you, my presence makes that a touch difficult." He let out another animated laugh.

"How wonderful." Miltiades said. "How long will he be staying?"

"He's arriving with a ship in three days and will be here for however long it takes for them to ready the boat for their next voyage. If I'd have known my son would live a life at sea, I'd have had another to keep me company and share my workload." Alexander stretched out his arms and linked his fingers behind his head.

Miltiades fiddled with the cup in his hands and looked at the sky wistfully. "To have a child – such a great gift. I envy you, my friend."

Alexander looked at him with surprised concern. "I didn't realise you thought of such things, friend."

"Now and then," Miltiades said, nodding. "I always thought I'd marry and have children, but it just… Well, it never happened." He took a sip from his cup. "I'm grateful for the life I have but I think there will always be a part of me wondering what it would be like if I had someone to share it with. A child – I think that would be a wonderful adventure."

Pandora walked silently up the steps of the porch and sat on the floor next to her father. She had never seen him like this. There was such longing in his eyes, such sadness. He looked so lonely, she desperately wanted to reach out to him but she knew she couldn't. "Father, I'm here," she whispered, desperate for him to hear her.

Alexander put a comforting hand on Miltiades' back. "Come, friend, you're still young, there is more than enough time to think of such things."

"I suppose. Who knows what the gods have in store for us."

Alexander laughed brightly and clapped. "Well, I suppose I should go and find the wife before she plunders your entire collection. How much do we owe you?"

"You don't owe me anything, Alexander. What are a couple of bowls between friends?"

The man looked at Pandora's father with kindness as he rose from his seat and stepped off the porch. "Gratitude, Miltiades. You're a good man. Believe me, it won't go unnoticed." The man held his palms together in thanks and looked at his friend.

It took a few moments for Pandora to realise that Alexander wasn't actually looking at her father – he was looking at her. She turned around to see if anyone else was nearby but there was no one. He was definitely looking at her.

The man spoke one final time, "Until we meet again," and winked.

Pandora froze and thought to herself, *Did he just wink at me?* She was sure he couldn't see her – Athena had said he couldn't – but she could feel his eyes meet hers. Unnerved, Pandora rose and stepped backwards into the house, the light soft and warm inside.

"I'm afraid he's not very subtle."

Pandora jumped out of her skin at the sound of the goddess's voice.

"Oh! Athena, I don't understand. He saw me. Alexander, I mean – he winked right at me."

"Yes, he did," she agreed with a sly smile. "But that's impossible, isn't it?"

"Well, I…"

"I think you can work it out yourself."

"But the only person who can see me is you."

"Hmm, correct. And what am I?"

"You're a goddess…"

Athena raised her eyebrow trying to prompt the girl.

Pandora's eyes widened and she looked back out through the front door. She drew in a quick breath of realisation. "Hephaestus?"

The goddess smiled. "I told you he was watching over you."

Pandora thought back to all the times she had seen him: fighting jovially with his wife, talking to her father, even playing games with her when she was small. Living so close, she had crossed paths with Alexander and Zina many times. They were avid travellers and often spent months away from home, which Pandora now realised was simply a clever ruse. They had always been so kind to her but she had never truly understood why they of all people were so accepting of who she was. It warmed her heart to know that Hephaestus had been watching over her all this time and yet she was saddened to realise that she had never truly met him. A thought caught her attention for a moment.

"Athena, if your brother was Alexander then… who was his wife?"

The goddess bowed deeply. "One of my finer roles, I must admit. She was always fun to play, especially because I got to tease my brother so." She grinned. "We had to make sure we could keep a close eye on you. Giving you to Miltiades was the best decision. He proved to be a wonderful father."

"Yes," Pandora mumbled, "he was."

Athena took her hand and squeezed tightly. "I am truly sorry he's gone."

Her worst fears confirmed, Pandora knew that whatever had happened at her home, her father hadn't survived. She had hoped she would never hear those words, never have to face what she knew to be true, but they were inevitable. Her father was gone and there was nothing she could do. The emotions overwhelming, Pandora flung her arms around the goddess and buried her head into her chest. Quite taken aback by the gesture, Athena was touched by the girl's grief. She wrapped her arms around her and held her close.

"I can't even cry for my father," Pandora said bitterly. "I feel so empty, so alone. I just want to cry."

Athena shushed the girl and stroked her hair. "Come now, child, he knows how you felt about him – how you will always feel. He loved you more than anything in the world. Nothing will ever change that."

~

Pandora eventually calmed herself and drew back from the embrace. Glancing around, she realised they were back on the steps of the temple. So much of her had hoped to stay in that world, to live in that dream and never return to the horrific reality she had caused. She realised it must be very late as the dark night sky was littered with glints of starlight.

Pandora turned towards Athena in exasperation. "So, what do I do now?"

"I am afraid your journey has only just begun, sweet child," Athena said with sadness. "The box has been opened and all the terrors it contained have been set upon the world. A world that is ill prepared to face them. This needs to be rectified, or I fear it will mean the destruction of mankind."

"I'm sorry… you want me to… the box? I have to…" Pandora could hear the panic in her own voice as she babbled incoherently.

"You are far stronger than you think," Athena said. "When you were created, the box was tied to you; it is a part of who you are. You are the only person that can stop the coming darkness set to consume the world."

Pandora wasn't convinced. She wasn't a hero or warrior. She thought of all the stories she had heard about the soldiers and kings who had fought evils in the world. None of those stories had featured a girl made of clay.

"I… I can't." She heard the sound leave her lips and lowered her head in shame. "I want to help, I really do, but what can I do? I'm just a girl."

"Just a girl?!" The goddess said, throwing her arms up in the air. "Pandora, I was unaware that being a young woman meant that you were unable to fight. Why hasn't anyone told me this before? *I'm* a girl too!" She threw herself sarcastically against her statue with the back of her hand pressed to her forehead. "Gods help me, I hope my father doesn't find out, otherwise he'll take away my pointy stick." She ended her rant with an expert flourish of her spear and a scathing look at Pandora who couldn't help but snort in amusement.

"I'm sorry, I didn't mean it like that." She was quick to realise her mistake and threw her hands up apologetically. "I just meant, I know nothing of fighting, or of swords, or anything like that. I can't possibly stop this – how can I?"

Her words were spoken in earnest and she stared at the goddess, desperate for guidance.

Athena shook her head and beckoned for Pandora to come closer. "Young lady," she scolded lightly, "I have seen you display courage, kindness, loyalty, fearlessness and a number of other noble attributes throughout your lifetime. Do you mean to tell me that a true hero is not made up of such characteristics?"

"Well no, but I—"

"Even the greatest warriors of all time didn't come out of the womb ready for combat. Not every hero is born into greatness, some," she encouraged, tilting Pandora's chin up with her fingers, "are made. All it takes is a little training and determination."

"Training?"

"Well, I'm not going to have you gallivanting around Greece in my name without training you first, am I?"

Pandora pursed her lips and her jaw became taut. Athena saw the fire ignite in her eyes. This is what she had been waiting for.

"When do I start?"

Athena shot a satisfied smile at the fierce, youthful girl standing before her. "Well, now you must rest. You've been through so much, you could do with a decent night's sleep. Then in the morning, I shall take you to a friend."

"A friend?"

"In the morning, child, this day has been so long. It is definitely time for bed."

THE TREE IN THE CLEARING

When Pandora woke the next morning, her eyes were heavy with sleep. She sat up reluctantly and yawned. Feeling disoriented, it took her a moment to remember where she was. The dark room, a chamber off the back of the temple, was small and smelled of stone and earth. Pandora rose slowly, careful not to strain her limbs. She took a moment to stretch before getting up. Scrabbling for the handle of the door, she swung it open. On the floor in front of her lay a small bowl of wine next to a rather delicate plate of barley bread and figs. Still a little blurry, Pandora picked up her breakfast and walked through the temple towards the steps. She sat down on the highest one and looked out to the sea while she ate. Her heart was heavy but Athena's words the night before had given her strength. She would do all she could to help, all she could to fix what had happened.

Hearing soft footsteps behind her, Pandora turned to see the goddess walk serenely towards her.

"So, are you ready, child?" Athena asked.

The young girl sighed deeply and stood up, turning to face the beautiful deity. "Yes. I mean, I think so," she said, nodding her head in a reserved but determined fashion.

The goddess smiled kindly. She could see Pandora was nervous and patted her shoulder encouragingly. "It will be alright, Pandora. I have spoken to my friend. He is expecting you."

"Where?"

"Pfft, let him worry about that," Athena said. "All you need to do is travel north into the hills. Just like you have done so many times before. Enjoy your time there. I cannot say when you might return so savour it, my girl."

Pandora narrowed her eyes in mild confusion. She didn't really understand what to do, but she didn't wish to appear foolish or ungrateful so she accepted the instructions and nodded. "I almost forgot," Pandora added, "I brought this here for you." Out of her tunic she pulled the piece of vase that had encouraged her to begin this rather unexpected journey. With a sorrowful smile, Pandora lightly traced the carved signature of her father's name and offered it to Athena.

Athena looked at the gift and then at the young girl standing in front of her. "That is a very precious thing, one which I believe would be of better use remaining in your possession." The goddess gently folded the girl's hands closed around it.

Pandora nodded, feeling a lump catch in her throat. "Thank you for everything you have done, Athena. I… I don't know what I would have…"

The goddess put a reassuring hand on the girl's shoulder. "Don't fear, dear one. We shall be watching. Remember, you are strong, Pandora, you can achieve anything."

From behind her back, Athena revealed a bag full of provisions and gave it to Pandora. "Just a few things to help you on your way."

Pandora took the offering gladly and gently slipped the piece of vase inside. As she turned to begin her journey, she realised there was one thing she hadn't thought to ask. Perhaps she had been too afraid to. "Athena, who was he?"

"Who was who?"

"The… the man that did this?"

The goddess's eyes went dark and cold. No sooner had the expression arrived than a dazzling smile flashed across her face and she returned to her normal self. For the first time in her presence, Pandora felt frightened. It unsettled her, and she wished she hadn't asked.

"That is a question for another day, darling girl. Come, you must be getting on. He'll be waiting."

Pandora decided it would be best not to press her further. She smiled, appreciative of Athena's kindness, gathered her belongings and began her walk down the steps of the temple towards the hills.

~

Pandora knew the land so well, it was comforting to be going somewhere she felt at ease. She strode quickly past the lines of cypress trees, admiring their stalwart nature. It was a beautiful day, the air was light and a calm breeze drifted lazily through the leaves. When the trees that flanked the path ended, Pandora turned away from the temple road and began her walk into the woods heading north. The grass was soft underfoot and the thick canopy of trees provided welcome protection from the sun. In the safety of the forest, she soaked up the familiar surroundings. With all that had happened in the last twenty-four hours, she felt relieved to see that at least a part of her childhood had remained unspoiled. Unsure of exactly where to go, she decided to make her way to her favourite spot as it was in roughly the right direction. She knew it wasn't far – a couple of hours' walk was all it would take.

Pushing her way through the dense foliage, Pandora felt comforting relief as she passed through the bushes into the clearing. It was a small glade in among the chaos of the forest, the floor littered with white clover and chamomile. As she walked, the beautiful snowy flowers gave off a soothing aroma that enveloped her in a veil of nostalgia. The thing that Pandora loved most about this place was its most ancient resident. In the middle of the clearing stood a redbud tree. Its blossoms had just come into season. The bold pink petals hung like precious gemstones adorning every branch. The tree was so old that with every passing year, the flowers had slowly travelled further south, so much so that now hardly any of the trunk was visible. It was a magical place, a magnificent sight that filled Pandora with hope and comfort.

She made her way over to the tree and dropped her bag at its base. Placing her palm reverently on the trunk of the tree, she felt the delicate blossoms caress her skin. Taking refuge in the tranquillity of the moment, Pandora let her thoughts wander. She was anxious about what might lie ahead of her, what trials she might face, who she might encounter. She thought of her father and all that she had lost. The sorrow in her heart weighed so heavy, she didn't know if it would ever lift. In the haze of reflection, she almost didn't notice the sudden flurry of falling petals that had begun to dance gracefully on the wind. She sat down and eagerly unwrapped her bundle to take out some of the food that Athena had packed.

Not knowing what she was supposed to do, Pandora didn't see any harm in stopping to rest for a while. Tearing off a chunk of bread, she eagerly popped it in her mouth and began stretching out her limbs. She massaged her calves to prevent any scizing that might slow her down and rested her head against the tree trunk. Enjoying the shade, she began to doze lightly. Before she could drift off completely, she was woken abruptly by the sound of a twig breaking. Eyes darting around the clearing, she couldn't tell where the noise had come from. Pandora thought it best to collect her things in preparation for a quick departure. She could now hear a rustling in the undergrowth directly in front of her no more than a hundred yards away. Whoever or whatever it was must be near. Before she could move, Pandora heard a coarse angry voice shout from the thicket.

"Bloody thorns. Walking all bloody day, hotter than Apollo's backside – gods damn these thorns. Oh Zeus' thunderbolt!"

Quite to Pandora's surprise, a man fell rather ungracefully through the bushes and staggered a few steps into the clearing before righting himself with a very satisfied smile, holding his arms out in mock celebration.

"No one can say I don't know how to make an entrance, eh?"

Pandora stood, feet firmly apart, ready to run if necessary. She was totally confused by the man's introduction. In fact, seeing another human being after what had come to pass the day before took her completely by surprise. She stood still and waited for him to speak again; meanwhile, he awkwardly adjusted his belt and cleared his throat in such a vulgar manner that Pandora had to seriously think about keeping her lunch down.

The intruder marched abruptly over to the girl with so much force in his stride he practically shook the ground as he walked. As he got closer, Pandora could see his features more clearly. His unkempt hair was black as a raven, slicked back with sweat. Every so often the light caught on a silver strand tucked in among the dark ones. His beard was partially shaved, leaving a thick ring around his lips and chin. As someone who must be an adventurer of some sort, he looked well qualified in terms of age and build. He was in fact, in terms of build, enormous. His bare torso was something unlike Pandora had ever seen before – the man looked to be made of bronze, his rippling muscles shining in the sunlight. Scars of battles fought laced his arms and stomach. Around his neck hung a tattered sheepskin cape, and underneath it Pandora could see the faint sparkle of arrow heads, resting in their quiver. *He must be a warrior*, she thought to herself as she felt her pulse quicken.

"Don't fear, little lady," he shouted, raising a palm as he spoke. "I'm just passing through. The name's Polemides, greatest warrior this side of the Aegean." The man flexed his muscles sarcastically, and Pandora couldn't help laughing.

"I'm not afraid," she said, sticking her chin up slightly.

"Oh, is that so?" The man sprang forwards so that they were only a few feet apart. Pandora flinched a little but held her ground. "Hmm, I guess I must be losing my touch," he said with a wry smile.

Raising one eyebrow at her, Polemides circled Pandora, eyeing her up and down. She didn't feel threatened; in fact, his presence was so commanding, she corrected her posture and straightened her back.

"You're a lithe little thing, aren't you? Like a baby bird. I daren't cough in case I blow you away."

Pandora pursed her lips and scowled.

"Ooh, now that is a face. I bet that's got you into trouble before. Look, little lady, I don't suppose you've seen a man come through here at all? I've been searching all gods damn day for him. The only tracks I found were yours."

"No, I'm sorry, I haven't seen anyone."

Polemides looked at Pandora, unable to hide his confusion. "Say, why are you here anyway? I haven't seen another soul for miles and then – poof! – you show up. What's a little lady like you doing all the way out here?"

"I'm waiting for someone. I mean, I think I am."

"Waiting for who?"

"I… I don't know. She told me to—"

The man furrowed his brow. "She?"

Pandora looked down in embarrassment, sure that her words would sound ridiculous. "A-Athena."

Polemides stared for a moment, a look of sheer disbelief on his face. Pandora knew it was crazy to say it out loud. No one like her ever met the gods. No wonder this man didn't believe her.

She waited for him to question her, laugh or call her a liar. The words that came out of his mouth were not in any way what she had expected.

He strode off a few paces and shook his head in an agitated fashion, then looked up and shouted, "I'm going to kill her! Oh that bloody woman. I'm going to kill her!"

Pandora was quite taken aback by the bellowing man. "I'm sorry, I don't—"

"She said a warrior. I was going to train a *warrior*, not look after a gods damn baby bird!" In his anger, the man took a swing at the tree trunk with his gigantic fist as he walked back past it, causing a storm of petals to flutter to the ground, some of which made the mistake of landing on him which only added to his annoyance at the situation.

Pandora looked at him with a mixture of confusion and anxiety. *"You're my trainer?"*

He threw his arms up in frustration, shaking off most of the petals. "Well apparently so, little lady. Damn her to Hades."

"I'm sorry, you don't have to—"

"No, no, come on, come on, grab your things," he ordered, abruptly marching off back the way he had come.

Realising that Pandora was not following, he turned on his heel, crossed his arms and looked at her incredulously. She stared him down, angry at his obvious disappointment. The scowl she had perfected made a reappearance on her face.

Polemides sighed deeply and looked up to the sky. "Look, this is going to go one of two ways. Either you march your tiny self over to me and we walk this journey together or I will carry you. What's it going to be, little lady?"

Thoroughly annoyed by the whole encounter, Pandora grabbed her things and stomped over to the man, the scowl firmly planted on her face. "The petals in your hair really add to your look by the way," she muttered as she barged past him.

Her unwavering attitude made Polemides crack a smile. He shook his head, laughed under his breath and clapped her on the back with such force she stumbled forwards a couple of steps. The man walked a few paces, turned back and pointed an authoritative finger in Pandora's face. "Here's your first lesson: *never* owe a god a favour."

~

Polemides walked in silence, and his large frame and long strides were difficult for Pandora to keep up with. She scurried along behind him, unsure of what to say, the silence between them feeling awkward. She had expected to meet someone eager to train her. His obvious annoyance at their introduction had left her feeling not just uncomfortable but also a little self-conscious. It only solidified her belief that she was unfit for the tasks ahead of her.

"I'm sorry that I'm not what you had expected," she mumbled. "Didn't Athena explain who I am?"

Polemides let out a snort of derision. "She was wise not to. I doubt I would have agreed to it, not that I would actually have had any choice."

Pandora's heart sank. She stopped in her tracks and looked down at her feet. "I told her I wouldn't be any good," she said to herself, clearly just as frustrated at the entire situation.

Polemides turned back towards the girl, his stern expression quickly changing to concern when he realised how his words had affected her. He shuffled awkwardly. "Don't take it to heart, little lady. I didn't mean to upset you. I just…" He sighed, clearly floundering for the right words. "I can shout at men all day, instil fear into even the bravest warriors. I've trained men for years." He laughed as he pointed towards Pandora. "Never in all my time, however, have I been given a candidate quite like yourself. My methods are harsh but they get results. I fear it will be too much for a little bird like you." He turned back and continued to walk.

Pandora mulled over his words for a moment before clenching her fists and shouting out to the man, "Well, if you've never trained someone like me, how can you know that to be true?"

Polemides laughed quietly. "You have a point there, girl," he said, clearly impressed by her determination. "I guess this will be training for us both then." He beckoned to her with encouragement. "Come on, little bird, we're setting a good pace. We should arrive at the camp just before nightfall."

Stomping her way through the undergrowth, Pandora passed him and stuck up her nose in jest. "I'm Pandora, by the way," she called back to the man nonchalantly.

"Well, Pandora, let's see if you can keep up with me," he taunted as he set into a jog to try to resume his lead.

Her years in the forest had been priceless preparation. Pandora had grown accustomed to the ways of the woods, careful to avoid bare roots and stones, and now that they were in the densest part, Polemides with his large frame struggled to keep up with her. She was exceptionally nimble on her feet, like a doe, gracefully scampering along an invisible path. Despite his initial irritation, Polemides was won over by her agility and determination. He was not used to such a restrictive environment and was impressed by how well she knew the terrain. The journey took them all day. During their brief moments of rest, Pandora explained her situation to Polemides. The story surprised him and he was taken aback by what she had been through. The longer they walked, the more they spoke. Pandora began to find herself becoming comfortable in his company. She was actually starting to enjoy having a companion to travel with. Despite his lack of interaction with women, she thought him to be kind. In some ways, he reminded her of her father and it gave her much comfort being with someone like him. After a steep incline, the pair arrived at the top of a crest and looked out over the canopy.

Polemides pointed to a break in the trees. "There, nearly home. Don't worry, little bird, not long now."

Pandora could see what looked like a small village: an oval of wooden buildings surrounding a large arena of dirt. When she squinted, she could just make out the outlines of people. "I didn't realise there would be others," she said, genuinely surprised.

Polemides put a reassuring hand on her shoulder. "You're not the only one who needs training." He chortled. "The place we are going is a school by any other name. Myself and a few others set it up a long time ago. We've had all sorts come through our gates, but no one quite like yourself."

Self-doubt crept back into Pandora's mind. She tensed slightly and her lips formed a slight frown.

Polemides smiled and spoke as sympathetically as he could manage. "You can do this, little bird. Anyone gives you trouble, just scowl at them and stomp your foot. It certainly scared the life out of me."

Pandora rolled her eyes before marching on towards the camp.

~

The gates were made of enormous sharpened logs, tied together with rope thicker than Pandora had ever seen before; they opened with a creak as the pair walked up to them. A man shouted a greeting at Polemides from atop the gatehouse and Polemides waved a hand in recognition. Pandora, now consumed with nervousness, walked close behind Polemides, desperate not to attract any attention. As subtly as she could, she marvelled at the sights in front of her: men of all shapes and sizes were going about their daily life as warriors in training. Some sparred with swords in the middle of the arena, while another walked past her cheerfully, carrying two huge jugs of water. A man, sitting by the steps of one of the huts, was so enormous Pandora wasn't even sure he was a man, rather a giant. Looking up, his eyes met hers and he gave her a hearty smile and a wave. Pandora giggled and waved back.

Spotting the interaction, Polemides nodded. "Gigamn, he's a gentle soul. Not a warrior by any means."

"Is he—"

"A Giant? Yes," Polemides said casually. "A fine friend to have, though by the gods, don't let him hug you."

He marched her through the throngs of men that had now begun to gather at the spreading news of Pandora's arrival. Polemides walked her through the training ground and they came to a halt at the door of the largest building. Polemides walked up the steps of the building and turned to face the men who had now gathered in a crowd at the bottom of the steps.

"Friends," he said with bold authority, "allow me to introduce our newest recruit. This is Pandora." He held his arm out towards her. "She has been sent to me by Athena. This girl's journey will be long and she is to face many things that few of you could even begin to dream of. She has come to us to learn the skills of war. I suggest that for the duration of her stay, you lot make her feel welcome, or else you can take it up with the goddess herself."

Polemides' words were met with silence. The crowd of men stared at Pandora, murmurs of confusion and disapproval rippling through them. She looked at Polemides with uncertainty as he stared ferociously at his students.

From the back of the crowd, Gigamn pushed his way forwards through the men, standing twice if not three times the height of those around him. Growling under his breath he scanned the crowd, until they were silent. With a roar, he punched his fist into the air, and separating the three syllables, called out her name, "PAN-DO-RA!"

This encouraged others to do the same. Soon the entire throng of men were cheering and clamouring in enthusiasm, welcoming the new recruit. Polemides let out a long, subtle sigh of relief.

He whispered under his breath, "Well, that went better than I expected."

Pandora smiled and waved in thanks at Gigamn who was now clapping, a dopey smile on his face.

Polemides opened the door behind him and beckoned to Pandora to follow him. As he did so, he shouted over the sounds of the men, "Second lesson: always make friends with a Giant."

THE DANCE

Pandora squinted as she adjusted her eyes from the daylight to the muted darkness of the large hall. Entirely made of wood, the building seemed particularly utilitarian in its construction. Thick columns ran in two parallel lines the length of the room and the roof beams were narrow and closely packed. Pandora heard Polemides shut the door behind her and felt herself relax a little as he did so, letting out a long sigh of relief.

"I'm sorry," she said, "I guess I wasn't expecting to meet so many people."

"You've had a long journey," Polemides said. "It's alright to be tired."

"But I have so much further to go," she said, feeling overwhelmed by the situation.

"Well, yes that's true, but that is not tonight, little bird. Let tonight be an introduction to your new home."

Pandora noticed that the darkness in the hall was easing. Spotting small flickers of light appear, she saw that candles were being lit around her. A herd of young boys ran around playfully, seemingly in competition with each other to see who could light the most.

"May I remind you boys that this hall is made of *wood*," Polemides chastised. "Won't be any good earning the right to train if you set the bloody place on fire first."

Pandora snorted under her breath and Polemides rolled his eyes, shaking his head at the young apprentices.

"They get sent here at a young age," he explained, "usually from families who can't afford to keep them. I take them in and look after them until they are ready to train. Then, they can go and make a name for themselves."

Pandora was surprised at her mentor's generosity.

It must have shown on her face as Polemides said, "I don't do it for nothing, mind you. They do the work that is necessary to keep this school functioning. It is a mutually beneficial understanding. Very few miss the life they had before this became their home."

There was a part of Pandora that envied the boys. She wondered if she would pick up the training quick enough or if she was too late starting. Again, she must not have disguised her feelings well as Polemides patted her reassuringly on the back.

"Don't fret, little bird. The men will be coming in any minute for the evening meal. Enjoy this night – get to know people. Then, in the morning your training will begin in earnest."

~

As soon as the last word left his lips, the doors flew open and the rabble of warriors piled in. Led by Gigamn, the men carried in tables and stools, laughing and joking as they set them down in groups around the outside of the hall. A ring in the middle left bare, each warrior found his place among his comrades and together they eagerly awaited their food. Polemides gestured to Pandora to join the company as he made his way through the crowd, catching up on the events of the day.

She glanced around her at the throng of men and felt incredibly out of place. They seemed loud and unruly, a rather intimidating bunch, and she had no idea how to fit in. As she felt herself start to become overwhelmed by the whole ordeal, a delicate finger tapped her on the shoulder. Spinning round, Pandora was surprised to see a man who looked just as out of place as she was.

He was the same height as her and nearly as slender. His face was soft and his jawline a delicate oval. He had enormous eyes like discs of blue agate which sat either side of a gracefully thin nose. The man smiled at Pandora and jumped up and down a little in excitement which caused the mop of golden ringlets on his head to dance quite endearingly. When he spoke, his voice was surprisingly beautiful.

"How very exciting," he sang. "You can't imagine how pleased I am that you're here." The man held out a hand in greeting and Pandora took it with a slightly confused smile on her face. "So very lovely to meet you, Pandora. I'm Orpheus. I do believe your presence has rather taken the attention away from me and for that I thank you."

"Oh, I, well—"

"Come sit, sit with me." His voice leaped an octave in enthusiasm. "I'll introduce you to the rabble."

Orpheus took her abruptly by the arm and began marching her over to a table at the far corner of the hall. Once closer to the table, she spotted two unclaimed stools in among a group of young men already deep in conversation, two of them clearly in a heated debate. Pandora thought them so similar in build and face that they must surely be related. As they approached, the two men stood up, fuelled by their discussion.

"I'm telling you, if the sun hadn't got in my eyes, I'd 'ave 'ad 'im."

"Ha! You wouldn't have hit him if he was two feet in front of you."

"Oh yeah? Want to try your luck, eh?"

The larger of the two men grabbed the other in a playful headlock which resulted in an eruption of laughter from the table.

"Gentlemen, will you *please* behave yourselves," Orpheus chimed in, clearly embarrassed by his friends' behaviour. "We have a new addition. Make room, you ugly savages." He stuck his tongue out playfully and the two men sat back down, not forgetting to poke each other in the ribs as they did so.

"Calm down, Orpheus," one of them teased, "it's all in jest."

"Hmm, well, most of it anyway," the other retorted with a final quick jab to the gut.

More laughter consumed the table. Pandora couldn't help but get swept up in it and began to laugh too.

Orpheus turned to her with a slight look of disapproval. "Oh really now, I thought you might be slightly more civilised company for a change."

The man sitting next to one of the empty stools beckoned welcomingly to Pandora. "Don't mind this lot, they're loud but harmless."

Pandora sat eagerly, only now realising quite how exhausted she was. "Thank you, I'm—"

"Pandora? Yeah, I think we got that already," he said, smiling and nodding his head towards Gigamn across the hall. Pandora lowered her head, a little embarrassed.

Orpheus claimed the last stool, waving dismissively at the man that had just spoken. "This is Perseus – he's here because of a rather unfortunate run-in with a less than pleasant king."

Pandora nodded her head in greeting to her new acquaintance, and Perseus mirrored the gesture before remarking with a smile, "Little tip: always bring a horse to a wedding."

Not quite sure what to make of this, Pandora thought it best to just nod in agreement which caused Perseus to laugh heartily. Unlike Orpheus, he was the epitome of a warrior. His jaw was strong and square, his light brown hair was cropped short and it had clearly been a few days since he had last shaved. Even sitting, Pandora could tell he was tall and broad-shouldered. She was impressed by the magnitude of his presence.

"So, what brings you to train then?" he asked, his tone cheerful.

Pandora thought for a moment, unsure of how much to divulge. "Athena sent me." she explained nonchalantly.

Perseus raised an eyebrow. "So we've heard."

"I guess you could say I'm going to be assisting her with somewhat of a crisis." Pandora mumbled the last couple of words a little. She could see Perseus hold back a smile.

"Well, I think a crisis worthy of the gods' attention trumps most of our reasons."

"I *told* you she was important," Orpheus chimed in, clearly pleased that he had commandeered the newcomer.

"Have you been here long?" Pandora asked the question openly to the table.

"Most of us just come here when we're a bit out of practice," Perseus explained. He pointed a finger to one of the men sitting across from him. "Or when we need to come get some sleep apparently."

The man he had pointed to rubbed his dark-circled eyes and yawned. "What did you say, Perseus?"

Pandora looked at the man intently. She recognised his face but couldn't place him. "I'm sorry, do I know you?"

He looked at her with slight confusion. "I… I don't think so. Where do you hail from?"

Pandora felt a slight twinge in her heart as she thought of home. "Kyparissi, it's a small trade port on the eastern coast, only a few hours away by foot."

"I'm sorry," he mumbled, "I think you might have me confused with someone else – never been there before." The man fell silent again. He appeared close to drifting off, before shaking his head a little and blinking harshly.

Perseus coughed under his breath. "Don't mind, Echion. He's a quiet one. Went home to help with the family business but I guess he missed this life. Half the time, however, it's a struggle to keep him awake."

"Oh, okay," Pandora said, not really concentrating. She couldn't shake the feeling that she knew the man but she decided to leave that thought alone for a while. She was only just beginning to feel comfortable and the last thing she wanted to do was hound her new friends trying to figure out something like that. Perseus nodded towards a door at the back of the hall.

"Looks like food's up."

The rabble of young boys began running around the room with cups, bowls and plates, dodging and weaving their way through the raucous men. Not long after, a group of older men and women appeared carrying jugs of wine and huge platters of meat and bread. The smell of the food was met with a hearty cheer from the awaiting warriors.

Pandora suddenly became aware of just how hungry she was. It had felt like an age since she last had a proper hot meal, and her stomach let her know it was eager to eat.

"Who are those people?" she asked, nodding towards the servers.

"Oh, most of them are parents of past and present warriors," Perseus explained. "If they have no duties at home, they offer themselves to help here. Polemides does good work raising the young and we all try and do our part. We all want to see this place continue to stand even after we have fallen."

Pandora scanned the crowd to find her mentor who was now sitting at the top table with the other teachers. He appeared to be deep in discussion with an elderly man sitting by his side.

"He's a good man, isn't he," Pandora remarked offhandedly.

"Pfft! Don't let him hear you say that. You'll probably end up doing laps all morning to show you he's not soft," Perseus said with amusement.

The food and drink warmed Pandora. With a full stomach, she felt far more at ease in this new environment. The men tore at the plates like a swarm of locusts. By the time they had finished, the meat had been picked to the bone and the plates practically licked clean. Pandora found conversation soon flowed naturally. They all made her feel so at home, she soon found herself eagerly participating in their discussions. They spoke of their adventures, their skills, and even the occasional run-ins with the gods. The men were all very impressed to hear of Pandora's encounter with Athena. It didn't take very long for her to feel less like an outsider.

When the meal was done, Polemides rose from his chair and held his hands in the air; the room settled and fell silent.

"Friends," he boomed, "I hear you have worked hard today."

A thunderous cheer swept through the crowd. All eyes were fixated on him.

Pandora was impressed by how much his presence affected the men around her.

"I thank you all for welcoming our newest recruit." He gestured towards Pandora's table. "I see you haven't scared her off quite yet. Castor, Pollux, I'm looking at you two." Polemides pointed to the two men who had been fighting when Pandora was first introduced to the table.

She had been right in her assumption that they were related, for as twin brothers, they were constantly at each other's throats but always by each other's side in a fight. They now looked at her with mirrored grins and raised their cups in unison.

"Tomorrow will bring some new challenges," Polemides explained, "however, tonight we will show our new friend the sort of family we are… Tonight, we dance."

This statement was met with deafening approval as the men applauded and cheered eagerly.

Pandora turned to Orpheus. "A dance?"

He smiled slyly back at her. "In a manner of speaking."

Polemides raised his arms up and the crowd fell silent. "Who offers themselves for the first pairing?"

"I do!" a voice boomed out from the other side of the hall. Pandora saw a rugged man with a full dark beard stand as volunteer.

Polemides smiled. "Leitus, of course, come forwards."

The man made his way through the crowd and paced around the empty space in the centre of the hall. He flexed his arms and roared, the crowd cheering in encouragement.

Polemides glanced around at his comrades. "Who shall be the one to dance with Leitus?"

"Polemides," another voice called out, "I challenge Leitus!"

The man who stepped forwards was identical in build to the first. He had white-blonde hair and his beard was plaited into three thick braids.

"Kleitos has accepted the challenge. Come forwards and meet your opponent."

The two men stood like columns opposite each other. Pandora didn't understand what was happening. She had a feeling that her limited knowledge of dancing would probably be of no help here.

Perseus took a sip of his wine and sighed. "You're in for a treat." He turned to look at her. "These two have been at each other for the last month, both arguing who's better. It's about time they settled it."

Pandora looked over at Polemides, who had raised a hand above his head. The crowd fell silent. The two men who had just finished having their hands wrapped stood in the ring, poised in braced positions opposite each other, grimacing.

Polemides lowered his hand. "Dance!"

In a blur of fury, the men ran at each other. Kleitos lowered his shoulder and when they collided, he forced it into Leitus' chest, causing him to stumble backwards. The crowd cheered in encouragement. Shaking his head, the now angered Leitus roared and stepped forwards. With an almighty upward swing of his hand, he struck his opponent under the chin. The impact threw Kleitos off his feet and he landed hard on his back, causing the dust from the floor to billow around him. Hoping to make the most of his attack, Leitus raised his leg and drove it down towards the man but Kleitos had already recovered his senses and rolled to the side before the enormous foot made contact with what was now just the ground. Swiftly, Kleitos picked himself up, took stance and lunged at Leitus, crashing into his left side and lifting him off the floor in a bear hug.

"Good move," Perseus said knowledgeably to Pandora. "He took a spear to the stomach last year. Some would consider it a cheap move but I'm not one of them."

The collision caused Leitus to yell out in both pain and frustration and he struck down hard with his elbow on the man's shoulder until he was released. Landing hard, he stepped backwards and shook his head before bending into a low crouch, his face burning with anger fuelled by the residual pain that still radiated from the old wound.

"How do you know who wins?" Pandora asked with a slight hint of panic in her voice.

"Don't worry," Perseus said before grinning, "you'll know."

Both men were now circling each other, knees bent and arms poised to make an attack. Each tried a few attempts at grabbing the other but all were blocked. Pandora couldn't see how this would ever end – they appeared so evenly matched. With a growl, Kleitos flung himself towards Leitus and both men locked into a grapple. Each had his hands around the other's biceps. They appeared fused together, neither one's strength bettering his opponent's. Pandora turned to see Polemides staring intently at the match. His eyes were narrow with concentration as he studied the techniques of his students.

If she hadn't looked back to the men in that moment, she would have missed it. As she turned, she saw Leitus move his head in towards Kleitos then in a sudden fast movement, he ducked back under Kleitos' right arm, moving himself behind his opponent, wrapped both arms around Kleitos' waist and, letting out a roar, lifted him clear off the ground, throwing him backwards over his head. Kleitos seemed to hang in the air for several seconds with a slightly bewildered look on his face before both men landed hard on the ground. This was met with an eruption of triumphant cheering from the audience. Perseus stood up abruptly and clapped.

Pandora just stared in amazement at the sheer power and skill of the two men. She struggled to process what she had just witnessed. These warriors were like a pack of wolves, training together and eating together, like true brothers in arms. It was incredible to watch the change that happened when they were pitted against one another. Leitus stood and raised his hands in the air triumphantly before offering one out to his opponent. Kleitos, still lying on his back, a little dazed, laughed heartily as he accepted his friend's assistance. Once he was back on his feet, they both made their way to their seats arm in arm, like nothing had happened.

Polemides stood, clapping slowly. "A fine match, gentlemen. So, who thinks they can top that?"

Pandora glanced around to see who would volunteer next. She noticed the crowd moving opposite her and saw a man, like a predator skulking through long grass, slowly appear at the side of the ring. He was very tall and muscular, and had the palest skin she had ever seen – it seemed translucent in its quality. The man said nothing; he simply walked into the middle of the ring and snarled. He was completely bald and had a jagged red scar that ran from his forehead, across his eye, and all the way down to his cheekbone. The scarred eye was completely white while his other eye was a dark brown. As he snarled, Pandora could see the discolouration of his teeth clearly against his pale skin. Something about this man made her feel incredibly uneasy, a feeling clearly mirrored by the men who were now awkwardly silent as they watched the monstrous warrior pace around the ring.

Polemides stared at the man with intense authority. "Very well. Who will take on Phobos?"

The silence was deafening. Men turned to each other in encouragement but none seemed any more comfortable around this man than Pandora did. From her side she heard a sing-song voice chime out, "Oh, I will, me, me!"

Orpheus sprung up, waving his arm erratically in the air, desperate to be noticed. Perseus laughed unsubtly into his cup, spraying wine over the floor.

Polemides shot a piercing look in Orpheus' direction. "Always the wallflower, eh, Orpheus?" He nodded his head as a signal for Orpheus to enter the ring.

Orpheus shot Pandora a dazzling smile and winked before prancing out into the ring.

Pandora grabbed Perseus' arm. "That man is twice his size, he'll kill him."

Perseus coughed, clearly trying to hold back a smile. "Here's hoping."

Pandora frowned but looking at the others around the table saw that they were all laughing under their breath. She felt very much like she was missing the joke.

Perseus patted her arm in encouragement. "Just watch."

As intimidating as Phobos may have seemed, it didn't appear to faze Orpheus one bit. He skipped jovially towards his opponent, circled around him once before settling himself in a feline crouch about ten feet away from him.

Polemides raised his hand once more, and brought it down to signify the beginning of the match. "Dance!"

This time the crowd stayed completely silent. It was as if the entire hall was holding its breath at once. Orpheus swayed lightly from left to right in his crouched position, his fingertips brushing against the dirt, his eyes never leaving his opponent's. Phobos snarled, spit flying from between his teeth. Orpheus grinned brilliantly, and then he pursed his lips, blowing a kiss in his opponent's direction. This action enraged Phobos so much that with a silence-shattering yell, he lurched forwards, arms outstretched. In response, Orpheus darted gracefully towards his match. Moving to the left at the last second, he linked his right arm with Phobos'. This sideways movement combined with his opponent's momentum allowed him to swing his body up and around behind Phobos until he had managed to lock his legs around the man's neck. Still using their combined momentum, Orpheus then corkscrewed his body around Phobos' neck and tucked himself in as he reached the apex of his arc. The force of this caused Phobos to fall into a very ungraceful and uncontrolled roll right over his opponent and straight into the dirt, the top of his head slamming into the floor with a thud. Once Phobos had stopped sliding, Orpheus finished the move by swiftly jabbing two fingers just under the right clavicle and twisted them upwards underneath the bone. This caused Phobos' look to move from surprise at finding himself on the ground to intense pain before, finally, he fell unconscious.

Pandora's jaw dropped. The palpable silence in the room was broken instantly by an eruption of noise from the men. The cheers, yells and laughter were so loud the room practically shook. Perseus whistled through his teeth as he clapped for his friend. The group of men sitting around Pandora all banged their cups on the table and stomped on the floor in celebration of his triumph.

Orpheus bounded gracefully around the circle and then stopped to give a bow, a huge smile on his face as he took in the applause. As he did, two men, both bald and pale like Phobos, skulked through the crowd and, glaring menacingly at Orpheus, picked up Phobos, dragging him out of the hall. Polemides laughed softly under his breath.

"Congratulations, Orpheus, once again you have shown that even those light of foot and weight should be considered formidable opponents," Polemides said, glancing subtly towards Pandora before continuing, "Though, maybe next time try and wait more than ten seconds before showboating."

The men carried on their dancing for the rest of the evening. Pandora watched eagerly as she saw match after match take place. The twins who had been sitting across from her took on five men in one dance, only to succeed quite spectacularly using some obviously well-practised moves. They dispatched each of their opponents with precise teamwork, the last instance of which saw one of the brothers use his twin as a launch pad. He came down with his full weight on the heads of the final two men who couldn't have looked more confused at the now aerial combatant just before being flattened. This move was met with huge amounts of applause and an uncharacteristic yell of admiration from Orpheus who had apparently helped them perfect it.

The later it got, the more wine the men drank and the more hilarious the dances became. Perseus refrained from taking part; instead, he stayed by Pandora's side and talked her through some of the more interesting moves. She enjoyed her time with him and found him kind and light-hearted. She felt an instant connection with him. After a while the dancing stopped and the men turned to more relaxed frivolities. Orpheus – who, Perseus explained, was well known for his beautiful voice – sang a melancholy song about a man whose wife was killed by a snake on the day of their wedding. Whether it was the beauty of his voice or the sadness of the tale, there wasn't a dry eye in the hall. That is except, of course, for Pandora, who dabbed frequently at her eyes with her hand in order to avoid seeming out of place or heart.

After a time, Polemides rose from his seat once more and addressed the crowd. "Friends," he boomed, "tonight has been a fine example of what this school can do. Tomorrow we will start our training early. I suggest you all find yourselves a bed."

The men agreed with nods and laughs before slowly, one by one, they made their ways out of the hall.

~

Polemides shouted towards Pandora's table, "Orpheus, I trust you can assist Pandora?"

"Of course, sir," Orpheus yelled in response. He took her arm gently. "Come on, you, let's get you some rest."

Pandora said her goodbyes to the new friends she had made that evening and followed Orpheus out of the hall. Walking across the training ground, she watched as groups of men staggered back to their sleeping quarters, the air full of conversation and chatter. Her stomach knotted a little at the thought of where she might be going. She had never shared a room with anyone before, let alone a group of warriors.

Orpheus noticed her anxiety and squeezed her hand reassuringly. "Don't worry, we're going somewhere special."

If it had been said by anyone else, Pandora would have felt all the more concerned but Orpheus' smile was so genuine she sighed as she felt her body relax a little.

They walked past several large barracks and heard shouting and singing as the men continued their jovial evening.

Further across the yard, Pandora saw a door fly open and Phobos marched out of what appeared to be the medical cabin, flanked by his two friends, his body language dripping with anger. Pandora stopped where she was and Orpheus cleared his throat as the three men marched towards them.

Orpheus moved subtly in front of Pandora, shielding her from the approaching warriors, and his face turned cold. Phobos came to a halt a few inches from him and, leering down at him, a sickening grin spread across his face.

"Well fought, *little* man," Phobos said in a low hoarse voice, his accent not one that Pandora recognised.

"Oh well, you were a fine opponent, Phobos," Orpheus replied, his tone hard and firm.

Phobos grimaced and spat at the floor. "Next time, you might not be so lucky."

"Well then, till next time." Orpheus spoke confidently, unaffected by the threatening nature of the three men in front of him. Pandora was surprised by his authority as it seemed so far removed from his otherwise light-hearted character.

With a word in their native tongue, Phobos signalled to his friends to follow him and the three of them stepped past Orpheus and walked towards the barracks. Once they were far enough away, Pandora felt her body relax.

"Gods, Orpheus, he looked ready to kill you," she said under her breath.

"He can try," Orpheus muttered darkly before turning to Pandora and linking his arm in hers. "Right," he sang in his familiar soft voice, "shall we get you off to bed, my dear? That's quite enough action for one day."

Pandora couldn't help but laugh at his instant change in character and, nodding in agreement, the two of them set off again.

~

At the far side of the school, Orpheus guided Pandora towards a cabin, much smaller than those she had seen already. It was laced with ivy and the roof was covered in moss. He stopped and waved towards the door. "Your quarters, my lady."

"What, just… just mine?"

"Well, you didn't think I was going to let them put you in with those *animals*, did you?"

Pandora smiled with gratitude. "Thank you, Orpheus. I… I am so glad to have met you all."

Orpheus patted her gently on the head. "Us oddballs have to stick together, eh?"

Eager to sleep, Pandora walked up the steps towards the door and opened it with a creak.

"Everything should be in order," she heard Orpheus call from behind her. "It's one of our guest quarters normally reserved for visitors. We don't often have women come through here, though we always make sure to have provisions for when we do. Well, unless of course the Amazons pay us a visit, but they just tend to take over the entire place. I hope you like it. I, uh, added a few homely touches. Try and get a good night's sleep. I'll see you, bright and breezy in the morning."

Pandora waved from the doorway as her new friend skipped away to bed.

Walking into the little room, Pandora saw what Orpheus had meant. The bed, pressed up against the left-hand wall of the cabin, had a charming bouquet of wild flowers neatly laid on the blanket. A shelf above the window was adorned with a variety of candles that gave the room a warm, inviting glow. In the far right corner sat a small wooden chair upon which had been laid a variety of clothes as well as the parcel of her belongings that she had brought with her to camp. As she checked through her belongings, Pandora heard a knock at the door.

"We're lucky you came, to be honest," a voice spoke gently from behind her. "We were all getting a bit sick of the flowers on our beds."

Pandora turned to see Perseus standing on her doorstep.

"He is so very kind," she said as she stroked the petals.

Perseus nodded in agreement. "Yes, he is. I know he seems like a rather frivolous character but there's more to him than you might think. You wouldn't know it by looking at him but he's been through a lot. He finds it easiest to let it out through song. I think that makes him stronger than all of us put together."

Pandora looked down at her feet. "I can relate to that." She thought back to the song he had sung at dinner and replayed the tragic story in her head before turning to Perseus, eyes wide. "Wait, you mean…"

Perseus nodded. "His bride, his loss – that was his story."

Pandora clutched a hand to her heart. She couldn't believe that a man who had experienced so much pain could be so positive. In a way, it made her hopeful that she would one day be able to manage her pain as well as he did.

Perseus glanced at her with mild concern. "I wish you would tell me more of your story. I feel you have a lot to say, though something makes me think you haven't quite found the right words yet."

Pandora sniffed. "Mmm, something like that."

The pair of them stood for a moment in silence before Perseus clapped his hands together awkwardly. "Right, well, we can leave that for another day then. I better get some rest. I have a feeling I'm probably going to be the one showing you the ropes tomorrow." Feeling he had outstayed his welcome slightly, Perseus turned briskly and walked back towards the hall.

"Goodnight, Perseus."

He heard the light voice travel across the air towards him and smiled in relief. Without turning around he called back, "Goodnight, Pandora."

SABOTAGE

Sleep came quickly to Pandora but it wasn't long before the nightmares started. Tossing restlessly, she clung to the sheets as she dreamed. She found herself back in her home, surrounded by the blazing fire, stumbling desperately as she tried to find her way out. The voices from her memory were agonising: her father's cries, the sound of her panic, all consumed by the hoarse rasping laugh of the con man. His voice echoed menacingly and the more she struggled, the louder his laughter became. Falling to the ground, Pandora crawled across the floor, through the flames and debris towards an open door. In the doorway stood the outline of a man. As she dragged herself towards him, the voice of the con man rang in her ears.

"You killed him – you killed them all."

"Stop this, please. My father… where's my father?"

"So many will die – all will be consumed."

"Please, why are you doing this? Who are you?"

No matter how far she crawled, the doorway and the figure never got closer; she held out her hand but he was beyond her reach.

"Please, help me."

"You could not save him. You will not save them. Wake up and realise the truth."

"No, help, please!"

"Wake up, wake up…"

"WAKE UP!"

Pandora was jolted awake by a firm grip around her shoulders. The room still dark, she could just make out the features of Orpheus as he shook her vigorously.

"O-Orpheus? What's—"

"You have to get up, Pandora. We have to go."

"Go?"

"There's a fire, Pandora, there's a gods damn *fire*. You have to get up."

Orpheus dragged her roughly out of bed and pulled her towards the door. Lurching down the steps, Pandora's eyes widened as she came to her senses. The school was in complete chaos. Men were running in every direction, shouting instructions at each other as they moved. She could see Perseus leading a group of warriors towards the great hall which, to her horror, was now billowing thick, black smoke. Pandora froze and her heart dropped to her stomach as the familiar swell of panic began to wrap itself tightly around her body. Orpheus pulled her arm, trying to get her to follow him but she couldn't move.

"Pandora, we need to get you to safety. I need to get you away from here."

His words were muffled in her ears and she stared blankly into space as he shouted at her. She stood in that moment for what seemed like an eternity, unable to process what was happening; she could do nothing. Orpheus shook her desperately, and with incredible effort, she finally managed to turn her head and meet his gaze. His face was white with concern. She could see his mouth moving but the words that came out sounded distant and faint. As she tried to decipher what he was saying, a voice in her head called to her softly.

"Pandora?"

The sound made her flinch. It was her father's voice, his soft, loving tone making her heart ache.

"Pandora, you can help them."

She turned to look at the flames, watching the men run with buckets of water, desperate to try and stop it engulfing any more of the hall.

"Remember who you are, my girl, remember what you are... Help them."

"Help them…" Pandora mumbled incoherently, before pulling herself out of her panic and nodding to Orpheus. "We have to help them," she cried abruptly and began racing towards the hall.

"No, wait! I have to get you to safety," Orpheus called after her but she didn't stop. She ran past the men, towards the flames with determination. If this had anything to do with what had happened to her home, she wasn't going to just stand by and watch.

As she got closer to the scene, she scrambled through the men to try and find out what was happening. The blaze was intense and despite their best efforts, they were struggling to fight it. Feeling a grip around her wrist, Pandora turned to see Perseus looking at her with worried anger.

"What are you doing?" he said, his tone harsh as he shot an exasperated look at Orpheus. "I thought I told Orpheus to get you out of here!"

"You try stopping her," Orpheus said defensively.

"I'm not running – I can help," Pandora shouted, surprised by the boldness in her voice.

Perseus was about to argue when he was distracted by cries of anger and disbelief from the men. Turning to the hall, they saw two figures emerge from the doorway. Carrying enormous torches, out walked Phobos and one of his followers, swords raised, snarling grins printed on their faces.

Polemides stepped forwards from the group of warriors and bellowed, "How *dare* you desecrate this place? Lay down your weapons!"

Polemides' words were met with cruel laughter from the two men.

"Step aside, old man," Phobos roared, "before I cut you down where you stand."

All around her, Pandora heard the noise of swords being unsheathed as the warriors prepared to protect their teacher and their school. She couldn't believe that two men would be so foolish to take on an entire army of soldiers.

Polemides stepped forwards and held his hands out to caution his men. "Pollux, Castor, help me see to these criminals. Perseus, take the men and do what you can to stop this fire spreading. We may have lost the hall but I will be damned to Hades before I let this school fall."

With confident smirks, the twins walked forwards and flanked their mentor, weapons drawn readily, eager for blood.

Perseus shouted orders to the men around him, "You heard what he said, MOVE," and the majority of them left to try and contain the fire. A few men remained, hands on their swords, ready to step in to assist their mentor if necessary.

Orpheus tugged at Pandora's arm. "We have to go, Pandora."

She shrugged him off. "We can't leave Polemides. I won't leave."

Her eyes burned with such ferocious determination, Orpheus knew there was nothing he could do.

"Alright, but stay back," he said through gritted teeth. "You'll do more harm than good if you get in the way."

With the burning hall behind them, Phobos and his partner stepped forwards and lowered themselves close to the ground, readying for the fight. The terrifying man spat on the ground and beckoned to Polemides to attack.

When he didn't move, Phobos sneered at him. "You will be but the first to fall. The earth will turn red with the blood of those who stand in our way."

He pointed his sword towards Pandora and the men with a twisted smile before running towards Polemides, his blade trailing behind him. He swung it up in attack at the last minute, hoping to surprise his opponent. Polemides, however, was ready and bent low, blocking the assault with his shield. Pushing his weight behind it, he threw Phobos off balance before lunging towards him. He moved his sword with well-practised precision, each move executed with skill that could only have been acquired from years of experience. At his side, Pollux and Castor met with the other man, their weapons a blur of movement. Phobos and his ally fought relentlessly, like cornered wild animals, fuelled by rage. Pandora watched as the fight became more and more intense. She wanted desperately to intervene but she knew there was nothing she could do.

Phobos screamed in rage, pushing his body forwards, and thrust his sword towards Polemides. With superb reflexes, Polemides anticipated the move and spun away from the attack; his blade extended, it sliced through the side of Phobos' thigh. With another carnal roar, Phobos staggered backwards but the wound only made him more ferocious and he charged at his opponent again. Their swords clashed against each other, the sound of metal on metal cutting through the noise of the crowd as Polemides blocked attack after attack. Pandora had never seen anything like it. The way they moved, the aggression in their fight was more powerful than anything she could have imagined. The two men drew back from one another before Phobos once again initiated an attack. Simultaneously, the two men locked swords, but Polemides clearly had better footing and pushed Phobos back, then drove his foot into the man's chest, causing him to fly backwards. As Phobos landed in the dirt, he heard the unmistakable sound of metal sliding through flesh. He turned his head to see his ally, pinned against one of the log piles by Pollux, as Castor drove his sword through the man's stomach until the blade became lodged in the wood behind.

"Brother, no!" Phobos screamed as the man slumped, his body held up by the blade. Now blind with rage, Phobos lurched to his feet and lunged desperately at Polemides, who deflected the uncontrolled attack with ease, and responded by slamming the hilt of his weapon on the side of the man's skull, causing him to once again fall to the ground. The twins reformed ranks at their mentor's side and the three men closed in on their enemy. Rising to his knees, Phobos recognised defeat and threw his sword to the ground. He stared at the men with unrelenting hatred.

"You will not win," he said, spitting a mouthful of blood at them.

"It's over, Phobos," Pollux shouted. "Look around you, there's no escape."

"You cannot win," Phobos retorted as he turned to stare at the crowd.

Pandora felt his eyes bore into her and anxiety once more tightened its grip around her throat. He only looked at her for a moment but the smug, knowing expression on his face frightened her.

"What's he talking about?" she whispered to Orpheus.

"I… I don't know." His brow furrowed in concern as he watched.

Polemides stepped forwards and bent down until his face was inches away from Phobos', staring at the man with authoritative intensity. "Go," he said, his voice low and dark, "leave here and do not ever return."

"Sir, we can't let him go. He—"

Pollux tried to argue but was silenced with a wave of his hand.

"You can't even kill me?" Phobos snarled. "You are naive and weak, old man. There is a storm coming, a darkness that will consume you all."

"Then we shall defeat you then too. Now go."

Polemides' authoritative voice echoed through the air. When the man didn't move, Polemides picked him up by the scruff of his neck and dragged him towards the gates. The gates were opened and with a growl, Polemides threw Phobos out of the school.

With one final glare, Phobos stared at the men and laughed menacingly before staggering away into the forest. After a few moments, Polemides whistled through his teeth and a young man ran towards him. A few whispered words were spoken and the man shot off through the gates.

~

Pandora was about to question the young man's exit when she felt a strong grip on her shoulder and turned to see Perseus, his face contorted with frustration and anger.

"Gods damn it, Pandora, what are you still doing here?"

It was clear he had been trying to stop the fire: his face and arms were covered in soot and ash, his brow dripping with sweat.

She shrugged his hand off her shoulder and scowled. "Why can't I stay? I can help."

"We've got it under control. You have to go, it's not safe here. Polemides ordered me to protect you – you *must* go."

Pandora wanted to argue but could see from his expression that he wasn't going to let her stay there and help. With a reluctant sigh, she turned and followed Orpheus away from the hall, hearing Perseus bark orders at the men.

She looked at Orpheus who gave her a reassuring nod. "They'll be fine, there's really nothing you can do, the men can handle it. You need to be kept safe. Polemides was very clear we are to protect you."

Pandora rolled her eyes but accepted that she couldn't do anything to change their minds. She walked a few paces further and stopped. Something had seemed off about what had happened. The fight happened so quickly, it almost seemed too easy.

"You will not win," she muttered under her breath.

"Hmm?" Orpheus replied, clearly eager to get Pandora away from the chaos.

"That's what he said to Polemides. 'You will not win.'"

She studied the school, watching the men running around her, all directing their attention at the burning hall. A thought flashed through her head from the night before.

"There were three of them," she whispered.

"What?"

"When they came at you after the dance, there were three of them. Where's the third? What if that was a distraction?"

She scanned the scene, narrowing her eyes as she searched for the third man. Out of the corner of her eye, she saw a thin trail of smoke coming from further back, behind the hall.

"What's over there?" She pointed at the smoke and Orpheus hissed through his teeth.

"Oh gods, that's the boys' cabin. The children are in there."

Pandora didn't stop to think. She began sprinting towards the cabin, Orpheus in quick pursuit. Once they got closer, Pandora saw the outline of the man as he stepped out of the hut, torch in hand. Skidding to a halt, Pandora and Orpheus watched as he smiled their way before throwing the torch back in through the door, closing it behind him. Orpheus drew his sword and pushed Pandora behind him.

"Go, find some help. We have to get the boys out of there. I'll deal with him."

He strode boldly towards the man before breaking into a run and flying at him with his sword raised. Watching Orpheus' attack, Pandora could see that the bald man was an adequate warrior but it was clear Orpheus was the better swordsman. She thought about running to get the others but she knew there wasn't time to go for help – the cabin was already ablaze and if they were going to save the children, she needed to act fast. Pandora moved slowly to the side to avoid getting embroiled in the fight and once out of reach, she ran to the back of the cabin. She could hear the children inside screaming. Without thinking, she jumped up and pulled herself in through the window.

~

Inside the room, the flames had started to take hold but were still confined to the front of the cabin, blocking the exit. Smoke had filled the air and the children were panicking, but Pandora could see that none of them were hurt and there was still a clear path for them to reach the safety of the window.

"Hey, HEY!" she shouted above the noise. "It's going to be okay but you need to follow me."

The children were afraid, but the oldest, tallest boy ran to her and, beckoning to his brothers to follow, jumped out the window.

"I'll help you get them out," he shouted back up at her.

Seeing their brother escape unharmed, one by one, the children ran to her and Pandora passed them out through the window to the arms of the boy. When no more children came, she scanned the room and saw that it was clear. By this point, the fire had taken hold of the bedding along either side of the room and was spreading rapidly.

When she was sure the room was empty, she jumped back through the window and ushered the children away from the building. Pandora turned to the older boy. "We need to get you all to safety. Run and see if you can find someone to help."

The boy nodded and sped off but nearly crashed into a man running towards him.

"What in Zeus' name are you doing?" Pandora heard a shout and turned to see Perseus storming towards her. "I thought I told you to—"

"The children were in danger. There was another man, Orpheus—"

Perseus held a hand up to silence her. "Orpheus is fine. He disarmed the man but the coward fled. He's gone to track him down."

"We need to get these children away from the fire."

Pandora herded the children into a tight group and Perseus signalled to some of the men to help.

"How many should there be?" she asked, panting a little.

"Fifteen."

Pandora counted each child in front of her and hissed through her teeth. "Gods damn it, there's only fourteen here."

She turned to the cabin to see that it had now been nearly completely engulfed in the flames.

She moved to go back in but Perseus grabbed her arm. "Are you mad? You'll be killed."

She shrugged him off and sprinted back to the hut. She knew what she was capable of but if she was to have any chance of saving that child, she couldn't stand there and explain it to him. Covering her face protectively, Pandora slammed herself into the now burning door, causing it to splinter as the flames burst out around her in an enormous fireball. She staggered through the front half of the cabin, barely even noticing the flames as they licked at her arms and legs. She could hear shouts from outside but didn't have time to worry.

Pandora called out as she walked through the fire, "Hello? Where are you?"

As she made it to the rear of the cabin, she could hear muffled crying but she couldn't see the child anywhere.

She moved quickly towards the sound, the fire closing in menacingly behind her now. In their panic, the children had knocked into the beds, pushing them against the wall. Pandora couldn't see anyone but she could still hear the noise.

"I'm here, where are you? Don't worry, I'm here."

She kept talking as she searched, and following the muffled responses, she dropped to the floor to see a small child stuck behind the bed.

"Oh, little one, don't worry, I'll get you out. You're going to be okay."

Pandora dragged the bed away from the wall and jumped over it to the child. He was a little boy, no more than four or five years old. Petrified by fear, he was unable to move. Pandora gently picked him up and cradled him to her chest, and he grasped her tunic tightly.

The flames had almost completely consumed the hut now. The only way out was the front door and that was too dangerous for the little boy as he was. Pandora scanned the room and saw a large jug of water. She knew it wasn't enough to quench the fire so instead, she poured it on one of the blankets. Talking constantly to the small boy to calm him, Pandora covered him in the wet cloth and with a deep breath in, she ran with him held close to her through the flames and out the doorway into the fresh night air.

Running straight to the children, Pandora put the little boy down and threw off the blanket. She could see that he was breathing but his eyes were closed and he was limp on the ground.

"Help! We need help over here!"

Immediately two older men ran over, picked the boy up and took him away towards the medical cabin. Pandora went to follow but one of the children pulled on her hand.

"Is he okay?" a little voice cried.

"I hope so," Pandora said through staggered breaths before lowering herself to the children's level. "What about you, are you alright? Is anyone hurt?" As she tried to catch her breath, she studied the children. No one seemed to be in pain; they looked shaken and frightened but at least none of them were hurt. As she examined them, she realised that they were all watching something behind her. Turning slowly, Pandora felt her chest tighten for behind her stood a large crowd of men, led by Polemides and Perseus, all of them watching in silent disbelief.

Pandora looked towards the burning building, down at her charred clothes and then back over to the men.

Before anyone could say anything, Polemides walked forwards, his expression dark. Stopping in front of Pandora, he glowered at her sternly before unbuckling his cloak and wrapping her in it. "Walk with me – *now*." His voice was hard and unwavering as he steered her away from the crowd.

Pandora looked back to the group of children anxiously but Polemides gripped her elbow and pushed her forwards.

"They will be fine, keep walking."

Pandora realised that he was directing her back to her cabin. As they walked through the grounds, she could see the men were still frantically trying to put out the dining hall fire.

Polemides noticed her concern. "We may not be able to save the hall but the men have contained the fire so it won't spread further."

~

When they reached her room, Polemides gestured to her to enter and once the pair of them had stepped into the small space, he shut the door behind them. The night air was beginning to make way for morning and the room was just light enough to see in. Pandora went to her bed and sat down. She wasn't sure what Polemides wanted to say but from his body language, she knew it wasn't good.

"Do you have something you want to tell me?" His words were quiet and his tone was dark.

Pandora shifted her weight anxiously. "What… what do you mean?"

"Don't play games with me, girl. I took you in, welcomed you into my family and on the same night we were attacked. Do you really think I'm supposed to believe those things aren't related."

"I had nothing to do with it. I swear!" Pandora stood up, gesturing to the hall. "I'd never seen those men before. You have to believe me."

Polemides walked towards her and glared at her. He stood there for a moment, studying her face before sighing. "I'm sorry, little bird. I just… We've never been attacked like this before and I just don't understand why."

Pandora could hear the concern in his voice.

He rubbed his eyes and threw his arms down exasperatedly. "What you did for the children – you just ran in. That should have killed you."

Pandora bit her lip. "I just… I couldn't leave them. I had to do something." She couldn't bring herself to tell him the truth. She was scared of what would happen to her if they found out.

Polemides was quiet for a moment but stepped towards her and put his hand on her shoulder. "What you did was incredibly brave. I don't know how you survived it but I am glad that you did. Athena was right to choose you."

Pandora breathed a sigh of relief. "Thank you, Polemides. I… I just came here to learn. I swear to you I had nothing to do with those men."

He nodded gruffly and opened her door. "I sent a tracker to follow Phobos."

Pandora had wondered why he had let him go but before she could ask, he answered her. "I don't believe he was working alone. If we can find out to whom he pledges allegiance, maybe we can gain the upper hand. I don't believe this is the last we will see of him. I want to be prepared."

"I want to help. I want to fight." Pandora's voice was small but determined.

Polemides smiled at the headstrong girl. "Well then, we'll have to get started. Once the school is safe, we will begin training. You should get some more sleep. Once we've got the fire sorted, we'll come and get you." he said, heading towards the door. Turning back to her, he smiled. "Next time he comes, I'll let you take the lead." And with a laugh, he left her cabin.

Pandora shrugged off his cloak and changed into fresh clothes. She was about to get back into bed when she heard a faint knock at the door. Upon opening it, she saw a very bedraggled-looking Perseus sitting on the steps of her cabin. Shutting the door behind her, she joined him on the steps. He looked exhausted, his clothes and skin were covered in ash, and his hair was slicked with sweat.

"Are you okay?" she asked softly.

"You are *really* bad at doing what you're told. You know that, right?" He raised an eyebrow at her and smiled weakly.

Pandora smiled and nudged him. "I know. I'm sorry but I just couldn't run away, not when there was something I could do."

"Well, that something was one of the most stupid things I've ever seen."

"Thanks," Pandora said, shifting her weight awkwardly.

"Stupid will only get you so far." Perseus' tone dulled a little and he picked nervously at his hands. "I don't want to see you get hurt. You need to be more careful."

Something about his tone made Pandora's stomach tense. She hadn't expected to see him so affected by her actions and she wasn't sure how it made her feel. With a sigh, she stood up and pointed to the door. "I should probably—"

"Oh, of course, go rest. I'll see you later."

Perseus held a hand up awkwardly before turning away to walk back to the grounds.

The fire had shaken Pandora and as she fell into bed, she felt the weight of anxiety push heavily on her chest. Whoever Phobos was working for wanted to hurt the people around her. She had already experienced so much destruction in the last few days, she dreaded to think that the things could somehow be related, but she just couldn't shake the way Phobos had looked at her. Only one man had looked at her that way before and that man had brought nothing but death. Whatever was going to happen, she had to be ready. The fear of the unknown became too much for her and clutching her blanket, she drifted back into the turbulent dream she had woken from.

Sword & Spear

The next few days at the training school were filled with activity. The fire in the hall was eventually stopped and reconstruction began immediately. The first few days were the hardest. Placing the larger logs was a task, even with the help of Gigamn, but eventually the skeleton of the hall stood tall. There were plenty of people to help with the building of the new structure and Polemides asked Pandora to keep an eye on the children. At first she had felt a little worried that he didn't think her useful but she soon found that she enjoyed spending time with the boys. They had been so shaken by the events of the fire that she felt personally responsible for their care and they followed her instructions religiously. The small boy she had saved was particularly fond of her and once he'd fully recovered from the ordeal he would find any excuse to spend time with Pandora.

Once the larger construction work had finished, Pandora joined in with the work at the hall. Despite the events that had caused the fire, the men were cheery in their work and Pandora spent the days laughing and joking with her new friends. The children became more confident around her and she would frequently be seen chasing them through the grounds, chastising them humorously. The fire had delayed the beginning of her training but Pandora never became restless. There had been no news from the outside world regarding the box or its contents and for now, Pandora was content with helping restore the school to its former glory.

It wasn't long before the refurbishments were complete. The hall stood even greater than before and its construction signalled the beginning of the new training season. After a celebratory feast, full of food, wine and dancing, the warriors staggered back to their beds ready to begin their tuition.

~

After the feast, Pandora woke and was eager to start her training. Making sure to stretch before she stood up, she walked over to her chair and assessed her clothing. A light-coloured tunic had been laid out for her. It was simple in design and fitted her comfortably. She found her comb on the shelf and gently teased the disaster that was her matted curls. In all the frivolities of the night before, she hadn't realised quite how monstrous it had become. What started off as gentle teasing soon turned into frustrated tearing as she desperately tried to tame it. Eventually Pandora got so cross with her hair that she threw the comb onto the bed in frustration. Spotting a thin leather strip dangling from the arm of the chair, she scooped her hair together and tied up the disastrous mass of curls with a firm knot. *If so much as one of you falls out of place, you're all getting chopped off,* she thought to herself.

Stepping out of her cabin, she saw several men already at work, though there were many who seemed barely functioning. Glad she hadn't joined them in their imbibing the night before, Pandora spotted Gigamn sitting on the steps of one of the men's quarters and went over to join him. As she walked towards him, she was greeted with a warm grin.

"Good morning, Gigamn."

"Mor-ning." The Giant's voice was slow and gravelly. Spending most of his time in silence, the few words he said were straight to the point. With an enormous hand, he waved to Pandora to join him. Willingly she climbed the steps and sat herself next to her friend. He had an entire bucket of milk in front of him and Pandora looked at him in mild confusion. Gigamn took out of his pocket a cup that looked comically small in his hands. He dipped it in the bucket of milk and offered it to Pandora.

"Thank you, Gigamn," she said, beaming kindly.

As she drew the cup to her lips, she saw him do the same with the bucket. The Giant began to drink and as he did, Pandora became so fixated on him she entirely forgot about her own cup. In a matter of seconds, the bucket was empty. Gigamn turned to his new friend with a look of childlike happiness on his face, his beard soaked in milk. Pandora couldn't help but laugh. This caused him to laugh too, the sound of which resulted in several shouts of annoyance from inside the barracks as hungover men tried to get a few more precious moments of sleep.

"Good morning, you two," a silvery voice floated through the air as Orpheus bounded eagerly towards them. "I trust you slept well?"

Pandora nodded. "Oh yes, very well, thank you."

It had taken Orpheus a while to get over the fire. After the fight with the third man, he had chased him into the woods but had lost him. Orpheus prided himself in his tracking ability and his failure that night weighed heavy on his heart. Pandora was pleasantly surprised to see him so cheerful.

Orpheus rubbed his temples. "Honestly, count yourself lucky. Try sleeping in the same room as those brutes. The snoring was so loud I could have sworn I was sleeping next to a cyclops." Orpheus shot a nervous look at Gigamn. "Sorry, big man, no offence."

Gigamn frowned and very slowly lifted himself to his feet. He stood nearly three times the size of Orpheus. Orpheus glanced at Pandora with a look of apprehension.

Gigamn pointed a finger to his own chest. "Not Cyclops. Giant!" He growled so loudly that Orpheus' curls fluttered slightly and he scrunched his face up in response.

"Quite right," Orpheus chirped, a hint of hysteria in his voice. "How very marvellous you Giants are… Um, Pandora, would you mind…"

"Gigamn," Pandora called out in a soft voice, and with one hand she held onto his finger, "he didn't mean to upset you. Orpheus is very sorry." She stared at Orpheus and widened her eyes in encouragement.

After a moment he caught on. "Oh, yes, yes I am so terribly sorry. How awfully ignorant of me. I can be quite chatty, you see, and when I start, sometimes I just tend to prattle on until someone" – Pandora shook her head at him as a signal to wrap it up – "stops me." Orpheus finished with an audible gulp.

Softening at Pandora's touch, Gigamn's expression lifted and he sat down again. With a nod and a grunt, he accepted Orpheus' apology. Unsure whether it was safe to speak or not, Orpheus twiddled his thumbs and whistled.

Pandora smirked. "So, what's first?"

"Ah, we'll be doing sword training first."

"I've never even held a sword before," she mumbled with a hint of apprehension.

"Don't worry, you can be my partner." Orpheus offered his arm. With a wave to Gigamn, Pandora linked arms with Orpheus and he led her over to the training ground. Several men were already stretching and preparing themselves for training. Pandora spotted Perseus among them, stretching his arms, and he smiled warmly at her.

Finding herself a space among the men, Pandora thought it best to begin stretching out her muscles too. She looked around and took notes from what the others were doing and was surprised to see that it wasn't dissimilar to how she stretched every morning. Excitement coursed through her: she was eager and nervous all at once. She had grown close to the men since the fire but this was all new territory. She was terrified she would look a fool. So much was riding on her, she couldn't afford to fail. This was the beginning of her road, a road she wasn't sure she was ready for. She didn't have long to dwell on these thoughts as, finally, she saw Polemides step into view. As soon as he came to a halt in front of the group, all the men stepped over to one side of the ring. Pandora followed suit.

"Right. I trust you are all feeling refreshed this morning." Polemides smirked. His words were met with groans and quiet laughter from the students. "Hmm, that's what I thought."

Pandora could feel her heart beating – this was all so new to her she couldn't help but get carried away with the excitement.

"Today has been a long time coming." Polemides' words were solemn. "You have all excelled yourselves as members of this community. Now, you must prove yourselves as warriors." He shot an encouraging look at Pandora. "We will be starting with the sword today."

One of the young boys brought forwards a barrel of wooden swords. Polemides drew one and rolled it around in his palm. "Often considered a secondary weapon, I have seen many a warrior fall as a result of neglecting his swordsmanship." He began to brandish the sword in a figure of eight pattern. The wooden blade swung with timed precision from one side to the other. He continued moving the weapon as he spoke. "I will not have one of my soldiers die before their time because they didn't receive the proper training." Every so often he moved his wrist so the sword would swing backwards by his side before returning to the figure of eight. "Do you understand me?"

"Yes, Polemides!" The men around Pandora shouted so loudly, she nearly jumped out of her skin.

Polemides caught her eye and raised his eyebrow slightly. There was no humour in his voice now. He was playing his role. She knew she would receive no special treatment in this arena. He had warned her of his training methods and she had been bold in her answer. Now was her chance to prove her worth. He called out once more, "I said, do you understand me?"

This time Pandora was ready. Her eyes hard and determined, she shouted along with the others, "Yes, Polemides!"

Polemides finished cutting the air with a strike sideways, the tip of the blade pointing in the direction of one of the boys. With a nod of his head, he gestured to the boy to hand out the swords.

"Pair up," Polemides ordered.

Orpheus was quick to grab Pandora's hand and she couldn't pretend she wasn't relieved. As eager as she was, some of the men around her looked like they could snap her in half.

She smiled at the boy who handed her the sword. He was the oldest child that had helped her get the others to safety during the fire. He gave her a cheeky smile as he handed her the sword before running off to arm the other men. She felt the smooth wood in her hand, the blade chipped and worn from constant use; it felt light in her grip. Opposite her, Orpheus waved his around with elegant ease. He shot her a concerned look but she nodded her head to convince him she was ready. She wasn't entirely sure he believed her but there was nothing she could do about it. Once all the warriors were equipped, they stood in silence. Polemides took his place in the middle and stared at his pupils. With a wave of his arm, he commanded them. "Begin."

The morning was spent with the sword and Pandora learned to attack and defend. Orpheus was a good partner: he was patient and skilful and happily demonstrated the moves to her, though he did not hold back when it came to putting them into practice. Halfway through the training session, Pandora began to feel the strain in her muscles. Her legs began to shake at the constant movement, though she refused to let it show. By the end of the morning, she was completely exhausted and it took all of her focus to stay upright. Once the session was ended and the swords had been collected back in, the students reformed the line in front of their teacher.

"A satisfactory start to the morning," Polemides acknowledged, "we will break for food. Make sure to get plenty of water. We will begin the afternoon session shortly." He glanced at his newest recruit. She could see from his expression that he wasn't sure if she would be up for it. Breathing deeply, she held her head high, straightened her back and nodded quickly towards him, signalling she wanted to continue. Polemides smiled to himself, proud of her stubbornness and strength.

~

The boys returned to hand out bowls of water and bread. Pandora took hers eagerly, noticing that the child had slipped her an extra piece of bread, and joined her friends under the shade of a tree nearby. The twins were already berating each other.

"You'd have never guessed you'd even held a sword before."

"Oh yeah? I'm sure that was why you were too afraid to be paired up with me."

"Afraid I'd be poked in the eye, sure."

The men laughed heartily and Pandora concentrated on her lunch, drinking eagerly.

"Slow down, there. You don't want to choke," Perseus teased lightly.

Pandora gulped dramatically and stuck her tongue out.

"I must say, you did well to keep up with me, young lady. I won't go so easy on you next time," Orpheus chirped in eagerly before turning to Perseus. "How are you feeling, young man? Looking a little parched."

"Well, I'm not here to relax, that's for certain." He ran a hand through his sweat-slicked hair and flicked it playfully towards his friend. Orpheus let out a sound of disgust.

Pandora tore her bread into small chunks and popped one into her mouth. "What are we doing next?"

"What, not tired yet, girly?" Pollux taunted her with a wicked grin which was met with an unceremonious punch to the arm from his brother. "What?" he yelled defensively. "Look at her – she hasn't even broken a sweat."

Pandora didn't want to highlight the fact that she couldn't actually sweat even if she wanted to, in the same way she couldn't cry. Luckily the twins were more interested in fighting with each other.

"She wielded her weapon a hell of a lot better than you did, brother."

More laughter ensued as the pair of them fought childishly.

"I may not be tired, but someone sure is." Pandora nodded to Echion who was now dozing.

Pollux gave him a whack on the back of the head. "Come on, mate, pull it together."

"What…" he mumbled, rubbing his eyes and yawning. "Hey, what was that for? I was just resting my eyes."

Perseus scanned the training ground and pointed towards the young boys. "Looks like they are setting up for spears."

The apprentices had brought over several straw targets and now a dozen or so straw men stood ready to be attacked.

Orpheus could see the apprehension on Pandora's face. He patted her knee encouragingly. "The first time I held a spear, I nearly fell over when I tried to throw it. Don't worry, this is just the beginning for you. Nobody expects you to become a warrior in a day."

"I can do it." She spoke with such determination that the men around her glanced at each other humorously.

"See" – Castor nudged his brother – "a morning of training and she's already more of a soldier than you."

They were not given long to relax. Pandora barely had time to finish the last of her bread before she heard a horn sound from across the training ground.

The men around her stood up and stretched their limbs.

Perseus offered her his hand in assistance and she took it willingly. "Come on, time to show those two what you're made of." He nodded towards the twins who were now barging each other out of the way.

~

Standing back in line, the afternoon sun was nearly unbearable for the men.

Polemides strode out into the ring, a huge spear in his hand. "I hope by now you all know what we will be working on this afternoon, though I really wouldn't be surprised if some of you were still oblivious." He pointed towards the twins, which was met with sniggers from the cohort. "For most of you, the spear will be your first line of attack." He balanced the weapon in his hand. "It is a powerful weapon, but only when used correctly." Raising his hand up and back, in one swift motion, he threw the spear. With a whistle, it cut through the air and pierced directly through the centre of one of the targets. The men stared at their instructor, simultaneously impressed and intimidated by his skill. Polemides smirked to himself, happy with his throw. "You will practise your form with the weapon. Those of you who are already skilled may begin running through drills."

The young boys began to hand out the weapons again. Several men grunted in appreciation. Pandora quickly realised she was by far the least practised of the bunch as all of these men had seen war in some form. She reached out to take a spear from the boy when her mentor called out. "Not you. You are with me."

This was met with quiet jeers from the men around her which caused her to scowl, her eyes dark with frustration. She didn't understand why she had been singled out. She had already proved she was determined. *Does he think I'm not capable?* She thought, *does he think I can't do this?*

Polemides narrowed his eyes at Pandora and beckoned her to come forwards. She stomped over to him, unable to hide her obvious annoyance. He opened his mouth to speak but became aware that the men around them were clearly eavesdropping.

"I'm sorry, were my instructions not clear? Move!" he yelled, and the men quickly scattered and began training.

Once again Polemides went to speak but Pandora cut him off before he could start.

"I can do this," she said, a little harsher than she had planned.

Polemides replied curtly, "I don't doubt that, little bird." He whistled through his teeth, causing a boy to scurry over with a spear that looked different from all the others. The leaf of the blade was slightly finer and the colour of the wood was a beautiful dark red. Polemides ran the shaft through his hands before handing it to his new student. "Cherry wood," he explained. "It feels different in the hand to the ash that we normally use. I had this made for the daughter of a friend a few years back, designed so that it would not be as intimidating an introduction to the weapon. You should be able to wield this with little trouble. Once you are confident with this, we can move on to heavier spears."

Pandora felt the weapon in her hand. The wood felt strong yet light, smooth to the touch. She could see that it had been made with care. She felt embarrassed for having assumed Polemides' intentions. "I'm sorry, I—"

He rolled his eyes at her with a hint of a smile. "Don't even go there." He pointed towards the men. "Go on, go see Perseus. He'll assist you this afternoon."

Still feeling guilty for her behaviour, Pandora gritted her teeth, nodded and turned on her heel. With her new weapon in hand, she marched back over to the others. Perseus had commandeered a target and was practising his swing. She could see he was very skilled, and the spear seemed to move as an extension of his arm. For such an enormous weapon, he wielded it with graceful finesse.

Perseus saw her from the corner of his eye and turned to face her. His smile was encouragement enough for her to let go of her feelings of embarrassment. He pointed at the weapon in her hand. "First time you've held one?"

She nodded, looking a little sheepish.

"Don't worry," he said cheerfully, stepping to her side, raising his spear up so that it ran parallel to his ear. "You want to hold it so that it is balanced. It should always be pointed where you want it to go."

Pandora followed his lead and drew the shaft up close to her ear. She could smell the warm wood, feel the weight of it in her palm.

"Good." He nodded with confidence. "Keep your knees bent a little. You should feel comfortably weighted, and the movement of the spear should be fluid with your body." He began to move the spear backwards, then forwards in the motion it would travel. Pandora copied him to gauge the feeling of the movement. She could see how it could easily put her off balance if she wasn't concentrating.

Perseus pointed with his other hand to the object in front of them. It was a circular target with a ring painted in the centre. "When you feel ready, use your body to help push your arm forwards. Don't let it dip, keep the shaft straight." He drew his arm back and with impressive force threw the spear. It pierced the target just left of the centre. "Hmm, that would have been much more impressive if I'd hit it dead on." He chuckled light-heartedly.

Pandora smiled. She focused on her stance, feeling the earth beneath her feet. Her knees felt loose and relaxed.

Perseus moved closer to her and gently raised her elbow a little. "Remember, keep it straight. Visualise your target."

Pandora narrowed her eyes, took a deep breath, pulled her arm back and released. She watched, her mouth open slightly as the spear flew gracefully through the air and landed with a light thud about five feet in front of the target. She let out a sigh of frustration just in time to hear the men around her howl with laughter. Furious, she spun around and stared at them with fire in her eyes. They immediately returned to their exercises, not wanting to bear the brunt of her rage.

Perseus chuckled under his breath. "Well, I suppose you could just scowl them to death."

Pandora turned to face him but couldn't maintain her steely glare long enough to make it count. She laughed and shoved him so he stumbled sideways. "I will kill you, I swear," she said in mock anger, her jaw clenched.

"Hmm, well, I'll make sure to just stand further back, that should do it." He anticipated her attack this time and skipped lightly out of the way before she had time to hit him again. One of the boys brought her spear back over to her and she took it begrudgingly. "Come on," Perseus said, "again."

For the most part, Pandora's efforts that afternoon went in a similar vein. She found the spear to be incredibly difficult. It felt so alien in her hand, she couldn't understand how to make it find its target. Time and time again she threw it. A few times she managed to graze the side of the target but it never hit true. She was concerned her efforts were irritating her friend but if they were, he never let it show. He remained positive and encouraging the entire afternoon. It gave her the confidence she needed to persevere. A few times Orpheus came over to offer his advice and once even the twins sauntered past to offer words of encouragement. Pandora realised that the men around her were on her side. Despite their laughter, they wanted her to succeed. Her determination impressed them. She struggled even more when the light began to fade. Perseus turned to Polemides, who nodded in response.

Pandora knew he would end the session soon. She wanted so badly to succeed. Taking a moment to rest her weight on her spear, she took in her surroundings. It really was a beautiful place. Past the walls of the school lay a blanket of lush woodland. The late afternoon sun filtered through the canopy and scattered across the training ground.

It was at that point that Polemides clapped his hands. "Right, you lot, I think we're done for the day. Hand in your weapons, it's time for— Pollux, Castor, for the love of Hades, stop it!"

The twins had somehow managed to grapple each other to the ground and were now scrabbling about trying to gain the upper hand. Polemides rolled his eyes exasperatedly and waved everyone off to the new hall for dinner before marching over to deal with the brothers. Pandora reluctantly handed her weapon back to one of the boys. She was frustrated with what little she had achieved but she was now too tired to care. Perseus patted her on the back.

"You'll get better," he said enthusiastically.

"I guess." She sighed. "Come on, I'm starving."

Orpheus came bounding up and linked arms with her. "You and me both, young lady."

The three of them marched eagerly back with the others to eat and rest.

~

The evening meal was a quieter affair than the night before. Pandora could tell that a lot of the men were clearly suffering from the previous night as the wine was far less free-flowing. She enjoyed each bite of her food. Sitting down, she felt her muscles screaming for rest.

Choosing not to stay late, she took herself back to her room and collapsed with a sigh on her bed. She closed her eyes and bathed in the tranquillity of her own company. She felt the knot of hair against the pillow and knowing that she would regret it if she didn't, she rose begrudgingly from her bed and grabbed the comb from the shelf. Untying her hair, she laboriously picked through the mass of curls until they flowed softly once more, then massaged her scalp and lay back down to rest. She fell asleep to the images of what she had learned that day and in her mind she continued practising the attacks she had learned with the sword, playing out the training session over and over again, ensuring she'd taken it all in.

It wasn't until she was in the deepest realm of sleep that the horrors she had witnessed came back to haunt her once more. She saw the same scene over and over again: the man with his twisted grimace watching her as her whole world decayed around her. She woke several times that night. Each time she prayed for the dreams to stop, prayed to rest, but each time they came back stronger than ever. She wondered if they would ever stop, if anything she could do would ever mend what had happened that day.

Revelations

Despite the challenging start, Pandora soon found her skills began to improve. The days turned into weeks, weeks into months as the daylight hours of the sweltering summer slowly began to shorten. As time went on, the pain that Pandora felt in her heart began to heal. The raw wounds forged from that fateful day that started it all had begun to scar and although it would never stop hurting, she had started to accept how to live with the pain. The school had recovered from the fire and training had now become the sole thought in her mind. Undeterred by the initial struggles she encountered, Pandora had become proficient in her abilities. Her nimble frame aided her in swordsmanship and it didn't take her long to become quick and deadly with a blade. Archery too came naturally to her. From all her years in the woods, she found it the most organic weapon. She would often go out hunting with Orpheus and the skills her father taught her never went unused. They were both experts in exploring the land and hunted well together, regularly bringing home prizes of rabbit and deer for the kitchen, simultaneously honing their skills and strengthening their bond of friendship.

As she had expected, the spear was her biggest hurdle. It took her a long time to understand the weapon. It felt so alien in her hands, and she often grew frustrated with her lack of skill. It was while training in the spear that she bonded with Echion. Perseus and Orpheus did all they could to help her but she knew they were at the school for their own purposes. She felt guilty asking for their tuition and it was during this time that Echion stepped in. As far as Pandora was aware, he was not at the school for any particular reason other than to get some respite. She was awkward in his company at first, thinking that he was not too fond of her though she soon learned this was not the case. He was quiet but friendly and was very accomplished with the spear. Despite their new-found friendship, she never shook the feeling that she knew him from somewhere. She hadn't asked him since their introductions as she figured it would probably come to her eventually.

They spent several hours together, often early, long before camp rose for the morning meal. With his help, Pandora could now not only hit her target but carry out a strike that would result in a fatal blow; even Echion seemed impressed by how much she had improved.

~

Pandora had now settled into a comfortable routine. She woke at sunrise, dressed and tied back her hair. Her small cabin had become a true home to her. Opening the door, she saw Echion sitting on the steps holding two spears, one the cherry wood weapon that Polemides had given her on that first day. She had tried heavier versions of the weapon but felt her skills were better suited to the more nimble spear. Echion's voice was soft and he always spoke with an air of slumber, as if he were only seconds from falling asleep.

"Good morning, Pandora, did you sleep well?"

She smiled at her friend. "Yes, thank you, Echion. How are you feeling?"

He yawned as she spoke. "Hmm?" A quizzical expression formed on his face.

"Never mind." Pandora laughed. "Come on, I feel good about today."

Although she hadn't noticed, those around her saw a change in Pandora's disposition. Her once serious nature had softened as she became more comfortable with her new life. She never lost her determination though, and the warriors commended her for it.

As they walked to the training ground, Echion pulled two chunks of bread from his pocket. Offering one to Pandora, he took a bite out of his own.

"I wish I could be as bright as you in the morning," Echion mumbled sleepily, "I don't understand how you do it."

Pandora smiled and turned the bread around in her hand. "Echion, why… why are you here?" she voiced the thought that had been in her head for a while.

"Hmm, that's a complicated one." He laughed uncomfortably. "I'm sure you can understand."

Pandora nodded in response.

"Let's just say I had gone home with the intention of assisting my father with his business, though it wasn't quite what I thought it would be. I missed my old life and my friends."

"What does your father do?"

"Oh." Echion looked shifty and Pandora was quick to notice him fumble over his words. "Well, I guess you could say he's in the business of acquisitions."

"Acquisitions?"

"Yes… I… look" – he pointed his spear to the sky – "the sun is rising. We should get on if we want to train before the morning meal."

Pandora knew he was holding back. Her curiosity was strong but she could tell that it would do no good to press him.

They trained together until they saw the first of the men begin to move to the dining hall for breakfast. Pandora was pleased with her improvement. She took her spear one last time, raised it to her ear and, with all the force she could muster, threw it towards the target. The weapon sailed elegantly through the air in a silent attack. The leaf-shaped blade tore through the centre of the target effortlessly, as if it had cut through silk. Echion smiled and let his pride at his teaching and her display of skill show with a satisfactory nod.

From the men's quarters, Pandora heard someone clapping. She turned away from Echion with an accomplished grin still fixed on her face to see Gigamn clapping and cheering as he sat in his usual spot on the steps of the men's cabin. Pandora waved eagerly to him, the childlike expression on his face warming her heart.

Echion walked over to the target and with one hand placed on the hay next to the spear, he pulled it out with a slight grunt of effort. He turned to see Pandora's interaction with the Giant and raised a wary eyebrow. "They're quite temperamental, you know?"

Pandora narrowed her eyes in confusion. "Who?"

Echion nodded towards Gigamn. "I'll admit he is gentle compared to others I have met but still, you should be wary of him. They are very difficult creatures to understand."

Pandora looked back to her enormous friend who was now guzzling down his morning bucket of milk. "I understand him." Her voice was hard and defensive. She knew how cautious the others were around Gigamn but she didn't care. She saw him differently. He was such a gentle soul, she knew he would never hurt her.

Echion shrugged, obviously not particularly bothered by her answer.

Pandora clenched her jaw in frustration. "I certainly thought he was nicer than you when I met him."

Echion shrugged. "That doesn't surprise me. You're not the first person to tell me I don't make a good first impression." He grabbed onto Pandora's spear in an attempt to get her attention. "Look, I'm sorry, I didn't mean to offend you. I know you have a good relationship with him. I just… I don't want you to get hurt. You can't get hurt."

Pandora didn't understand. "What do you mean I can't get hurt?"

Echion's eyes darted as he tried to find the words. "Oh, I, uh, I just meant that none of us *want* you to get hurt. You're doing so well here." He clapped her on the back. "We've got used to having you around. Would be a shame for you to get trampled."

Pandora could tell from his tone he was teasing and she let go of her stubborn defensiveness. "Well *I'm* going to go and have some breakfast with my scary Giant friend. You coming?"

Echion rolled his eyes. "I think I'll just go to the hall. Might have time to catch a few moments' sleep." He took her spear and darted off in the direction of the weapons shed. Pandora let go of the comments about Gigamn and went to join him on the steps. She often sat with him for the morning meal. They rarely exchanged words but she felt safe with him. It hurt her to think that others didn't see him the same way she did but she brushed it off. She only had a short while before training was to begin and she needed to rest.

~

Her appetite satisfied by breakfast, Pandora strolled back over to the training ground. She spotted Polemides already there, giving instructions to the gaggle of young boys that followed him everywhere. He turned towards her and smiled curtly. Pandora had grown used to his brash personality. He was not very good at showing his emotions in front of his students. A curt smile was usually the best they got.

"Good morning," he called out, distracted by the boys running around him.

"For the love of the gods, boys, *walk*. You're giving me a headache." The boys slowed to a walk and giggled to each other.

"You know they do it on purpose?" Pandora said.

Polemides grunted. "Well, I'm so glad that I'm such a source of amusement. What do you want?"

"Just wondered what's first today, sir?" Pandora hardened her tone to match her teacher. It was clear he was not in the mood for pleasantries. This didn't bother her; in fact, she found it helped her prepare for her training, and perhaps that was his intention. It actually felt good to be treated the same as the other students.

"Ah, well, today will be a little different." Polemides smiled suspiciously. Pandora raised an eyebrow. "I thought you lot were getting a little soft. It's about time we had some real competition. Get you back into a warrior's mindset."

Pandora didn't like the sound of that. She was confident in her progress but she had never truly faced off with one of her peers. In training there was always an air of caution, especially around her. She knew the men held back – now was her chance to prove she should be taken seriously.

Pandora didn't have time to question her teacher further as the other men began to arrive. She found her place among them and waited for instructions.

"Excuse me, pardon me, coming through." Orpheus pushed his way through and took his place next to her. He could tell from her body language that she was nervous. "What's got you all shaken up then?"

Pandora shifted her weight from leg to leg. "I don't know. Polemides said—"

"Let me guess, trials?"

She nodded.

"Ah, don't worry, just remember your training. Sure, some of these guys could snap you in two but you've got your own advantages. Just remember what we've taught you and you'll be fine."

"I… I don't think that's helping."

"Sorry, just don't overthink it. You'll be fine."

She looked down the line to where Perseus was standing. He caught her eye and winked at her. She smiled briefly but her anxiety took over and she lowered her head.

Polemides marched out in front of his students, his eyes cold and calculated. "Today, we see how much you have learned," he shouted. Gesturing to his side, Pandora saw his apprentices bring out the weapons. Seeing the steel glint in the sun, she realised they wouldn't be using the usual training equipment.

"Real swords?" she whispered under her breath.

One of the boys ran over to Polemides with a leather bag. Not taking his eyes off his students, Polemides put his hand in and drew out a small stone. "Pollux," he barked.

Castor shot a glance to his brother but didn't say anything. Pollux cleared his throat and stepped forwards. Pandora saw no evidence of nerves in his stance.

Polemides put his hand back in the bag. "Cadmus."

A short, stout man at the far end of the line stepped forwards with a grin on his face. Pollux sneered at his opponent and cracked the bones in his neck in preparation. One of the boys ran to the men and handed them each a sword and a shield. Pollux swung his weapon around, gauging the weight of the blade, while Cadmus stood completely still, watching his opponent intently.

Polemides held his palms up. "Now let's keep this clean. This is not a brawl. I want to see what you have learned here." He pointed to the line of men. "Castor, if you move an inch, I will cut you down myself."

Castor growled angrily, his loyalty to his brother absolute.

Polemides turned to the two opposing men. "Ready?"

They both nodded.

"Begin."

Pollux was the first to strike. He ran towards his opponent and brought his sword down hard, though Cadmus anticipated the move and blocked the attack with his shield. The sound of metal on metal was not something that Pandora was used to. The knot in her stomach tightened. Breaking apart, Cadmus spun and attacked with a backhand blow. Raising his shield, Pollux intercepted it, though having to bend low left him vulnerable and Cadmus kicked his shield, causing him to stumble backwards. Castor growled from the line and the men standing either side of him prepared to restrain him if necessary. Pollux jumped up and swung again; this time, Cadmus met it with his own blade and the two became locked, their heads nearly touching, grimacing at each other. With an enormous push, Pollux forced his opponent back and a second swing of his blade cut into the man's stomach. The wound was only flesh deep but the blood came almost immediately. Pandora gasped, and Orpheus took her hand in his and squeezed.

Staggering backwards, Cadmus clawed at his stomach and shouted in frustration. The wound was not fatal, barely a scratch really, but Pandora could see from his face that it was causing him pain. Yelling, Cadmus advanced once more, leading with his sword. Pollux deflected the blow with his shield but this caused the blade to glance sideways, cutting through Pollux's arm near his shoulder. Pollux cried out in pain and anger, raised his foot and kicked Cadmus in the cut across his stomach. The man fell backwards and hit the ground hard, his shield falling beside him. Pollux was quick to take this opportunity – he stamped on the man's arm, causing Cadmus to let go of his sword. Straddling the now disarmed man, Pollux held his sword to Cadmus' throat. Cadmus looked as if he was about to try and free himself but Polemides had seen all he needed.

"Enough," he shouted, signalling the end of the fight.

Castor was the first to roar, and the rest followed suit, clamouring at Pollux's victory. Pollux stood, grabbing the arm of his opponent and bringing him up with him. The two shook hands and laughed, evident that there was no bad blood between them. They had both fought well and praised each other for their efforts.

"That'll leave a nice scar, you brute." Cadmus punched Pollux in the arm near where his blade had struck.

"Ah! Well, I'm sure your wife will be pleased with yours," Pollux taunted.

"If I didn't come home with a new scar, she'd be suspicious," he said, laughing.

Polemides clapped his hands. "You two go get cleaned up." He whistled for the boy to come forwards with the bag once again. The crowd of warriors fell silent in anticipation. Polemides drew a stone from the bag and held it up to the light. His eyes darted to the crowd, a slight look of concern on his face. "Pandora."

She felt her heart drop to the pit of her stomach. Her mouth dry, she gulped heavily. She knew she must step forwards but her feet refused to budge. She was frozen where she stood. With a gentle nudge, Orpheus encouraged her forwards. She turned to him and saw a pained smile on his face.

"Go," he whispered, nodding his head gently.

Pandora walked slowly; it took all her effort to keep her feet moving. She could feel her entire body shaking. Glancing under her lashes at her instructor, she saw the concern on Polemides' face which certainly didn't give her any optimism. She was conscious of the men's eyes on her, could feel the anticipation in their stares. Her breathing quickened a little as she waited for her opponent to be called. Polemides sighed deeply, clearly wary of what was to come. Without looking, he delved into the bag and pulled out the second stone. "Perseus."

Pandora looked at Polemides with disbelief. Of course it would be her friend, just her luck. How could she fight someone she had grown so close to.

She couldn't stand the idea of hurting him. Perseus laughed under his breath and strode forwards. Coming to a stop a few feet away from her, they stood face to face, motionless. Pandora's face was cold, hard. She knew there would be no excuses for refusing to fight. In this moment they were not friends. All the evenings they had shared in conversation and laughter, the time they had spent training and working together, it all meant nothing. In this moment they were enemies.

One of the boys ran forwards and equipped them with their weapons. The weight of the metal was different from the wooden sword and shield that Pandora was used to. She took a moment to familiarise herself with the balance of the weapon, determined that it wouldn't affect her skill. Perseus stood calmly wielding his sword in preparation. Pandora turned to the crowd and saw Orpheus, a look of apprehension on his face. She gave him the same comforting nod he had given her just moments before.

Turning back to her opponent, she saw Perseus smile and wink with wicked amusement. This irritated her a little, fuelling the fire inside her. She had a feeling he had no doubt he would win the fight and she would do everything she could to prove him wrong.

Polemides raised his hand once more; he knew it was vital that Pandora get the chance to use her skills, but at the same time, the fondness he had developed for her made him wary of what would happen. "Begin."

Pandora lowered her stance, her shield held in front of her, sword poised, ready to anticipate a strike. She had fought Perseus many times but always in the vein of training; she had never seen him in the reality of battle. She was wary of this and waited to see how he would attack.

Knowing he would have to strike first, Perseus moved forwards, broke into a run, jumped and with an arching blow brought his sword down on Pandora's shield. She gritted her teeth and crouched below her shield to brace for the impact. His weight caused her to slide backwards in the dirt. Turning to the side, Pandora quickly moved behind her opponent and kicked him in the small of his back, making him stumble forwards. The move took Perseus by surprise. He had not anticipated she would be that quick. Turning to face her, he smiled at her skill and winked again. She didn't know why but this angered her and she ran at him with her sword raised. They sparred against one another, and every time their swords met, the sound of the metal clashing rang out into the atmosphere. Perseus had strength on his side but Pandora's reaction time was quicker and she successfully parried his strikes with ease. Realising that the fight would not be as easy as he had originally anticipated, Perseus let out a laugh of surprise. Swinging his sword towards her, Pandora once again met it with her own. The blades locked and Perseus used the momentum to pull her towards him. Their faces inches away from each other, he taunted her, "I guess Orpheus and I did our job."

Pandora could feel the laughter in his smile. He didn't take this seriously – he didn't see her as a threat at all. The anger bubbled up inside her and with a cry of frustration, she brought her head forwards sharply and cracked her skull against his. This move was met with noises of surprise and laughter from the crowd. Orpheus snorted under his breath in amusement.

Perseus shook his head, stumbled backwards a little dazed and laughed openly. "Okay, I'll give you that one." He narrowed his eyes. "No more holding back." With a snarl, he ran at her, his sword tucked in, then as he got close, he drew it in a backhand arc and slashed at Pandora.

She deflected the blow with her shield and dodged away from a second blow. She could feel the force in his moves; he was serious when he said he wouldn't hold back. If he kept this up, she didn't know how much longer she would be able to hold him off. Perseus was relentless, his attacks fierce, blow after blow. Pandora parried them efficiently but Perseus could tell that her strength was waning. The red haze of war had taken over his brain: he was in battle. No longer conscious of who he was fighting, Perseus yelled defiantly and kicked Pandora's shield with such force she spun wildly. She felt something hit her back hard and she dropped her to her knees. She assumed he had kicked her again, which was a low move in her opinion. She rolled to the side and jumped up to prevent a further blow. Slashing the air towards her opponent, she stopped the blade at his neck. It was only at that point that she realised he had dropped his weapon.

Perseus stood frozen, the colour drained from his face. His eyes met hers and she saw something in them she hadn't ever seen before: fear. Pandora looked at him with confusion, panting from the exhaustion of the fight. She turned to look at the crowd and saw they were silent, open-mouthed. Orpheus had a hand to his lips in shock and a few had begun to murmur to each other, pointing and whispering. Polemides stood stone cold, his eyes narrow, his lips taut. Only Echion didn't seem surprised. Instead, he was looking at the reactions of those around him.

Pandora was utterly confused. She didn't understand what had happened and turned back to her friend. "Perseus, what… what's wrong?"

He could barely get the words out, and when he did, his voice shook. "Pandora. I'm so sorry, I don't know what happened. I… Your back, I don't…"

Pandora looked at where his sword lay on the floor and then she saw it: the blade was covered in dust, a rust-coloured powder she recognised all too well. He hadn't kicked her – it was the sword she had felt. Slowly she reached around to her back and with a deep sigh, she felt the ravine that the blade had cut. Her fingertips were covered in dried clay and she knew the wound was large, large enough to cause her friend to panic. She hadn't expected to have to explain herself, especially not like this.

By this point, the men watching were talking rather loudly. They couldn't believe what they had seen. Some of them were shouting her praises for winning the fight but most were understandably wary.

"Perseus, I'm fine, it doesn't hurt."

"I don't understand. How are you standing? You should be—"

"Look, it's a long story, but I'm fine."

Polemides raised his hands but this time the men were so worked up they didn't notice. "Silence," he bellowed, and the men stopped immediately. "You two, get cleaned up. NOW." He pointed to Pandora, fury etched on his face.

Not wanting to antagonise him, Pandora moved to leave the arena but Perseus didn't budge. She grabbed him by the arm and with all her force dragged him with her back to the camp.

~

He didn't speak. He couldn't speak. Pandora dragged him all the way to the medical cabin. As they approached, Pollux and Cadmus exited, their wounds bandaged.

"Alright, you two?" Pollux grinned. "Who won then?"

"Can't talk," Pandora spluttered, "injury."

Pollux looked Perseus up and down. "He looks alright to me."

Pandora marched Perseus up the steps, past the two men. It was then that they caught a glimpse of her back.

"Well," Pollux exclaimed, "that's new. How did that—"

Pandora slammed the door in his face before he had time to finish his sentence. She heard him laugh and waited for their footsteps to grow fainter before letting go of the door handle. Perseus had walked forwards on his own, his back to her. Unsure how to address the situation, Pandora tentatively put her hand on his shoulder. He shrugged it off immediately, the force of it making her flinch. She had expected people to be surprised, wary even, but she had begun to think her new friends would understand. She had hoped Perseus at the very least would let her explain.

"Perseus, I—"

"I hurt you."

She stopped in her tracks. "What?"

"I… I hurt you, you should be dead. I got so worked up, I don't know what happened. I just, I hurt you. How are you not dead?"

Pandora felt unprepared for this reaction. She stepped in front of him and held her hands out. "Don't panic. I'm going to turn around, okay?" She turned slowly and held his hand up to her back. "Touch it, tell me what you feel."

Perseus pulled his hand away. "I can't, I'll hurt you."

If you'd hurt me, don't you think I'd be acting a bit more… I don't know, hurt?" Pandora said.

Perseus held his hand up tentatively and gently ran his fingers over the long wound in her back. There was no blood, no torn skin or muscle. Perseus felt the jagged edges of the chip. He rubbed his fingertips together and raised them to his nose. "Clay?"

Pandora turned to face him, smiled and nodded. "Now, I need you to do something for me."

"Anything."

"I need you to go to my cabin. Under my bed there's a leather pouch. Can you bring it back here?"

Perseus narrowed his eyes but didn't argue. He must have run the entire way because he was gone mere moments and when he returned he was panting heavily. Pandora sat on one of the beds and held out her hands. Perseus passed her the bag and stood awkwardly, clearly not sure what to do.

She pointed to a bucket of water on the table. "Grab that and come and sit behind me. I'm going to need your help."

Perseus took the bucket and gingerly sat behind her.

Aware that she would have to do something about her tunic, Pandora ripped the fabric around the wound and tied it around her neck so that she could keep her modesty. She could feel his breath on her back. It formed a knot in her stomach and she suddenly felt a wave of nervousness wash over her. Trying to shake it off, she pointed to the bag. "Right, now this might sound crazy but I'm going to need you to fill the wound with clay."

"You want me to what?"

Pandora turned and gave him such a scathing look that he decided it was probably in his best interests not to argue.

Breathing deeply, Perseus dipped his hands in the water. Taking a small lump of clay from the bag, he gently pressed it into the wound. He started out incredibly hesitant, but as soon as he saw that Pandora was not in any pain, he became more confident with his movements. Relaxing a little, he couldn't help himself asking questions. "So… so, this doesn't hurt?"

"No."

"And you're made of this stuff, this… clay?"

"Yes."

"Right, okay then."

Pandora smiled to herself. She had heard these questions before, but they had always been dripping with an air of judgement. Perseus' innocent curiosity was refreshing.

"Incredible." Perseus whispered softly.

Pandora couldn't help but smile to herself at the word. Perseus' hands were gentle and every touch on Pandora's skin made the knot in her stomach tighten. She had been so worried about sharing this part of herself with another person. Now, none of that seemed to matter.

LINEAGE

For someone who had never encountered such a situation before, Perseus did a surprisingly respectable job patching Pandora up. Once he had filled the wound, he gently smoothed the edges with water, and his eyes widened as he watched the colour slowly change until once again Pandora's back was a smooth plane of unblemished olive skin. Prodding the area rather inelegantly, he couldn't contain his amazement.

"It's just gone. Look at that. I can't believe it, that's amazing."

"Yeah, would you mind easing up on the poking a bit," Pandora scolded, gently batting his hands away.

Perseus threw his hands up in compliance. A flash of worry darted across his eyes and he stumbled over his words, "I really am sorry about this, Pandora. I never meant to hurt you."

"Really, Perseus, everything is fine. I'm just worried what the others will be saying about me." She glanced timidly at the door. "By the gods, whatever must they think of me."

Perseus rolled his eyes. "You do realise we have a literal Giant living with us, right?"

"I know but—"

Before she could finish, Orpheus came bounding through the door with a cautious smile on his face. "Perseus, if you could try not to maim the fun ones, that would be much appreciated." Though said in jest, Perseus looked down at the floor in shame. Orpheus realised he had misjudged the tone of the room and

Pandora threw him a look. "Oh dear," Orpheus said, "it's all rather gloomy in here." He scampered over to the two of them and spotted the bag of clay on the floor. His bright eyes widened in clarity. "So *that's* why you were collecting that stuff."

On their frequent hunts, Pandora would often stop at the nearby stream to collect small deposits of clay to take back to her cabin. She had learned that it was always sensible to keep an emergency supply just in case. In that current moment, she was very glad to have done so.

Perseus was still looking at his feet, and Pandora wondered how long it would take him to get over what had happened. She had already forgiven him but she could see it would take him much longer to forgive himself.

Orpheus spun his finger in a circle to encourage Pandora to turn around. Willingly she moved so that he could inspect her freshly healed back. "Not even a scar," Orpheus shrieked in excitement. "Oh, my dear, you are just marvellous. Perseus, look. Look how marvellous she is."

Perseus mumbled something nondescript under his breath and, standing abruptly, marched out of the cabin.

Pandora's eyes followed him, her face full of concern, but Orpheus shrugged it off.

"Oh, don't worry about him. He'll get over it eventually." He walked over to one of the chests in the corner and rifled through it until he found a fresh tunic. "Here, my dear, pop this on."

Pandora took the parcel of clothes and stood awkwardly in front of her friend.

"Umm, Orpheus—"

"Oh gods, where are my manners!" He skipped back towards the door. "I'll be right outside."

Pandora was glad to have a few moments alone. As far as revelations go, it really couldn't have been any more dramatic. She rolled her eyes as she relived the embarrassment: *You stupid girl*, she thought to herself, *you should have told them sooner.*

She went to change into her new robes but realised that she was still filthy from the fight. In the corner of the room was a basin full of water. Eagerly she washed off the muck and dust before changing into the fresh clothes. She untied the leather band holding back her hair and let the curls fall naturally. A gentle knock at the door reminded her that she had left her friend waiting. She hurried over and opened it, only to find that Perseus had returned and was now standing sheepishly next to Orpheus.

"Oh! I thought—"

Standing in silence, it took an encouraging nudge from Orpheus for Perseus to speak. "I thought you might be hungry so I went and got us some food." He held out a bowl full of bread, cheese and fruits. Pandora smiled at his kindness.

"And I brought wine." Orpheus grinned so foolishly that Pandora couldn't help but snort. She glanced over their heads back towards the training ground. Orpheus shook his head. "Polemides has instructed us to make sure that you're alright. He doesn't expect you to return to training today. Don't worry, he was impressed with your skill this morning. I'm sure he'll discuss it with you at some point."

"Oh, lucky me," Pandora mumbled with more than a hint of sarcasm. Perseus snorted under his breath, which made her grin in his direction. She felt the tension in the air lift a little and she sighed before gesturing behind her. "So, do I need to stay here or can we go eat somewhere else?" The afternoon was mild and the air fresh, so Pandora was in no hurry to go back inside. Not waiting for an answer, she strode confidently past the two men and marched towards the main hall. Orpheus and Perseus were quick to follow suit.

The three friends set up camp outside the main hall. The building had weathered over the past few months and it had settled naturally into the environment. It was nearly identical to the previous hall with the exception of an additional outdoor seating area to the side of the entrance. Large carved logs surrounded an enormous brazier and it was here that Pandora headed. Though it was afternoon and the fire wasn't lit, it was still a pleasant place to sit and watch the world go by. Pandora sat wearily on a log and the two men placed themselves either side of her. While they ate, Orpheus filled them in on the rest of the morning. There had been a few more trials after theirs but Orpheus clearly hadn't been paying much attention as he was sparse in his descriptions.

They sat in silence for a few moments and the air once more felt tense. Pandora could tell they were holding back. It didn't take long for Orpheus to crack. "So, um, Pandora?"

"Mmm?"

"I completely understand if you don't want to," he said, tripping over his words in his hurry to get them out, "but we're dying to know." Perseus shot him a dangerous look, and Orpheus corrected himself. "Sorry, *I'm* dying to know."

Pandora could tell where this was going but she was having far too much fun watching her friend squirm.

"How, um…"

Finally she gave in. "How am I the way I am?" she clarified with a slight smirk.

Orpheus grinned at her innocently. "Please don't take offence. I think you're magnificent. We just… it made us realise how little we actually know about you."

"It's okay, Orpheus." Pandora sighed and began her story. She told them how she was created, and how she came to live with her father. She told them of her childhood and her life in the village. She told them of her life right up until that last fateful day. Then something made her stop. She could feel a lump in her throat, and it was as if the words wouldn't come out whether she had wanted them to or not.

Sensing that she was struggling, Perseus cleared his throat. "You know, most of us here have had run-ins with the gods in one way or another." Pandora picked mindlessly at a bunch of grapes as she listened intently. Perseus shifted uncomfortably in his seat. "I mean, technically I'm a demigod," he mumbled almost inaudibly.

Pandora paused, a grape lifted halfway to her mouth. "Sorry, what?"

"He is too, you know?" Perseus pointed at Orpheus, desperate to draw the attention away from himself.

Pandora sat in awe as the two men argued.

"Yes, but your story is far more interesting." Orpheus laughed. "My mother is a muse so I have a pretty voice. Big deal. *Your father*, on the other hand…"

Perseus threw a piece of bread at him but seeing Pandora's shocked interest, he humoured her and carried on his story. His shoulders tensed a little and he looked at the ground as he spoke. "I don't really talk about it much. My mother was imprisoned by her father to prevent her having children. Little did he know that Zeus would decide to pay her a visit and… well… here I am."

Pandora looked in disbelief at Orpheus who solemnly nodded, corroborating Perseus' story.

"When my grandfather found out, he cast us out to sea to die," Perseus continued. "We ended up on an island just off the south coast. It was there that a man, Dictys, took us in and cared for us. He became more of a father than I could ever have hoped for."

Pandora felt her heart ache. She had spent months analysing her birth and her adoption by her father. She hadn't even considered that there may be others who had shared similar fates.

"I would have had a good life there," Perseus said, sighing, his eyes cold with melancholy, "if it hadn't been for the king."

He paused his story and the three of them watched as a large group of warriors ambled raucously past them, up the steps and into the hall. The light had begun to dwindle which meant the evening meal would be starting soon. Pandora turned back to Perseus, about to ask him to continue when Orpheus cleared his throat, signalling the arrival of Polemides, and they stood abruptly as their teacher strode over to them. He held out his hands in gentle encouragement to remain seated. A stern look on his face, he turned to Pandora. "Next time, bloody warn me, girl. I don't like being the last to know."

Pandora looked down in embarrassment. "Of course, Polemides. I am so sorry for—"

He cut her off with a wave of his hand. "I presume you will be fit to return to practice in the morning?"

She nodded in response though could see the concern in his eyes doubting her answer.

"Well, I suggest the three of you remain out here for the meal." Whistling towards the hall, a small boy came out with plates of food and once distributed proceeded to light the brazier in the middle of the log circle. "Make the most of the peace and quiet before the vultures descend. I'm sure they'll have plenty of questions." With a satisfied nod, Polemides turned on his heel and strode back into the hall, shutting the doors behind him.

Pandora stared at the plate of food on her lap while the two men either side of her eagerly tucked into theirs. "So, what made you come here, Perseus?"

He turned to face her, his mouth full of food, and grinned foolishly. "I told you, horse… wedding… essential."

Pandora looked in confusion at Orpheus, hoping he may elaborate. Orpheus rolled his eyes as he watched his friend stuff his face. "Really, you do give us men a bad name, you absolute animal." Perseus responded by opening his mouth to reveal the half-masticated food, which was met with a snort of laughter from Pandora.

Orpheus sighed and put his plate of food down in revulsion. "Well, my dear, you see, the king of the island Perseus lived on took rather a fancy to his mother" – he turned to Perseus with narrowed eyes – "and may I say I don't blame him, she is *quite* lovely." Perseus pulled a look of disgust and reached behind Pandora to take a swipe at his friend. "He set Perseus up at a banquet," Orpheus continued, "which resulted in the king demanding Perseus go off on some ridiculous quest just so that he could have Perseus' mother all to himself. I guess you could say Perseus came here first to brush up on his skills. Spending his days as a fisherman didn't really do a lot for his heroic capabilities." This caused Perseus to take another swing at his friend though Orpheus quickly dodged out the way.

Having finished his mouthful, Perseus continued, "I didn't feel ready to take on the task he had set me. I travelled here and sought council from Polemides. I had visited the school previously for training but never out of necessity. He suggested I stay here until I was ready to move on."

Pandora looked around her at the school she now called home. "I never thought I'd come to a place like this. I mean, I always dreamed about adventure…" Sadness swept across her face. Her heart ached and she folded her arms defensively. "If I had known the price I would have to pay, I don't think I would have been so eager for it to come."

The two men went quiet and looked at their friend with concern. Pandora could feel the emotions well up inside her.

If she were able to cry, this would be as good a time as any. "My family… my home… my entire village. They're all gone because of me." She felt her voice crack. "Because of what I did."

Pandora felt herself begin to drown in the memories of what happened: the images of her house ablaze, the sound of the roaring flames, the smell of her childhood burning to dust. All those things paled in comparison to the image of the man, laughing at her torment, his narrow, beady eyes piercing her soul. An eruption of laughter from inside the hall caused Pandora to return to reality. Looking at her friends, she saw the worry on their faces.

Orpheus moved back over towards her and put his arm around her. "Oh, my dear, you have suffered terribly. We heard news of a town near the coast that had come to ruin. We had no idea it was Kyparissi."

Pandora winced at the sound of it and nodded, her head falling wearily into her hands. A few moments of silence passed as neither man knew quite what to say.

At last, Pandora raised her head and sighed. "I don't even know why I'm here." She ran her hands through her hair in frustration and stood up abruptly. She began pacing back and forth, her agitated movements reflecting the confusion in her mind. "This is all because of that stupid box." She kicked the nearest log in frustration and a small shard of her toe chipped off and flew into the brazier, causing her to yell out in anger. She stomped over to the fire and fished out the fragment as her friends stared at her in shock.

"See?" She pointed at her foot. "It happens all the time."

Neither Perseus nor Orpheus knew what to say. They watched their friend with furrowed brows though it was clear from his clenched jaw that Perseus was desperately trying not to smile at her slight outburst.

"Didn't that hurt?" Orpheus asked, clearly a little concerned.

"No, not really."

"And the fire?" he added with a quizzical smile.

"Not at all, clay can withstand intense heat. I guess I'm lucky in that respect."

"So that's how you did it – saved the children, I mean." Orpheus clapped his hands together as if he had found the missing piece of a puzzle. "That has bothered me for so long. Obviously bravery played an enormous part in that but even the bravest of us wouldn't have made it out alive. You truly are incredible, young lady." He looked at her with such admiration, Pandora couldn't help but smile, shrugging awkwardly.

"What did you mean it's because of the box?" Perseus asked, picking at the bones on his plate.

Realising that her friends didn't have any clue about the box, Pandora rolled her eyes and attempted to explain. "When I was made, I was given to Epimetheus along with a vase. I don't know what was in it but it was bad. It was given to him as a punishment for his actions. When I was passed on to my father, the contents of the vase had to come with me. The gods decided that the vase was too fragile, so they transferred it into a box. My father agreed to protect the box so that he could have me."

Pandora squirmed awkwardly as she relived the horrific memories. "There was a man. He… he tricked me into opening the box. It all happened so fast. When I woke up, everyone was gone – my home, completely destroyed."

"So, what happened to the box?" Perseus asked, a serious expression on his face.

"I don't know," Pandora snapped back a little quicker than she had meant to. "Sorry, I didn't mean—"

"It's alright, I'm sure this is difficult to talk about." He smiled reassuringly.

Pandora concentrated on her breathing and sat back down to calm herself. "I don't know, it's just… My father had spent years protecting it and in a matter of moments I not only opened it but also potentially destroyed the world as we know it, all because I interfered with a worthless con man. So yeah, no big deal." She sneered at her own words and scuffed her sandals in the dirt.

"So it wasn't your fault."

"Yes it was. I opened—"

"You were tricked into opening it, my dear," he corrected her kindly; his eyes narrowed and he held his fingers up to his lips pensively. "The real question here is who this man was…"

"And how he knew you had the box," Perseus added.

Pandora's eyes widened. "I never thought of that." Her voiced raised a little in panicked realisation. "No one knew about the box. The only person I met who knew of its existence was told by a god and it wasn't him that did it."

"So, could this man have been told by a god too?" Orpheus asked.

Pandora thought for a moment. "If he had, it would have to be a god that *wanted* the box opened. But, who could want that?"

Perseus snorted. "Huh, you'd be surprised. Not all the gods are on our side. In fact, I can't think of a single one that hasn't decided at some point or another that we arc the scourge of the earth."

Orpheus tutted at his friend and leaned forwards, eager to get to the bottom of the predicament. "What did the man look like? We may have crossed paths before."

Pandora's stomach tightened as she spoke. "He was tall, incredibly thin. His skin was almost translucent it was so pale. His hair was like oil dripping from his scalp and his eyes were fiercely black." She looked away in shame and whispered under her breath, "He terrified me."

Perseus shrugged his shoulders. "I can't say I recognise him, and by the sounds of it, he seems like someone I wouldn't easily forget."

"So Athena didn't explain who this man was?" Orpheus patted her hand encouragingly.

Pandora thought back to the expression on the goddess's face when she had asked. "She wouldn't tell me. She looked... furious."

Her friends glanced at one another and nodded in agreement. Orpheus explained, "There's usually only one reason why a god would become so involved in a situation like this."

"Because another god already has," Perseus concluded solemnly.

The three friends sat in silence for a while. The night around them had grown colder. The brazier roared fiercely in front of them. The light breeze in the air made the sparks of the fire dance high in the air. Feeling mentally drained, Pandora sighed deeply. She could hear the men in the hall raucously singing and laughing and felt completely detached from everything around her.

Orpheus noticed the expression on her face and stood up, offering her his hand. "Come, my dear, I think it is time we got you to bed. Today has been rather eventful and I should imagine you are exhausted." Pandora turned to Perseus who nodded in agreement. She took Orpheus' hand somewhat reluctantly and together the three of them walked towards her cabin. Once closer she saw a warm glow filter through the window.

"Polemides must have sent one of the boys over," Orpheus explained. He skipped lightly up the steps towards the door and opened it gently before scampering back to his friends.

Pandora paused at the bottom of the steps. She looked at Perseus who stood quietly next to her, seemingly lost in thought. Orpheus shifted awkwardly on the balls of his feet. He could sense a tension in the air and quickly made his excuses to leave.

"I think I'll pop back to the hall and catch up on the day's events. Sleep well, Pandora."

She smiled and nodded as he turned to walk back to camp. Once he was out of sight, her attention turned back to Perseus. "Are you okay?" she asked kindly, pressing a concerned hand lightly on his arm. He flinched slightly at the contact but didn't pull away.

"I just… I can't stop thinking about what I did. What I did to you."

Pandora frowned, her eyes full of compassion. "Please don't."

Before she could continue, Perseus shrugged and smiled, the worry wiped from his face. Whatever he was feeling, Pandora knew it wasn't something that could be healed with words. She realised her hand was still resting on his arm and sheepishly pulled away from him.

Perseus turned towards her but kept his eyes on the ground. The air felt thick with tension but neither of them had the courage to break it. A sudden roar of laughter and noise erupted from the hall which knocked them both out of their daze.

Perseus grinned. "I guess that means Orpheus has made an appearance."

Pandora laughed lightly and knowing that there was nothing more for her to say, she slowly walked up the stairs towards her room. "I'll see you tomorrow?" she called over her shoulder.

"Of course."

"Perseus, I—"

"Pandora, it's alright. Get some rest." The smile on his face was genuine and she relaxed a little.

"Goodnight, Perseus."

"Goodnight, Pandora."

Part of her wanted desperately to stay with him. She could see the struggle in his eyes but she knew he probably needed some space. Reluctantly she walked into her room and closed the door behind her. Pandora stood against the door for a moment, resting her head on the cold, sweet-smelling wood; she could feel him still standing on the other side. She stayed there until she heard him walk away, the light footfall barely audible. Only then did she completely relax. She hadn't realised how tense she had felt. Something about the air between her and Perseus felt different, and she cursed herself for not having given him a warning before the fight. It hurt to know that he was struggling to cope with what had happened.

~

Lying in bed, Pandora struggled to fall asleep. She tossed restlessly for what seemed like hours. The brief moments she did slip away into slumber were filled with images of the man without a name, standing in her doorway, laughing at her as she lay amid the crumbling ruins of her home. Unable to take any more, Pandora flung herself out of bed and paced her room restlessly. She relit the candles on the shelf and briefly cast her eyes over the few belongings she called her own: a small woven basket she had made, a wooden figurine of a wolf that Gigamn had carved her and a little cup that held the latest posy of flowers Orpheus had left her. It did not bother her that she had so little. She had never been a materialistic person and since leaving her home, she had come to realise how little some things mattered when compared to others. She reached the end of the shelf where an unimposing pile of blankets sat. Tentatively she lifted the pile and, from underneath it, pulled out the piece of vase her father had made. Wrapping herself in one of the blankets, she took the trinket and the candle outside and sat on the steps of her home. It was still several hours before dawn. Pandora looked up to the star-speckled sky and wistfully traced the edges of the clay with her fingertips. She felt the indent where Miltiades had carved his name and shut her eyes. She felt desperately lonely. Even here among friends, the world seemed so very empty without her father.

"Do you mind if I join you?"

A voice came from the side of her cabin and Pandora jumped, her eyes wide in panic. A figure walked towards her and it wasn't until he stood near the glow of the candle that she realised it was Echion.

"By the gods," she said, scowling, "you scared me half to death, you fool."

Echion held his hands up apologetically. "I'm sorry, I didn't mean to startle you." He shot a look to the steps next to her. Pandora frowned but after a moment nodded and he sat himself down next to her. She became aware that she was still in her nightwear and pulled the blanket a little tighter around herself.

"I didn't think anyone else would be up," she mumbled.

"Mmm, well, I couldn't really sleep." Echion sighed. "I guess I'm not the only one."

"Yeah, well, I've got a lot on my mind." Pandora said.

She didn't realise she was still fiddling with the shard of vase in her hand.

Echion pointed to it. "What's that?"

"Oh, it's nothing, just something from home."

Pandora tucked the shard into her blanket, eager to keep it safe. It didn't take her long to notice that Echion seemed even more detached than usual. His eyes looked distant and his face was pale. Before Pandora could ask what was wrong, Echion broke the silence. "So, I, um, I overheard your conversation with the others earlier."

Pandora furrowed her brow and Echion raised his palms in innocence. "I wasn't really in the mood to socialise so I went to train by myself. It was while I was walking back over to eat that I heard you mention something that caught my attention."

By this point Pandora was thoroughly confused. She sat in uneasy silence as her friend explained. He lowered his head and bit his lip. Whatever he had to say was clearly difficult to talk about. Pandora leaned forwards and put her arm on his back.

"Echion, I don't understand, what's troubling you?"

"The man," he whispered shakily, "I… I know him."

Pandora froze, her body went stiff and her jaw clenched. "How?" she asked through gritted teeth, not sure if she wanted to hear the answer.

In a way totally out of character, Echion took both Pandora's hands in his and squeezed them tight. His eyes were dark with sadness, his face frightfully pale, even more so than usual. "Before I tell you, I need you to promise me you won't leave until I finish." Echion said.

Pandora squirmed, uncomfortable in the situation but Echion wouldn't let go of her hands. "Promise me." he said.

"Alright! I promise. Echion, what on earth are you talking about?"

Echion let go of her hands and wrapped his arms around himself, clearly struggling with the words he needed to say. The phrase that came out was barely a whisper. "He's… he's my father."

Pandora couldn't move. Of all the things she had expected him to say, that was not one of them. "Your father?"

Echion stood up abruptly and shook his head. "I'm sorry, I'm so sorry. I'm not… I'm not like him. I had heard your name before, heard him speak it, but I didn't put two and two together until the trials. Oh, Pandora, I'm so…"

Echion began to walk away, and Pandora stood up and followed him, desperate for answers. "I don't understand. Why would your father do that?"

Echion didn't stop. He ran his hands through his hair as he spoke. "Look, I can't say. If he knew…"

Pandora could hear the fear in his voice. "Echion, wait."

"I'm sorry, I'm so sorry." By this point he had broken into a run, heading towards the forest, and Pandora slowed, knowing she wouldn't catch him. Shaken by his words, she turned back to her room, her head filled with questions.

As she walked she could feel the weight of sleep wrap itself around her. Her lids heavy, she reached her bed and collapsed. Moments later she was asleep, her hand still clutching the shard of clay she treasured so dearly.

THE MESSENGER

Orpheus was the first to notice a change in the air that morning. He had gone to Pandora's cabin only to find it empty. Making his way back to the main hall, he heard noises coming from the training ground. As he got closer he saw her, spear in hand, practicing at a frantic pace. He couldn't tell how long she had been there but from the state of her he guessed it had been a while. Her tunic was caked in dirt, her hair was wild and knotted, and the expression on her face was hard and cold. Orpheus stopped in his tracks. He watched her as she went through her drills. Teeth clenched, she fuelled each move with immense power, yelling as she delivered each strike. He smiled sadly at the skill she had begun to show. With every move she seemed to slip further away from the nervous, awkward girl he had met all those months ago. Not wanting to startle her, he coughed quietly under his breath. She turned her head slightly to acknowledge his presence but didn't say anything.

"The men will be coming soon," he cautioned her kindly.

"Let them come." Pandora said coldly as she moved the spear in her hand.

Orpheus, now deeply concerned, called out in a calm voice, "Pandora, what… what happened?"

For a few moments she didn't say anything; the spear continued to move like an extension of her arm, then finally, she hissed the words, "I know who he was."

Orpheus' eyes widened slightly, but he didn't rush to speak.

Pandora continued, "The man who destroyed my home, killed my father…" She stopped the spear sharply mid movement, turned it upright and spun to face Orpheus. "Well, I know – no, *we* know his son." She spat as she bounced the spear in her hand before pointing it towards the target. With all her might she threw it so that it plunged deeply into the target's red centre. "His son was the one who taught me how to do that."

Orpheus took a moment before he spoke; he knew better than to let the surprise show on his face. Pandora turned to him, her brow furrowed at his lack of reaction. Walking cautiously towards her, Orpheus held out a hand. "I think we should speak to Polemides. He should know."

Pandora smiled bitterly. "You know him, don't you? You know Echion's father?"

Orpheus sighed and nodded solemnly.

"Will you tell me who he is?"

"It's not my place. Please, just come with me?"

Pandora muttered under her breath and threw her arms up in defeat. "Fine."

They walked together back towards the main hall. It was still early and only a few of the men had started their morning routines. As they walked, Pandora's expression slowly changed from anger to sadness. "Is Echion alright?" she asked softly.

"I don't know. Perseus went to find him."

Pandora looked out into the forest. "He's not at fault, I… I know that. He was so scared to tell me." She sighed. "I'm afraid for him, for what he might do to himself because of this."

Orpheus gently put his arm around her shoulders. "Come now, I'm sure he's alright. Telling you was dangerous but he believed it was the right thing to do. Whatever happens, we'll find him and we will keep him safe. I promise you that."

Pandora took comfort in his words and smiled wearily. "I'm so angry," she said, sighing again, the weight of her words heavy on her heart. "I feel like so much is expected of me and yet I can't even be trusted to know what I have to do."

"Of course you are. Come, the sooner we speak to Polemides, the sooner we can work out what to do."

As they got closer, Orpheus saw Perseus open the doors to the hall with defiant purpose and stride out. The look of surprise on his face made it clear he wasn't expecting to see them.

"Oh, I was just going to come and—"

Orpheus held out a hand in gentle warning. Perseus saw the expression on Pandora's face and fell silent. As they walked past, he turned on his heel and followed them back into the hall.

~

Polemides' work room was attached to the back of the refurbished hall. The three friends walked quietly through the dining area until they reached a door at the back. Orpheus knocked lightly and waited for a response.

"Enter."

Pandora hadn't been in the room before. Polemides was not a man for vanities: the walls of the room were plain and the only furniture served utilitarian purpose. It was fairly small and due to the lack of windows, rather dark. There were mismatched candles littering every surface, their warm glow making it feel more like evening. In the middle of the room stood an enormous table made of thick oak. On its surface sprawled maps, weapons and all manner of items used in the school. The room felt like it was in a perpetual state of organised chaos. Behind the table, Polemides was sitting in a large chair, carefully reading a small piece of parchment.

Orpheus gently grabbed Pandora's wrist and, spinning round to look at him, she immediately realised why. In the corner of the room sat a very dishevelled-looking Echion. Catching Pandora's gaze, he quickly looked away. Pandora's reaction was far less subtle. She moved swiftly over to him and grabbed him in a ferocious embrace. Clearly taken aback by the gesture, Echion couldn't contain his surprise.

"Pandora, I—"

"Don't, Echion. I don't care. I don't want you to do anything that will put you in danger." She smiled at her friend and he couldn't help but smile back.

Orpheus chimed in, "Perseus saw his bed empty in the middle of the night and went out to find him." Perseus rather unceremoniously jabbed Orpheus in the ribs with his elbow before shooting an awkward smile towards Pandora.

The minor commotion didn't seem to faze Polemides. Without looking up from the parchment he spoke in a low, calm voice. "So, now that we are all present and accounted for, we can sort this damned mess out." Pandora sighed deeply, ready to re-tell the story of the box but Polemides held up a hand to stop her. "If you're going to go on a long-winded tale about that cursed box, don't bother as those three have already filled me in." He waved towards her friends. "It's open, bad things came out, bad things need to go back in. That's the general gist of it, correct?"

"Well, I—"

"Correct?"

Pandora nodded, and Polemides continued, "And just to top things off, the whole thing happened because of this man's father, yes?" He pointed at Echion who coughed a little and nodded sheepishly. "Right. That's us all caught up then." Polemides crumpled the piece of paper in his hands and tossed it to the side. "So I guess it falls on me to tell you about him then?" Echion looked down at his feet, his body tensed up. Pandora patted his shoulder in gentle encouragement. "Well, I can say for sure that you already know him."

Pandora looked at her teacher with a quizzical expression. She turned to Echion who mumbled quietly under his breath, "Hermes."

Pandora didn't know how to react. "Hermes, as in the god Hermes?" she spluttered.

Polemides nodded. "The very same. Had a few run-ins with him myself but we've never been on opposing sides. For a long time he was known to be a protector of mankind, but for some reason, in recent years, his allegiances seem to have changed."

"It's why I came here," Echion said, his voice quiet. "Every time I saw him he was less and less like himself. I was afraid of who he was becoming." A look of relief crossed his face knowing that he could finally talk about it. "As soon as I heard your description of the con man in the streets, I knew it was him you were talking about. It's a guise he often uses when visiting the human world. He's not known as the trickster for nothing." His words stung with a bitter tone.

Pandora could see how the actions of his father had affected him. No wonder it had been difficult to come clean to her the night before. She realised now that the colour of his eyes was indeed similar to his father's human disguise. She knew there had been something about him that she had recognised – she had just never expected it to be that.

"So, what do I do now?" Pandora said in a quiet voice, turning to her teacher.

Polemides walked around the table, leaned against it and crossed his arms. "Well, when it comes to the gods, there is little we can do."

"One of the perks of being immortal," Perseus said, his tone bitter.

"The only way you are going to be able to stop this is by finding whatever was in the box and destroying it." Polemides reached across the table and grabbed the crumpled piece of parchment. "This came just before you walked in." He handed the message to Pandora. "I have received word from a town not too far from here. They have requested that you travel there. Apparently, they are playing host to someone who wishes to speak with you."

"Who?" she asked as she read through the short message.

"It doesn't say." Polemides sighed. "At first I was wary given what happened with that bald fool when you arrived. I had thought it might be a trap but judging by who brought it to me, I'd say it's pretty clear." Pandora watched as Polemides whistled through his teeth. From out of nowhere a small owl fluttered down and landed on his arm. He smiled and threw it a piece of meat.

"Is that—"

"Athena's owl? Yes," Polemides said as he scratched the bird's head.

"I should go," she said, her face full of determination.

Polemides nodded in stern agreement. "If I didn't think you were ready, I wouldn't allow you to go." He turned to the three men and shot a look towards the door.

Orpheus was the first to catch on. "Perseus, Echion, why don't we go and eat. We can bring something back for Pandora when we're done."

Echion was the first to move, and with a gentle smile towards Pandora he made his way out of the room. Orpheus followed a few paces behind but Perseus didn't move. He looked at Pandora in a way that she didn't understand. Orpheus coughed subtly and shot him a look, trying to encourage him to leave. If Perseus had something he wished to say, he kept it to himself, and with a grave expression, followed his friends back into the hall, shutting the door behind him.

~

Now that they were alone, Polemides stepped closer to Pandora and took her hand gently. She was surprised by the contact. "I'm so sorry, little bird."

Pandora's heart softened. He hadn't called her that since she had started her training. She had suspected it was to harden her nature, not wanting to ostracise her from the men. Though she had initially missed his sense of humour, it didn't take her long to become accustomed to Polemides' stern character as teacher. Hearing those words now took her back to how she felt the moment they met: a scared little girl with nobody left in the world. She wanted to speak but she was struggling to find the words.

Polemides patted her hand in a fatherly manner. "Your friends came to me early this morning," he explained. "Between them they pieced together the events that brought you here."

Pandora stood solemnly; the knowledge that the three of them had been talking about her stung a little but she understood why they had. Loneliness crept across her skin like cloying mud.

"When Athena came to me," Polemides continued, "I assumed you were just another toy, a plaything for her to entertain herself with. If I had known your purpose in this world…" He fell quiet, the anger at his own actions evident in his voice. Pandora was anxious to understand why.

Polemides gave a stiff nod of his head. "Hermes' involvement is grave news indeed. For a god to be involved in what happened can mean only one thing." He moved one of the maps across the table and turned it to face Pandora. "Whatever was in that box is powerful enough to change the course of our world in ways we can only imagine."

The sound of Polemides' words rang loud in Pandora's ears. *Why didn't Athena tell me?* she thought to herself.

Her questions must have been evident on her face as Polemides spoke, "You weren't ready to hear it, Pandora. Athena sent you to me to train you, to make you stronger in both your body and your mind." He smiled proudly at his student. "You have truly excelled yourself at this school. You show great skill but have not lost your compassion or the gods damn stubbornness that I saw in you when we first met. As Athena's witness, I can say with total assertion that you are ready now."

Pandora felt strengthened by his words. "When do I leave?"

"As soon as possible."

She took in a nervous breath. "Of course."

Polemides pointed to a marker on the map. "The town, Peleta, isn't far from here. If you leave within the hour, you should reach it by tomorrow morning." His eyes were full of kindness and a warm smile spread across his face. "I have grown rather fond of you, little bird. Always know you have a home here, even if it is with a bunch of animals like us."

Pandora snorted and rolled her eyes but smiled brightly at her teacher. She knew she had become complacent. A part of her wished she didn't have to leave but there was too much at stake for her to stay. "Thank you for everything, Polemides." Her voice was strained and quiet.

Her teacher swallowed and pursed his lips. "Thank you for everything you have yet to do." His voice broke a little as he spoke but he shrugged it off with a loud cough.

The parchment still clutched in her hand, Pandora reluctantly turned and walked out of the room, leaving Polemides standing alone in the candlelight. She was concentrating so hard on not looking back that she walked right into Orpheus.

"Oh!" she cried out in shock as he feigned injury. She gave him a playful punch on the arm. "What on earth are you doing?"

Orpheus held up a plate of food while Perseus stood nearby, cutting slices of an apple. "Well, if we're going today, you need a good meal before we leave."

"Sorry, before *we* leave?"

"You didn't think we were going to let you go on your own, did you? Besides, we heard word from that town a few weeks ago. They sent a message to warn us that a pack of wolves has been seen hunting in the hills nearby. It wouldn't be safe for you to go alone."

Pandora smiled weakly. She was moved by his solidarity but fearful of putting him in danger. "Orpheus, this isn't your fight. I can't ask you to come."

"Well then, don't ask me."

Perseus snorted. "I don't think you've got a choice," he said, waving his knife nonchalantly at Orpheus. "This one is almost as stubborn as you are."

Orpheus nodded with a foolish grin.

Pandora rolled her eyes but knew there was little she could say to change his mind. "Thank you," she muttered quietly.

"Right" – Orpheus clapped abruptly – "now that we've got that out the way, I suggest we get a move on."

The three friends ate quickly and were just about to leave the hall when one of the wards ran over and whispered in Perseus' ear. His expression darkened and he stood abruptly. "I... Polemides needs to speak with me."

Pandora and Orpheus nodded and watched as he turned to walk back. Orpheus shrugged and stood, offering his hand to Pandora. "Come on, we need to get our things ready for the journey. Don't worry, I'll sort Perseus' out."

~

It didn't take long for Pandora to gather her things. What little belongings she had fitted neatly in the bag Athena had given her, the shard of vase tucked safely among them. She went with Orpheus to the weapons shed to collect her spear along with his sword and shield. One of the wards handed her a sword, and she took it apprehensively. It was nothing special, one of the many they had at the training ground, but it was a sword nonetheless and she was grateful. By the time they were ready to leave, the men were walking over to the training ground, ready for the morning session. Pandora was met with a quiet embrace from Echion and crushing hugs from the twins, and even Gigamn came over to say goodbye. She was sad to leave the men she had come to call friends, but the parting was made better knowing that she wouldn't be travelling alone.

As she scanned the crowd, she realised she couldn't see Perseus among them. "Where's Perseus?"

Castor shifted awkwardly from side to side and looked at his brother for help.

"Uh, he… he left," Pollux mumbled sheepishly.

Pandora turned to Orpheus, her mouth open in disbelief. "He left?"

Castor explained, "After he went to speak to Polemides, he walked out without a word. We saw him get his things and walk off into the woods. We don't know what happened, but he was certainly in a hurry."

"He's not coming with us? He… he didn't even say goodbye," Pandora whispered to Orpheus.

Orpheus' expression was full of concern. "Whatever news he got, it must have been urgent. Don't worry, I'm sure he'll be fine. Come, we have to go."

Pandora lowered her head. She knew they didn't have time to waste but she couldn't ignore the knot in the pit of her stomach.

~

Their journey was as Polemides had predicted and they made good time through the woods. Although wary, they saw no signs of the wolf pack and Orpheus concluded that they must have moved on. The two of them didn't speak much during the day: Pandora was still trying to process Perseus' swift departure and Orpheus knew better than to push her. Every time she turned to her friend to speak, she stopped herself. Orpheus focused on keeping a swift pace. He was relentless, barely stopping to catch his breath; the entire journey he ploughed ahead, feet skipping lightly between the roots and vines. It was as if something had lit a fire within him, and Pandora could only assume that Perseus leaving had bothered him as much as her.

By the time night fell, they had made such good progress that Orpheus seemed in good spirits. He quickly assembled a fire and sat himself down beside it. Even though the height of summer had passed, the air was still mild enough to sleep in the open. They had not seen anything untoward on their journey so felt it was safe enough where they were. Pandora sat eagerly by the flames and shed her belongings, dumping them in a clattering heap by her feet. A screech from above signalled the arrival of Athena's owl.

"If it's following us, this meeting must be important," Orpheus explained, and the owl cooed in response. "Pandora?" he spoke her name quietly as he held his hands out towards the warmth of the fire. She turned to him and smiled. He continued, "I must be honest with you. I owe you a lot for letting me join you today. I'm ashamed to admit that my reason for coming was not entirely selfless."

"What do you mean?"

"Well, I don't speak about it often," Orpheus said, stumbling slightly over his words, "the reason I came to the school, I mean."

Pandora crossed her legs and picked at her fingers awkwardly. "Your wife?"

Orpheus could barely look at her. She could see how painful it was for him to talk about it. Ever since Perseus mentioned it after the dance, Pandora had been curious but had never asked for fear of upsetting her friend. She knew first-hand what grief could do.

"Her name was Eurydice." His face softened when he spoke her name. "She was so very beautiful and kind, every time I looked at her I fell in love all over again. She was my whole world. The day of our wedding was both the happiest and the most horrific day of my life. We were all dancing and she went further away into the field which is where she was bitten by a viper." Orpheus' voice broke. "I held her in my arms as I watched the life leave her eyes. There was nothing I could have done. I had spent years training, learning, bettering myself to save others and the one person I couldn't save was the person I loved above all others." He laughed bitterly and threw a handful of dirt into the fire. "I really just came to the school to get away from my life, to try and heal. I've known Perseus a long time and having him there helped me greatly. It wasn't until you came along, however, that my wound truly began to heal. Watching you train, seeing your determination and fearlessness gave me hope. It reminded me that I could still be of use, still dedicate my life to protecting others. Being here with you gives me purpose. I don't know how I will ever be able to thank you."

Pandora didn't know what to say. During their training he had always been so positive, so full of life, he had learned to hide his pain from the world so well.

"Orpheus, I—"

"Pandora, you don't need to say anything. I've spent so long ignoring my feelings, it feels good to be able to speak about her with you."

"I'm so sorry for what happened to you. I can't even imagine—"

"Have you ever been in love?"

The question surprised Pandora. Her life with her father had been so sheltered and she had felt so ostracised from society that she had never even contemplated the idea of love. Marriage had always felt so political, she'd never dreamed that love could have played a part in such things. Hearing her friend's story had opened her eyes to how the world could be. She shook her head and smiled awkwardly.

Orpheus sighed. "Oh, my dear, it's like nothing else. Love is… well, it's indescribable."

"I don't think I've ever really thought about it," Pandora said earnestly.

Orpheus reached out, took her hand in his and squeezed it lightly. "When you find it, you will know. I pray that one day you find someone worthy of your affection. You are magnificent."

Pandora smiled. "Thank you, Orpheus."

He shrugged lightly and yawned. "Well, I suggest we get some sleep and make our move at first light. We can't be too far away now." He stamped on the fire to put it out and lay down a few feet away from her. Pandora moved her belongings under her head and closed her eyes. In a matter of moments, she was asleep.

~

They arrived at Peleta early the next morning, the small owl gliding high above them as they walked. The town was surrounded by a lush green pasture, bordered by the treeline of the forest. Such a small place had no need for walls or gates. The residents were friendly and upon their arrival they were greeted immediately by an innkeeper who had been keeping watch. He said that it was one of his guests who had sent the message. He beckoned eagerly to them to follow him. The villagers stared as they walked past. Pandora assumed they didn't often have visitors that looked quite like they did. She became very aware of her weapons and did her best to appear non-threatening. The man stopped outside a small taverna and pointed to the door. With a gracious smile to the man, Pandora stepped past him and opened the door. The room was dark and with a swift nod to Orpheus to follow, Pandora stepped inside.

Pandora was surprised to see the room empty. Even at this hour in the morning, it was unusual for such a place to be so quiet. The owl shot through the door behind them and landed on a nearby table. She noticed the innkeeper didn't join them and she became instantly cautious. Turning to Orpheus, she gave him a look of warning and put one hand on her sword. They walked slowly through the room, stepping round the tables and scattered chairs. They soon spotted a single candle lit on a table near the back, at which a hooded figure sat with their back turned. Pandora gestured to Orpheus to stay behind; he nodded and stopped as she moved towards the person.

"Hello? I… I received a message to—"

The figure raised a cloaked arm and Pandora stopped immediately. "I can't tell you how wonderful it is to hear your voice, Pandora." The person rose slowly and turned towards her, lowering his hood as he did so.

"Alexander?"

In the light, the unmistakable face of Pandora's neighbour beamed widely at her. He opened his arms and without a second thought, she ran towards him and fell into his embrace.

Sacrifice

Pandora couldn't contain her happiness. "I thought I was meeting Athena," she said, still a little flustered by the shock of seeing Alexander.

The man smiled. "I'm sorry for not being more specific. It wasn't safe to explain in a message." The owl flapped its wings and screeched as if insulted by the comment; Alexander cooed apologetically at the bird. "But I knew if I used my sister's owl, you would come."

Orpheus cleared his throat. "Sorry, your sister?"

The man stepped forwards and held out his hand in greeting. "Pandora has always known me as Alexander. You, Orpheus, can call me Hephaestus."

Orpheus beamed and took his hand eagerly. "Oh, well, I must say it is just wonderful to meet you. I've heard a lot about you. I'm a big fan of your work," he gushed, clearly a little star-struck.

Pandora tried to process her neighbour's true identity. "I should really call you by your real name." she said.

Hephaestus shrugged. "Call me whatever you like, Pandora. I'm just so very happy to see you again. It has been rather a challenge these past few months not knowing how you were getting on. I have missed you so." Hephaestus pointed back towards the table he had been sitting at, only now it was covered in a vast array of food and drink. "Please, come and eat. You must be weary from your journey."

Orpheus didn't need to be told twice; he leaped over to the table as politely as he could and eagerly began eating. Pandora gratefully picked up an apple and tossed it around in her hands.

Hephaestus rubbed his temples wearily. "I'm sorry I couldn't go into detail in my message. I wish I could have prepared you better."

Pandora looked into Hephaestus' kind eyes and saw the concern in his expression. "Don't worry, I know about Hermes."

"You know? How do you—"

Orpheus shot her a look of warning, but Pandora was already aware of what she needed to say. "I can't say. It would put a friend in danger if I did."

Hephaestus nodded sympathetically. "Well, my dear, we can't have that. I am glad you know. It means we can speak freely about everything."

Hephaestus sat opposite Orpheus and waved to Pandora to join them. Slowly, he reached into his robes and brought out the small, octagonal box that had started Pandora's journey.

She had been preparing herself for this moment since her first meeting with Athena. She knew that at some point she must be reunited with it but, nevertheless, it still caused her stomach to flip. The box was so small in his hands, so unsuspecting. Orpheus paused mid mouthful as he watched it intently. Hephaestus slid it across the table towards Pandora, causing her to flinch.

"I know this must be extremely difficult," Hephaestus murmured, "Pandora, your father was a good friend of mine. I couldn't have found a more deserving man to raise you." She squirmed in her seat as he spoke, the wounds in her heart pounding. "You know that this box is the key to stopping what has been started. You must find a way to move past your fear and guilt, let it be the past."

Pandora took a deep breath and reached out over the table. Gently she took the box and moved it closer. It was so smooth, the wood polished and shiny, but she had never really taken the time to admire it.

Hephaestus smiled weakly. "I was quite pleased with it when I made it.

If I'd have known what would happen…" He said as he sat solemnly contemplating the past.

Pandora clenched her jaw as she stuffed the box unceremoniously into her bag.

Hoping to break the tension, Hephaestus clapped his hands suddenly, causing Orpheus to choke on the food he had just half swallowed. "Apologies, young man. Well, now we have that out the way, I can give you something much more exciting." He pointed to the table next to them, upon which now lay a blanket, clearly draped over something. The owl hopped over to the table and began to pick at the cloth. "No, don't. Don't spoil it!" Hephaestus ran over and shooed the bird away.

Composing himself, Hephaestus nodded to Pandora to unveil the surprise. Cautiously, she walked over to the table and lifted the blanket. There on the table lay two objects. The first was a delicate metal gauntlet, decorated with etchings of minute feathers, interlaced in a beautiful pattern, the likes of which Pandora had never seen. She picked it up and, turning it in her hands, was surprised by how light it was. Turning to Hephaestus, he gestured for her to put it on. It slipped easily onto her wrist, the metal cool against her skin. She was amazed by how well it fit her.

"Thank you. I honestly don't know what to say. It's… it's beautiful."

Hephaestus grinned. "That's not all…" He positioned her a few steps back, away from the tables. "Now, I want you to imagine that an attacker has just made a move towards you and they are about to attack with their sword. What would you do?"

Pandora shrugged. "Well, I—"

"No, no, my dear, show me. See it in your mind."

Pandora closed her eyes and pictured an opponent. She saw them flying towards her, sword raised high, and instinctively she threw her arm out across her body in protection. As she did, a circular shield of metal feathers unfurled like wings from the gauntlet in a blaze of movement. Orpheus' mouth dropped open and Pandora laughed in surprise and amazement.

The owl lifted its beak and raised its wings with a loud chirp. Hephaestus turned to it with a slightly smug look on his face. "Yes, that one was inspired by you – don't let it go to your head." He looked coyly back at Pandora. "What do you think?"

"I don't… I can't… *wow*," Pandora stuttered.

"It's alright I guess," Orpheus murmured, walking over to the owl and leaning casually next to it, "nothing special, I'm definitely not jealous at all." The little bird chirped again and pecked at his hand. "Ow! Gods, I was joking." Hephaestus gave him a humoured look and smiled warmly.

"I… I can't accept this Ale— Hephaestus," Pandora implored.

"My dear, I don't just make any old thing in my workshop. If I make something for you, I make something *for you*. It is tailored to predict your needs, sense your movement – not to mention it looks pretty good too." He chuckled.

Pandora couldn't help but agree as she swung her arm around, marvelling at the movement. The feathers created a shield that was solid and sturdy yet as light as the feathers it was modelled after.

Hephaestus pointed back towards the table. "You haven't even tried the best one yet."

Pandora could tell he was a man who loved his work. She could see why he had got on so well with her father, both being masters of their craft. A childish smile on her face, she scampered eagerly back to the table and saw the second item, a magnificent sword. It was small and ornate, the metal so thin it was almost transparent. The traditional shape was the only thing that was familiar to Pandora. The metal itself seemed other-worldly, engraved with elegant lines that emphasised the fluidity of the shape. The polished wooden hilt was wrapped in a rich, russet-coloured leather and looked soft to the touch. Pandora's hands shook, hovering above the weapon. She looked nervously at Hephaestus, who smiled encouragingly. With the tips of her fingers, she brushed the leather handle. Picking it up, she examined it momentarily before slashing it through the air. It felt so good in her hand, like an extension of her arm.

Orpheus stepped forwards to inspect it. "Such a delicate thing. I always thought a smaller blade would be a better fit for you."

Hephaestus nodded. "In the right hands, the size of the blade is an insignificant thing. Besides, wait until you see what it does."

Orpheus shot him a concerned look and unsubtly took a few large steps back. Pandora rolled her eyes at him and smirked.

Hephaestus stepped back too. "Now I want you to imagine yourself in combat. You have been sparring against an opponent and they begin to move away from you. What would you do?"

"Well…" Pandora thought for a moment. "I suppose I'd use my spear."

"Right, well raise up your sword" – Pandora did as commanded – "and squeeze the hilt." Wincing a little in anticipation, Pandora squeezed her grip on the sword. The blade shot forwards and the hilt shot backwards in an organic motion, the wooden handle elongating to form the shaft of a spear.

Orpheus let out an excited yelp. "Okay, that's not fair – I want that one." The owl pecked him again and he folded his arms in a playful sulk.

Pandora exhaled loudly in awe and Hephaestus clapped. "Well, I'd say from the looks of it you are… suitably impressed?"

Pandora was amazed to find that the spear felt the same weight as the one she had trained with; she knew she could control it with ease, but she was less sure how to control the transfiguration between sword and spear.

"How do I—"

"Again, it's all in your head, my dear. It'll know what you need."

Pandora closed her eyes and felt the spear change. Opening her eyes she smiled, satisfied that she could learn to understand it better and swung the sheathed weapon across her back. "How can I ever repay you?" she mumbled, overwhelmed by the god's kindness.

"Don't be ridiculous, sweet girl. So much has been asked of you, I just want to help you as best I can."

Pandora shuffled her feet awkwardly. "What if I can't do it?" she whispered, barely able to get the words out.

Hephaestus put a comforting hand on her shoulder. "You can survive this, Pandora. We all believe in you, now it's time for you to believe in yourself."

Pandora opened her arms and hugged Hephaestus in a loving embrace. The look of surprise on his face quickly turned into an affectionate smile as he held the young woman he had watched over so protectively for so long.

"I am so very proud of you, Pandora."

"Thank you, Alexander." She couldn't help using the name she had called him for all those years. "Thank you for the life you gave me."

Hephaestus pulled away gently and held out his arm to Orpheus. "And thank you, young man. I have no doubt Pandora is strong enough to handle the road ahead of her, but it is a road made easier when you have a friend to walk beside." Orpheus smiled, took the god's hand and nodded.

"So where do you suggest we go next?" Orpheus asked.

"Well…" Hephaestus stroked his beard. "Hades has said that he wishes to speak with you. Whatever destroyed your town hasn't reappeared yet and we aren't sure where it will go. At this moment, we still don't know what we are dealing with and that is a danger for everyone."

Pandora looked at the him sheepishly. "You want us to go to Hades?" Of all the gods, Hades, ruler of the Underworld, was notoriously one of the most terrifying.

"Oh, come on," Hephaestus said, smiling, "he's really not that bad. I've always said that with the correct anger management, he'd be the life and soul of any party, but hey, what do I know."

"Where do we meet him?"

Hephaestus bit his lip. "Well, he's not quite as comfortable around mortals as some of us. Athena always said he's agoraphobic but personally I think he just prefers not to get involved. It's a tough job down in the Underworld, though I must say ever since he met Persephone, he does seem to have a bit more spring in his step."

Pandora looked sceptical. "So, we have to go to the Underworld?" She turned to Orpheus who had now gone pale. He was staring at the floor, a cold expression on his face.

Hephaestus noticed the change in the air. "I know, not exactly conventional," he said, "but I have a way for you to get there, courtesy of my brother Ares." From out of his robes, he drew a small gold coin and turned it in his fingers a couple of times before flicking it to Pandora. She caught it clumsily and examined it. On one side was the bident, Hades' weapon of choice, on the other, Cerberus, his three-headed hound. "With this in your possession, nothing will harm you in the Underworld," Hephaestus said reassuringly. "You are there by invitation of the gods. You are guests not prisoners."

Pandora felt a wave of anxiety ripple over her. The Underworld was not a place for the living, she feared it just as any human would, but she knew this was a meeting she couldn't avoid.

Hephaestus noticed her concern. "Hades is fighting for the same cause we are," he said, letting out a frustrated sigh. "I don't know what my brother was thinking when he tricked you into opening the box, but I can assure you, from what we understand he is working alone."

"How can you be sure?" Pandora asked cautiously.

"Well, we can't be completely sure. None of us really know what is in the box but we were all warned of its evil. Zeus made it clear that whatever it was, it could do just as much damage to us as it could to the mortal realm."

"I didn't realise that was possible." Pandora's eyes widened.

"I'm afraid so, my dear, but that isn't something for you to concern yourself with right now. If anyone can shed more light on the situation, it's Hades."

Orpheus coughed, interrupting their conversation. "How are we supposed to get there?"

"Ah!" Hephaestus grinned. "One of my favourite creations." He pulled out a small black stone with a bright white streak across the top. "This little beauty, this will take you where you need to go. I shall accompany you to the outskirts of the village to show you how to use it. After that, you're on your own."

Pandora turned to Orpheus, and from his expression, she realised what he was thinking. She should have known that speaking of the Underworld would bring up painful memories for him. They may be able to come and go as they please, but his wife was stuck there for eternity. Tentatively she placed a hand on his shoulder. "I understand if you want to stay," she whispered, her tone soft but anxious.

Orpheus continued to stare into space but shook his head briskly. "No, I... I must come. I just... what if she—"

"To lose the one you love, well, that is pain beyond reason, dear boy." Hephaestus sighed. "You must decide whether this is a wound you are strong enough to reopen."

Orpheus' eyes filled with tears, his lips shook, and he clenched his hands into fists. "What if I could ask... if I could—"

"Bring her back?"

Orpheus hung his head, embarrassed for having asked.

Hephaestus continued, "I'm afraid that's not a question I can answer. Though if you have the courage to ask, ask it of Hades. You didn't hear this from me, but he has rather a soft spot for a beautiful voice." Orpheus lifted his head and Hephaestus winked at him.

Letting out a long sigh, Orpheus turned to Pandora and shrugged. "Well, someone has to look out for you."

Before Pandora could respond, Hephaestus motioned for them to gather their things. "Come, we mustn't dawdle. There is much to be done and I am afraid I have taken up too much of your time already."

~

Pandora adjusted the sword on her back and tucked the coin in her robes before checking that the box was safely secure in her bag. They were almost ready to leave when Orpheus snapped his head round. "Can you hear that?"

Pandora turned to listen. "Does that sound like—"

"Screaming," Hephaestus murmured, and with a sweep of his robes the god ran to the door of the taverna, flinging it open.

Nothing could have prepared Pandora for what she saw next. Stepping out into the street they were instantly hit by a wall of people running past them. Blood-curdling screams and cries of fear echoed through the street as villagers trod over each other to escape something moving close behind them. Hephaestus had stepped out into the crowd and now stood motionless in the middle of the road. Pandora and Orpheus pushed their way through the people to join him. Through the throng they saw it: a dark, oil-slicked mass of ash and smoke. It moved like a fog, its vaporous mass swirling through the village, consuming everything in its path. It was a mass of nothing and everything. Tendrils, organic vines of black and crimson protruded from the densest part, wrapping themselves around buildings, pulling its mass forwards, engulfing and consuming everything it could. Stone crumbled to dust, wood rotted away and Pandora watched in horror as people were swept up and pulled into it. Nothing could escape the sprawling, fibrous web. As it moved, waves of mechanical screeching washed over everything, a sound so terrible it shook Pandora to her very core.

"Mother of the gods," Orpheus whispered.

Hephaestus shouted above the cacophony of noise, "I don't know how it found us, but we need to get out of here now. Now run!"

By this point the villagers had begun to scatter, taking refuge in buildings, desperately scrabbling over walls. Pandora spotted a girl too small to reach her father's outstretched hands atop a nearby wall. Without thinking twice, she dodged her way through the crowd towards the child and lifted her to his open arms.

"Go, go now!" she shouted at them as she began to pull more people towards the wall. Orpheus saw what she was doing and ran over to help. Whatever it was that had attacked, it was clearly in no hurry as it moved at a haunting pace, slowly but unrelenting through the village. It didn't take long before only the three of them remained in the open.

"This way," Hephaestus yelled, pointing towards the gates. They sprinted down the road leading out of the village. Pandora was blind with panic, her expression mirrored on Orpheus' face as they ran. When they reached the pasture, Hephaestus slowed to a halt.

"Hephaestus, what are you doing?" Pandora cried, skidding to a stop. She watched as the tumultuous mass also slowed behind them. It stopped advancing and yet it was still constantly moving.

Hephaestus narrowed his eyes and whispered back to the two of them, "Wait for my signal. When I say go, you *must* go. Don't think, just do as I say. Do you understand?" Pandora went to argue but knew there was no point. She nodded meekly and waited.

Hephaestus turned back to face the Darkness in front of them and stepped forwards a few paces, just enough so there was now a few metres between him and his companions. Reaching into his robe, he pulled out an impossibly tall staff. It was shining gold and shaped like a tree bough, crooked and organic in its beauty. At the top shone a throng of golden twigs, covered in magnificent glass leaves and blossoms. In a swift, defiant motion, he brought it down to the ground, causing a tidal wave of force. "Show yourself," his voice boomed in a way that rattled Pandora's heart.

It was the first time she had truly seen him as a god. Watching with panicked eyes, she saw movement in the fog. Out of the centre of the mass stepped a creature, wolf-like in its form. Its eyes were pure glistening black, its fur wet, dripping with an oil-like substance. Up its legs, spidering tendrils crawled and wrapped themselves around its body, constantly moving along its form. A monstrous snarling thing, it stalked forwards, slowly, purposefully. Pandora gasped but she gritted her teeth, her eyes fierce as she reached for her sword. Hephaestus gestured to her to remain still and unwillingly she obeyed. She watched as out of the smoke followed more of the creatures, all advancing slowly but purposefully towards them. They stopped a few paces away from Hephaestus and snapped their vicious teeth.

"Leave this place," Hephaestus shouted in his terrifying voice.

For a moment there was silence. Pandora felt all her muscles clench in anticipation. Hephaestus stood tall and strong, his eyes fixated on his opponents. Then, it broke. With a deafening howl, the lead wolf charged towards the god and leaped into the air. Hephaestus stood motionless until the very last moment in which he swung his staff around and hit the wolf with a fluid strike, knocking it on its back until it slid across the dirt back to its brothers. The Darkness screeched painfully, angrily, and from its depths stepped more wolves. The creature got back up off the ground and bared his jagged teeth, now moving into position at the front of the ever-increasing pack.

Pandora couldn't see how they were going to escape this. She shot a look at Orpheus who was bent in a crouch, preparing himself for a fight.

Hephaestus sighed, gritting his teeth. "This is not going to end well," he said, and with another strike of his staff brought it back down to the ground. This time it stuck in the dirt. From the end shot a tangle of golden roots that embedded themselves deep within the earth. Pandora watched in awe as the golden bough of the staff began to grow. A delicate web of branches sprouted from the staff, and glass leaves and flowers bloomed magnificently as the tree stretched itself in a half-circle in front of the god. It was the most undeniably beautiful thing Pandora had ever seen, and for a moment she forgot entirely where she was. That was until the wolves began to howl in anger and frustration. The leader of the pack ran fearlessly towards the tree and hit it with its full force, only to be blown back in a spark of light. Hephaestus smirked as the staff shielded them from the attack and Orpheus cried out in surprised amusement.

Hephaestus held out a hand behind him. "We can't fight them off for long. You go, I'll hold them off for as long as possible." As he spoke, more wolves began to throw themselves at the shield, each one hitting it head-on with a deafening crack before being flung backwards.

"I don't know how long this will protect us." He turned to look at Pandora. "It's still in its primitive form – I haven't quite perfected it yet."

She shook her head stubbornly. "I can't… I can't leave you."

Hephaestus pulled the small black rock from his sleeve. "You don't have a choice, my dear, you *must* go. I will be fine."

Tossing the rock up in the air, the god caught it between his fingers and then threw it with all his might away from the village. Pandora watched as it soared past her, back towards the treeline of the forest. When it reached the trees, it hit something unseen and the air itself shattered like a mirror. Shards of the world fell to the ground to reveal sweeping grey desert. Pandora realised instantly where it led: it was their path, their way to the Underworld.

Hephaestus turned back to the shield; the pack of wolves were beginning to find a rhythm in their attack. He could hear the branches of his staff creaking and the dirt around the roots had begun to shift. "Orpheus, get her out of here, NOW," he yelled ferociously.

Orpheus nodded and grabbed Pandora's arm, desperately pulling her towards the woods. She screamed in anger at their defeat but knew they had to move. When she turned to run, she felt a part of her soul rip away from her. She had already lost her father, the thought of losing the man who had created her was agonising. Snapping her head back to the shattered rift in the world, she focused on running. She and Orpheus were now sprinting at full speed towards the woods. They were nearly there – she could make out the cracks in the grey earth beyond the rift. She knew she shouldn't but she couldn't help looking back.

She stopped dead in her tracks. "Orpheus," she screamed as she saw the golden tree snap at the roots, the branches disintegrate and the wolves engulf it. Hephaestus, now without a weapon, caught the first wolf with his hands and threw it aside; the second launched itself at him, then the next and the next, their numbers now overwhelming him in a terrible frenzy. From out of the middle of the hysteria pushed a lone wolf, its gaze fixed on the two of them, that instantly began a frantic chase towards them.

"Come on, Pandora, run. We have to run," Orpheus cried. They resumed their speed and pelted towards the broken world.

Pandora could now hear the snarls of the wolf hunting them and she felt her heart jump into her throat. They were almost there, metres away from the rift, when Pandora saw to her horror that it was beginning to close. Shards of the world were lifting from the ground and replacing themselves in the ever-shrinking gap.

"We're not going to make it," she shouted.

"Yes, we are. *We are.*"

"No, we can't, we—"

"Jump, Pandora, JUMP!"

Closest to it, Pandora leaped desperately towards the rift. Tumbling through, she hit the grey desert on the other side and rolled away from the hole. Turning her head, she saw Orpheus throw himself backwards through the world, slashing his sword towards the creature that was inches away from him. With a groan, he landed hard and seeing the wolf leap towards the portal, instinctively he threw his sword at it before jumping protectively towards Pandora, shielding her with his arms. As he did, the rift snapped shut and his sword fell to the floor with a loud rattle. The friends sat breathlessly, staring at the space where the rift had been. There was no sign of the wolf that had pursued them.

"Orpheus," Pandora said, "your sword."

They both looked down at the weapon, now rocking from side to side on the floor. Only half the blade remained, its jagged edge burned white as molten metal dripped to the ground.

A Coin For The Ferryman

Looking around them, Pandora and Orpheus realised they were at the bottom of an enormous ravine. The jagged rocks either side of them looked unscalable, the sky above was dark and bleak, and pockets of air whipped past them, picking up ribbons of dirt in swirling flurries. Pandora scanned the desolate surroundings, her heart still racing. She picked herself up, aware that she was still panting from the chase, and let out a long, slow breath.

Orpheus stood up, examining his sword. "Well, that's not ideal," he said, as he tossed it on the ground. "I liked that one."

"We just left him." Pandora sighed, looking up at the dreary sky where the opening had been.

"We had to."

"Did we?" She reached into her tunic and pulled out the coin Hephaestus had given her.

"He's a god, Pandora, he'll be fine."

"You don't know that. You remember what he said, whatever was in the box could hurt gods too. He could be—"

"He's not." Orpheus' tone was reassuring but Pandora could see from his face that he was as worried as she was.

She moved the coin around in her fingers. "Any clue as to what we're meant to do now?"

Orpheus assessed his surroundings and shrugged. "I'm guessing we just follow this pass until it pans out?"

"That's as good a plan as any, I suppose."

"Well, it's probably better than staying here and I really don't have any better ideas."

Pandora thought for a moment and realised that he was right. Nodding curtly, she gave her limbs a quick stretch and began walking.

~

They walked for what seemed like hours, the grim, monotonous surroundings sending them into a sort of trance; all they could do was put one foot in front of the other, not a word exchanged between them. Pandora replayed the events of the afternoon over and over in her head, the thoughts swimming around in a turbulent pool of emotion and guilt. Every time she turned to look at Orpheus, she could see her expression mirrored on his face. He was almost as grey as the landscape, his face sullen and his eyes dark. She knew this journey brought up other emotions, other fears for her companion that she couldn't begin to understand.

"What are we doing?" he mumbled, almost incoherently, his voice hoarse from thirst.

Pandora stopped and yelled up at the sky up in frustration, "I don't know." Growing impatient she clenched her jaw. "All we've got is this." She held up the coin. "What are we supposed to do with it?"

Orpheus took it gently from her and examined it closely. The wind had died down and the air around them was quiet and still. Pandora could hear nothing but the sound of her own breathing. With a curious expression, Orpheus flicked the coin off his thumb into the air and the metallic sound resonated forcefully in the silence before dissipating once again. Pandora sighed in despair, unsure of what to do.

Orpheus opened his mouth as if to say something when he felt the earth shake under his feet. "Did you feel that?" he whispered, and Pandora nodded frantically in response.

The rumbling under the ground was soft at first. Pandora felt the vibrations beneath her feet as the dirt around her began to fall through the cracks in the mud. As the sound grew, so did the fissures in the ground until the earth in front of them seemed to slip away like sand in an hourglass. It happened so quickly, they barely had time to react. Pandora and Orpheus watched open-mouthed as the earth fell away to reveal two perfectly formed rectangular holes. Standing by his side, Pandora looked at Orpheus with doubt in her eyes.

"They're—"

"Graves," he finished, his voice soft and tense.

He was right: the holes in the ground were the exact shape and size for a human burial. Nothing else around them had changed, but Pandora couldn't help feeling a little uneasy. "What do we do?" she asked, one eyebrow raised.

"This must be the way in," Orpheus reasoned.

"Don't you think it's all a bit… well, literal?"

Orpheus snorted, clearly not expecting her to say something so light-hearted. "Well, I'll let you be the one to tell Hades."

Hand on her sword, Pandora examined the holes and circled around them. "Do you think we're just supposed to lie in them?"

"I don't know, I guess so."

"And then what?"

Orpheus shrugged and gave her a look of frustration. "I don't think we'll know until we try it." Gingerly he stepped into one of the graves. "It's not like we've got any other options, unless you feel like walking aimlessly for a few more hours?" He sat down defiantly and crossed his arms. "I'm more than happy to wait for you." His voice dripped with sarcasm.

Pandora rolled her eyes and, pouting slightly, jumped into the remaining grave. Orpheus sighed and lay backwards, Pandora reluctantly doing the same.

"So, do we just lie here?" she called out.

"Mhmm."

She picked at the dirt. "This really doesn't feel good, I wonder if—" Her train of thought was broken as Orpheus let out a horrific scream.

Pandora shot up and leaned over to discover that the grave next to her was now filled with dirt. She dug into the earth but there was nothing there. Orpheus had gone. Lowering herself back into her grave, she was now panicking. Her breathing quickened and as she lay her head back, she moved one hand to the hilt of her sword. Eyes closed, she waited a few moments for something to happen, but nothing did. Slowly she opened one eye. From the side of the grave, a desiccated hand burst out from the earth and clawed at her tunic, quickly followed by countless others. Hand after hand broke out of the ground and began to scrape and scratch at her skin, her clothes, her hair. She screamed out, trying desperately to unsheathe her sword but the hands were so strong. All she could see were flashes of decaying skin and bone tearing at her, covering her in dirt and mud. Slowly they pulled her deeper into the earthen grave, burying her alive, entombing her. As she screamed, she felt the earth fill her mouth, pushing its way down her throat, suffocating her. Certain that this was the moment her life would end, Pandora watched in helpless terror as another hand brought down a final heap of dirt, plunging her into complete darkness. In that exact moment, the weight of the earth released, the pain in her chest eased instantly and she felt a cool breeze on her skin.

Cautiously she opened her eyes. The first thing she saw were dark rocks far above her head, followed by the shallow walls of the grave she was lying in. The air smelled strongly of damp earth and mould and she could hear the gentle rhythm of water not too far away. Feeling a little dizzy, she sat up cautiously and tried to focus her vision.

~

A deep voice travelled across the air towards her, "Whoa now, give yourself a second, that journey's never a pleasant one."

"I'm fine, I just need to…" She tried to stand but her legs were reluctant to comply and gave way. Wincing in anticipation, she was surprised when she didn't hit the floor. Instead, she found herself caught in the arms of someone who had predicted her fall.

"What did I just say?" The voice scolded with an air of humour, and this time Pandora could feel the speaker's breath close to her head.

"I'm sorry, I'm fine, really," she insisted as she shrugged away from the arms that had caught her and gingerly stepped forwards. Turning around, she saw a man, taller than her, muscular in build. He was dark skinned, the dreadlocks of his long hair were tied loosely back with cloth and he was draped in tattered black robes that swept around his body like smoke. Looking into his deep brown eyes, Pandora paused for a moment before scowling. "I feel that entrance would have been made a lot more straightforward with a simple warning, perhaps a signpost or two?"

The man snorted, clearly surprised by the audacity of the young girl standing in front of him. "Well, I'll be sure to pass your criticism along." He gestured behind her. "Your friend seemed to enjoy it." Pandora turned to see a very pale Orpheus stood bracing himself on a rock, still coughing and retching.

The man's sarcasm didn't amuse Pandora and she responded by glaring at him before running over to comfort her friend. "Orpheus are you okay?"

"Well, that was, um, different." He coughed some more, a somewhat haunted expression on his face. "Did you see the…" He couldn't finish his sentence as he turned away to retch some more, scraping the air and making a claw with his hand.

"Yes," Pandora said, nodding, trying not to relive the horror they had just experienced.

Sensing the level of distress, the man walked over to the two of them. "We don't get a lot of live ones visit, for… obvious reasons." He threaded his arm through Orpheus' and helped him stand up straight, "In all honesty, this is rather exciting for me. You must have a good reason for being here."

"We have been sent by Hephaestus to—"

"Oh no, don't tell me now" – he waved his arms emphatically – "save it for the journey." He pointed towards the water. "I always enjoy a little on-board entertainment. Now, do you have anything for me?"

Pandora frowned, and she took a moment to look around her, trying to understand what he meant. It was only then that she fully realised where they were. In what seemed to be an enormous cave, they were standing on the shore of a colossal river, its waters turbulently thrashing at a dark wooden boat that had been moored at a rotten, almost derelict jetty nearby.

"I'm just guessing," Orpheus said, rolling his eyes sarcastically, "but is this the river Styx?"

"That would be a correct assumption, yes."

"So, you must be—"

"Charon." The man beamed widely. He held out a hand to Orpheus which he took, albeit a little tentatively. The man then extended his welcome to Pandora who just stood and scowled. This only caused Charon's smile to widen. "Now it's all very well and good you've come here, but I'm afraid Hades is one for formalities so I must ask you again… Do you have something for me?"

Pandora turned to Orpheus and her eyes shot to his robes. He caught her glance and with a look of understanding, he pulled the coin from his belt. "Do you mean this?" He threw the coin towards Charon who caught it nonchalantly between two fingers.

"Hmm," he said, examining the coin, "haven't seen one like this in a long while. Important business I see." With a flourish of his arm, he gestured towards his boat. "Please, climb aboard."

Orpheus looked gingerly at the boat but followed the man and stepped on board. Pandora, however, didn't move.

Charon sighed. "You're more than welcome to swim, young lady, but trust me, you'll look far worse for it. There are plenty of unpleasant things in that river – just trust me on that one." Pandora rolled her eyes and walked towards the boat. Charon shot Orpheus a humoured look. "Your friend's a fun one, isn't she?" Orpheus bit his lip, and Pandora could see that he was trying not to laugh.

Once the three were aboard, Charon cast off and they slowly moved away from the shore. The river was incredibly wide, so much so that the other bank was barely visible. Pulling a golden apple from his robes, the god rubbed it on his arm before biting into it hungrily.

Pandora nodded to the fruit. "I thought the gods only drank ambrosia?"

"Well, ambrosia can take many forms – not that I'd expect you to know that. The purists like to keep it traditional but some of us less conventional folk prefer a little variety. Besides" – he waved the apple – "it's useful when you're always on the go." Charon grinned at her mid chew and she pulled a face of disgust. Clearly entertained by her irritation, Charon continued, "So what brings you to the Underworld?"

Pandora turned to look out at the river. "We're dealing with a sort of 'impending doom' situation," she muttered, trying not to think about what happened back at the village.

"Oh, impending doom." Charon waved his arms in mock fear. "Yeah, that'll do it, though normally you'd end up here after the doom part," he said with a cheeky smile.

Pandora was very quickly growing tired of this god's manner, finding him insensitive and crass. Sticking her chin up a little, she decided to test his character. "You don't look how I expected you to. People always said you were a stinking, festering old man."

Orpheus shot her a look of fear, for despite his jovial attitude, the man they were talking to was still a god and Pandora could see Orpheus was anxious about angering him. Charon stared open-mouthed for a moment, taken aback by the blunt statement, before laughing so hard he choked on the piece of apple he was eating. Pandora's frown deepened, and her eyes narrowed.

He slapped a hand on his thigh. "You do have a way with words, don't you? I did warn you that water's no fun to swim in, right? You come out looking a bit worse for wear – trust me. I swear, if I see Hercules again, I'm going to kick him right into the depths of Tartarus."

Orpheus snorted but quickly resumed his silence when Pandora shot him a look of derision.

Charon turned to Orpheus. "Bet he's telling everyone he threw me in, isn't he?"

Orpheus nodded.

"Yeah, I'm gonna kill him." Charon smirked and tossed the core of his apple into the water, which was instantly sucked under in an acidic froth of bubbles. "Sorry to disappoint you, young lady, though I must say you humans do use an awful lot of artistic licence when describing the gods. It's alright when it's just the colour of your hair or eyes" – he ran a hand through his dreadlocks – "but when you get turned into a dirty, grumpy old man… it hurts, you know?" Clutching his heart, he wept dramatically. Orpheus snorted again, this time trying unsubtly to cover it with a cough.

Pandora purposefully turned her head away, not wanting to participate in any more nonsense. She looked out across the water. The vast expanse of the cave felt empty and mournful and she couldn't help but find perverse amusement in how much it lived up to its name. The passengers sat in silence for a while, listening to the lapping of the waves as the boat smoothly cut through the river.

Eventually Charon came and sat next to Pandora. She felt a little awkward at the proximity but didn't show it. Clearly a little uncomfortable too, Charon cleared his throat. "Listen," he mumbled, "I didn't mean to offend you. I know I can be a little inelegant. It's just, well, there's not a lot of opportunity for fun in this job. Most of my passengers aren't particularly chatty. I really didn't mean to offend."

Pandora narrowed her eyes at him but could see from his expression that he was genuine. She let out a slightly strained smile. "It's alright. It's just, we've come from a…" She didn't know how to put it into words. "We were with Hephaestus, and then we were attacked."

"Attacked?"

"I thought I would be able to fight, but I just… froze." It was only then that Pandora really acknowledged the shame she had been feeling about the attack. She had thought that whenever she faced the enemy she had been sent after, she would run into the fray fearless and undaunted; she hadn't prepared herself for defeat.

Charon was a little taken aback by her honesty. The ferocity in her astounded him. "There's no shame in knowing when you can't win."

Pandora picked subconsciously at the wood on the side of the boat. "Hephaestus made us run but he stayed behind. Can he… I mean, is he—"

Charon smiled weakly. "He's a god. He cannot die. This I am sure of."

Pandora looked at him and saw the expression in his eyes. She couldn't help but hear a sadness in his tone that she didn't understand.

Before she could press him further, Orpheus called out, signalling that they were nearing the shore. Pandora stood up and walked towards the bow of the boat. Back from the shore stood huge rows of interlocking stalactites and stalagmites, and they made admittance to the passage beyond look like entering the mouth of a giant beast. In front of the gates stood the enormous three-headed dog known as Cerberus, snarling and barking in the direction of the incoming ship.

Orpheus turned to Charon, a look of mild panic on his face.

"Just don't try and pet him." Charon smirked as he jumped into the shallow waters of the river's edge and pulled the front of the boat up onto the shore. Getting out carefully onto the grey sand, Orpheus and Pandora walked along the rough path towards the monstrous dog.

"Wait," Charon called.

Turning around, Pandora saw him throw the coin towards her. She caught it effortlessly which was met with an approving smile from the god.

"You'll need this again. How else are you going to get back?" He winked, and Pandora smiled at him, this time with genuine warmth. She supposed he wasn't quite as terrible as she had first thought. There was something about him that wasn't like the other gods she had met. She watched as he pushed the boat away from the shore and with a quick wave to his two passengers, he jumped back on board and sailed away.

~

Cerberus was a terrifying creature. His three heads snapped at each other, spit flying everywhere. Spotting the two intruders, he strode forwards, a low growl emanating from each one of his heads. Pandora held the coin between her fingers and raised it above her head. The dog moved forwards and bent down, the central head sniffing the coin, before then turning around and making himself comfortable off to the side of the entrance, padding around a little before laying down.

The path now clear for Pandora and Orpheus, the stalactites and stalagmites opened with a slow rumble to reveal a moss-covered avenue. Tentatively, the two of them stepped past the dog who was now settled, the central head cleaning his paws while the other two heads partly dozed, partly watched the intruders. As they made it past the gates, the opening of the entranceway narrowed quickly until they were walking down a tight pathway.

Pandora took the lead and marched boldly down the passage. The further they got from the river, the darker it got until finally the light was all but gone. They felt their way along the rock with their hands and their pace slowed as they relied more and more on their other senses. It didn't take long before Pandora could see a rich, yellow glow coming from further down the passage.

"Come on, I think we're nearly there," she encouraged as she scrabbled forwards. The light got brighter and brighter until finally they reached the end of the path where they came across a large, jagged gap, big enough to fit through. Pandora squeezed through the crack in the rock and stepped into a cylindrical room, Orpheus following not far behind.

In front of them stood an enormous brazier. Behind it, three hooded figures stood side by side. "We are the judges of the Underworld." they spoke in unison, their voices deep and inhuman.

Pandora went to introduce herself. "My name is Pandora, I have come to speak with Hades."

The three figures each raised a finger to their lips, then pointed towards the flames in front of them. "Show us your truth."

Pandora stared at the flames and almost instinctively she held her arm out over the fire. Of course, this didn't hurt her, and she stared defiantly at the figures as smoke rose from the brazier. The smoke danced through the air towards them and they inhaled deeply.

"Welcome, Pandora," they said as one.

Raising her eyebrow a little, she removed her hand. Orpheus cleared his throat and stepped forwards.

"No, you'll hurt yourself," Pandora whispered but Orpheus thrust his hand into the fire before she could stop him. Never taking his eyes off the hooded figures, he grimaced at the pain but didn't move. The smell of burning flesh filled the room, smoke rose from the brazier once more and the three figures inhaled again.

"Welcome, Orpheus."

At the sound of his name, he removed his hand and clutched it to his chest, his face screwed up in agony only to gasp in surprise. He looked down at his hand to see that despite the reality of the pain and sensation, it was unscathed. He laughed, both impressed and relieved, and waved his hand at Pandora who did her best not to laugh too.

The hooded figures lowered their hands and the flames from the brazier went out, leaving behind only the cinders. Orpheus reached out to hold Pandora's hand and squeezed it gently in anticipation. In one voice, the figures spoke, "You share the same truth: reclamation. Proceed."

In a flash of movement, the figures threw their arms out in front of them, sweeping the smoke and ash from the brazier pit in a tidal wave that wrapped around the travellers. Orpheus pulled Pandora into his chest to shield her while holding his other arm protectively up to his face, the smoke swirling around them, obscuring their vision. For a few moments, the room vanished and they were surrounded by darkness, before the ash finally cleared. Somehow, they had arrived inside a magnificent throne room. The room had been carved out of the rock, everything flowing with the organic nature of their surroundings. The walls were covered in moss and vines, and water dripped from the ceiling which gave the whole place a damp, earthy smell. It felt natural and calm. They had appeared at the bottom of a flight of steps, and at the top, sitting on an enormous moss-covered throne, bident in hand, Hades watched intently.

Pandora could feel Orpheus' breathing accelerate at the sight of the god. She patted him encouragingly on the arm and stepped away from him towards the steps. Each step she took she breathed slowly, carefully. She wanted to appear strong; her fists tightly clenched and her teeth locked, she reached the throne. Of all the gods she had encountered, Hades looked the most intimidating. He was incredibly tall and broad, his skin a dark sallow grey, and his long black beard was plaited with ornamental beads that Pandora quickly realised were made of bone and teeth. Hades sat and watched the girl step forwards, his face sullen and dark. Finally, in an impossibly deep voice he spoke, "So, you're the pet my niece and nephew have grown so fond of."

An Invitation

Hades rose slowly from his chair and stepped towards Pandora. Scanning her up and down, he raised an eyebrow in curiosity. Pandora cleared her throat nervously. "My name is Pandora. I'm here to—"

"Oh, I know who you are, don't you worry about that," he said, laughing flatly.

Pandora frowned slightly. "Hephaestus told me you wanted to speak with me."

Hades stepped closer, towering over the girl. "Well, I never really *want* to speak to any of you," he drawled. "I find conversation rather exhausting, especially with *mortals*. Though in this case, needs must I suppose." His voice dripping with disdain, the imposing god turned and sat back down on his throne.

Pandora couldn't help but feel a little frustrated at his tone. "Can… can you help me?" she asked, trying not to let her exasperation show.

Hades let out a booming laugh. "*Help* you?" he cried. "I'm afraid this is not a fight for the gods."

Pandora's frown grew. "But Hephaestus—"

Hades slammed his fist down on the arm of his throne, cutting her off mid sentence. "Don't you think if we could have dealt with this ourselves, it would have been resolved by now? Trust you humans to expect us to do your dirty work for you."

Pandora was now finding it hard to hide her anger. "But this all happened because of Hermes," she said. "My father is dead, my home in ruins because a god chose to open the box."

"Ah" – Hades waved a finger at her – "but he didn't actually open the box, did he, my dear? You did."

"Well, if he hadn't—"

"My fellow deities unfortunately have a wonderful habit of orchestrating the follies of humans. We can influence, we can assist with advice or with gifts, but man is, and has always been, in charge of his own fate."

"We couldn't defeat it, even with Hephaestus' help," Orpheus shouted from the bottom of the steps.

Hades rolled his eyes and beckoned for him to come forwards. "I forgot there were two of you. By all means, young man, speak."

Orpheus ran up the steps two at a time and joined Pandora with a nod of solidarity. "If we couldn't defeat it with a god by our side, how are we supposed to defeat it now?"

"Well that all depends on what *it* is. Now that you have encountered it, perhaps you would care to describe it to me."

"Don't you know?" Pandora asked bluntly.

Hades shot her a terrifying look. "If I did, would I have asked?"

"No but—"

"Zeus was rather secretive when creating the box that was bound to you. I'm afraid not even I know of its contents. Nor, I thought, did any of the other gods."

Before Pandora could reply, the sound of an enormous door opening to the right of them caught her attention. Hades sighed and covered his eyes with his hand.

The sound of footsteps grew closer before a delighted squeal echoed through the cave. "Oh, guests!"

Pandora watched as a woman ran towards them and threw herself at her in a fond embrace. Pandora didn't have time to do anything as the woman pounced excitedly, knocking the wind out of her. Orpheus shot Pandora a look of bemusement.

"Persephone, my love." Hades sighed wearily and rubbed his temples. "Please meet my, um, *our* honoured guests."

Persephone let go of Pandora and took a step back, realising her forward behaviour had taken her by surprise. She held a delicate hand to her lips and giggled coyly. "Darling, why didn't you tell me. How exciting, this almost *never* happens." She moved her hand to speak behind it in a loud whisper, "He's not really one for company, you see, bit of a grump sometimes."

"Sephie, my love, I can hear you."

With another squeal, Persephone ran at her husband and jumped into his arms, showering him with kisses. He continued to scowl at his guests while his wife kissed him which caused Pandora to snort.

Whatever fear Pandora had felt being in this place had instantly dissolved at the introduction of Hades' wife. She was the complete opposite of her husband: she was even smaller than Pandora with elfin features, beautifully opalescent fair skin and long, flowing strawberry-blonde hair. Her face was delicate, and her blue eyes shone with a gentle purity. She was wrapped in light robes of green and gold that flowed effortlessly around her. The way she moved was playful and she had such an innocent elegance that Pandora and Orpheus couldn't help but smile, her personality infectious.

Climbing down from her perch on her husband's lap, she hurried back over to her new guests. "Oh, you poor things, the journey here must have been awful. You must be starving."

Hades rolled his eyes. "Darling, I didn't think we'd be—"

"Come," Persephone sang, clearly ignoring Hades' protest, "let me fix you something. Hades, you can talk to them while they eat. I'm not letting them leave without a proper meal. My mother always taught me to treat guests to a good feast."

~

Persephone led them into a room off the side of the great hall. It was beautiful in its simplicity. Like the throne room, it was carved out of the natural rock and the walls flowed elegantly with the shape of the cave. Compared to everything they had encountered so far, this place seemed much more inviting. The only furniture in the room was an enormous, thick ebony dining table which, to Pandora's surprise, was already groaning with food and jugs of glistening gold liquid. The raw, unpolished wood was laced with lichen and each chair had a thick blanket of moss. The floor and table were covered in candles and Pandora couldn't help but smile as she walked through the warm glow. Persephone danced through the room and encouraged her guests to be seated. She placed herself next to Pandora while Hades sat at the far end, clearly happy keeping his distance from the intrusive presence of the mortals. Pandora wondered how two people so completely different could be happy together.

"Oh do eat, please. Just help yourselves to anything you like." Persephone gestured eagerly to the food.

Orpheus didn't need to be told twice as he began to fill his plate with the bounty. Pandora sat and watched Hades as he stared blankly into the distance. Persephone tutted maternally and took Pandora's plate from her, filling it up with fruit and meats before setting it down again with an encouraging nod. Pandora knew she was hungry, but she was more concerned with speaking to Hades. The sooner she could leave this place – as nice as this meal was – the better. With a slightly strained smile, she took a dried fig and popped it in her mouth. This seemed to satisfy Persephone as she relaxed her posture a little and cleared her throat.

"You wanted to know what was in the box?" Pandora spoke, trying to re-engage Hades in the conversation that had been interrupted.

"Well, I'm sure you're going to tell me regardless of what I want." Hades rolled his eyes scathingly which was met with a terrifyingly stern look from his wife.

"*Be nice,*" she said, surprisingly menacingly. Hades scowled but nodded obligingly to Pandora to carry on with her story.

"It was like nothing I have ever seen before," she said. "We were attacked at the village where we met with Hephaestus."

"I had noticed his gifts." Hades pointed to her gauntlet and sword which made Pandora smile weakly.

"What we saw was like nothing I've ever seen. It seemed to be made of thousands of shadows. It was just… Darkness. It moved like a slow flood of black oil, with a thick fog or smoke, it had these tendrils, they came out of the mass and just consumed everything, pulling people and buildings into the oil. It destroyed everything." She tripped over her rambling words and became quiet as she relived what she had seen. "It didn't have a face, it was just this… evil. I don't know how to explain it better, I'm sorry."

"Tell him about the wolf things," Orpheus chimed in, his mouth full of food.

"Right," she said, her voice getting a little quicker, "out of the smoke came these wolves, but they weren't wolves. They were made of the same stuff, all covered in vines and black ash."

"They attacked Hephaestus," Orpheus added. "They would have got us too if he hadn't saved us."

Hades held a hand up and the room fell silent. "My nephew is too attached to your race. He's a fool," he said, disapproval colouring his words. "Why he even got involved, I have no idea." A furious expression on her face, Pandora was about to argue when Hades held up a weary hand once more. "I don't agree with his actions, girl, but I accept them. I simply don't understand his fixation on your kind. Though, having said that, from your rather exuberant description, it would appear that this is more interesting than I had first thought." He picked at his beard as he spoke. "Despite what I had initially thought, I fear that indeed I do know what is or rather what *was* imprisoned in the box."

Pandora took another fig from her plate; she needed to do something with her hands, the anticipation was too much.

Hades shared a concerned look with his wife, who Pandora realised had now gone very quiet: her eyes were painted with worry and she sat very still as she watched her husband.

"From what you have described, I can think of only one thing that could possibly create such a manifestation of darkness, but I…" Hades rose from his seat and paced lightly. Persephone glided out of her chair towards her husband and placed a concerned hand on his chest.

"I thought he was locked away in Tartarus," she said with a whisper.

"As did I." Hades took her hand in his to comfort her.

Pandora shot a look at Orpheus who by this point had stopped eating and was now avidly listening to the conversation.

"I need to speak with my brother," Hades said under his breath.

"They have a right to know, darling."

"I know, but I can't be sure until I speak with him."

"What if it is? What… what are we going to do?"

Pandora cleared her throat. Hades squeezed his wife's hand and encouraged her to take a seat next to him.

"Apologies, girl, it's just not what I had expected, and if it is what I think it is, then Zeus has kept us *all* in the dark."

Pandora felt an uneasy knot forming in her stomach. Whatever was behind all of this, the fact that it caused Hades to show concern and Persephone noticeable fear meant it was far worse than she could have imagined.

Hades took a deep breath and placed his palms on the table. "Aeons ago, there was a battle for control of the world, for Olympus itself. Despite what you humans may think, we weren't always the only ones with the power to rule. There were darker forces birthed by the primordial gods that threatened to rip the world apart. The greatest of these threats was a giant beast that went by the name Typhon." Hades appeared to shudder at the sound of his name. "An embodiment of all that is evil, he challenged Zeus for dominion over our world. They fought each other in a great battle that nearly destroyed everything. To this day, no one knows how my brother won, but he did. He told us that Typhon had been banished to the depths of Tartarus."

"But you don't know this for sure?" Pandora asked, confused. Tartarus was a part of the Underworld after all, a prison specifically designed to contain the very worst creatures, even imprison a god if needed.

Hades snorted. "My dear, there isn't a warden who manages Tartarus, no written log of its prisoners, no… guestbook as it were. Even I have no control over this place, none of us really do in case any of *us* need to be put in there." He poured a goblet of golden ambrosia and took a sip before continuing. "If Zeus really put Typhon in the box, and not in Tartarus, it wouldn't have been without good reason. He has in fact been safely imprisoned for an incomprehensible amount of time, so long that most of the gods haven't even spoken his name in centuries. Why my nephew wanted him released… I don't understand."

Pandora nodded solemnly. "Hermes."

Hades scowled. "Mmm, indeed. What could have possessed him to do such a thing, I do not know."

Pandora thought for a moment and raised a quizzical hand. "You said Typhon is a Giant?"

Hades nodded.

"But what we faced was no Giant." She shrugged. "I can't even be certain it had any real form."

The god sighed. "My only guess would be that after having been held captive for so long, Typhon's powers have diminished beyond recognition. I don't believe he is what you saw. Whatever it was, it was the form of whatever power he has left in this world."

"So, he's weak?"

"For now." Hades sighed. "For all we know, he could be gaining strength every second we don't find him. I would suspect he has fled and is in hiding while he regains his power. I must speak with Zeus and alert my brothers and sisters to this news." Hades turned to his wife and continued his train of thought in whispered conversation.

In that moment, Pandora felt incredibly small. Turning to her companion, she waited patiently for the gods to finish talking. If there had ever been a moment she had grown confident enough to believe she could win this battle, this was not it. In fact, never had she been more certain that this whole situation was now completely beyond her capabilities.

"What do I do?" she said sharply, her voice cutting through the tension.

Persephone squeezed her husband's hand and looked at him with concern. If he had heard Pandora, he didn't acknowledge it; rather, he sat and stared into space.

"What do I do?" Pandora said once more, this time barely above a whisper.

Persephone shot her husband a knowing look and swept up from the table to move to Pandora's side. Putting a comforting hand on her shoulder, she gestured for her to stand up. "I know this may all seem rather overwhelming at this point. Goodness knows, this was not what we had expected. I know what might just help you. Come, follow me."

With a defeated sigh, Pandora stood and followed Persephone towards the door. Orpheus rose too and began to move when Persephone held a hand up to stop him.

"I'm afraid not, young man," she chastised gently before moving closer to him to whisper in his ear. "Besides, I am sure you can think of something to talk to my husband about." With an encouraging nod, she pushed him back towards the table. Opening the door, Persephone led Pandora out of the room and away from her friend.

~

As the door closed behind them, Pandora watched Orpheus stand up from his seat and move closer to Hades. Sensing her reluctance to leave him, Persephone took hold of Pandora's hand as they walked. It wasn't until they had taken a few steps forwards that Pandora realised they were not back in the large throne room but instead were walking down a narrow corridor. The smell of the damp rock was intoxicating and as they walked, torches along either side of the hallway lit up.

Pandora looked at the goddess in confusion. "I thought we—"

"It'll save a lot of explanation if you try not to assume things work the same down here as they do on earth," Persephone chirped, amused by how easily humans were confused by such things.

Pandora rolled her eyes.

They continued down the corridor. The further they walked, the tighter the knot in Pandora's stomach felt. She could tell from Persephone's body language that wherever they were going, she was not hugely happy to be going there.

"You said this would help?" Pandora questioned.

"Help? Yes. Be pleasant? Not really."

"Oh, well, that's very reassuring."

"Mmm, I know, I'm sorry, and honestly I wouldn't have suggested it but they said they wanted to meet you so…"

Pandora tried to swallow the dry lump in her throat. "Um, who exactly wants to meet me?"

"The Moirai."

Pandora stopped in her tracks, entirely unprepared for that answer. "The Fates? The Fates want to speak to me?"

Persephone nodded, trying to make her smile as convincing as possible. "Come on, you don't want to keep them waiting."

They walked further down the dank corridor until they came to an archway. There was no light beyond the arch and it appeared to be filled with a thick grey fog that somehow did not seep back into the corridor; it just hung there as if held back by an invisible wall. Persephone stopped and stood to the side of the arch, gesturing for Pandora to continue.

"Oh, I'm definitely not going in there," Pandora said, laughing nervously, her jaw clenched.

"Shh! They can hear you."

Pandora shuddered as she felt a breeze pick up and blow towards the door.

"Look, I've met them before." Persephone winced. "It's not fun but if they ask for you, you go. Now just take a deep breath, relax and walk through the archway."

Pandora looked up at the ceiling in exasperation, filled her lungs with the damp air, composed herself and went to step forwards, only to suddenly have her path blocked by Persephone.

"I thought you said—"

"I forgot. When you walk through, walk in a straight line for exactly twenty paces then stop. And for the love of Zeus, don't touch *anything*!"

Pandora was now completely certain that she absolutely did not want to walk through that doorway. Every fibre of her being was telling her to just turn away but she knew she really didn't have a choice. With one last determined scowl at Persephone, Pandora marched through the fog into total darkness.

~

The sudden loss of vision made her panic a little. She froze on the spot and whispered, "Persephone."

A small voice whispered back, "Count to twenty."

Pandora counted her paces. Whatever the reason was for the instruction, she didn't want to find out what would happen if she got it wrong. As she took her final step, she braced herself, but nothing happened. She could see nothing, hear nothing, and most disconcertingly, she could smell nothing. She desperately wanted to wave her hands out in front of her, but she took Persephone's words to heart and kept her arms firmly rooted to her sides.

Trying to calm her breathing, Pandora shut her eyes. After a few moments she realised she could hear water, or at least she thought she could. It started off quiet, the sound of tiny droplets hitting a pool, like light rain on a lake. Slowly, she opened her eyes and gasped.

What she had thought to be a room was now a seemingly endless abyss. Pandora was standing on a platform in the middle of a metallic sea. The liquid shone and sparkled like molten iron. The surface of the water was completely still apart from the occasional droplets falling which created delicate ripples that fanned out across the sea. Curiously, Pandora raised her head up to the sky. Above her were thousands upon thousands of threads. Each one the thickness of a strand of hair, they moved together like seaweed. Every so often a droplet of the liquid metal would creep down a strand and fall into the pool. Some of them fell fast, some slow – there seemed to be no rhythm to the orchestrated cacophony. Pandora had never seen anything like it before. It was utterly breathtaking.

"H-hello?" she called out shakily.

Looking out across the sea, she saw large ripples form on the surface and they were working their way towards her.

Pandora stood, fists clenched, and before her eyes the liquid rose up sharply in front of her. Throwing her arms out in protection, she poked her head around to see the molten metal had formed the shape of a young girl. She had very few features, the liquid barely forming the outlines of a face, but the nature of her movements appeared playful.

"I know her," the form squealed with a playful laugh. "She's the girl." The liquid splashed and danced around the child.

"Well, I suppose I—"

Before Pandora could continue, the form of the little girl vanished, and the liquid crashed back down only to rise up again on the other side of the platform, this time in the shape of an old woman.

"Awfully skinny, isn't she," a wizened voice judged.

"Awfully," a third voice agreed, as the metal spiralled, and the face of the elderly woman was replaced with that of a younger woman.

"Can I play with her?" the little girl chimed in again.

"She's not here to play," the other voices scolded.

"Clay. She's made of clay."

"Oh, clay."

The iron sea sprayed and tossed as the forms of the women moved. Pandora could barely keep up with them, staggering as she spun. The voices babbled over one another in a confusing spiral of words.

"She's the one."

"What one?"

"She opened the box," the little girl said as the old woman appeared behind her.

"The human who opened the box?"

"She's not human," the young woman said and vanished, and the old woman turned to Pandora and winked.

"Clay, clay, clay," the little girl squealed, stamping her feet playfully causing sprays of liquid to splash up.

Pandora could feel her frustration building. "You summoned me. What do you want?"

"What do we want?"

"What do we want?"

"What do *you* want?" the young woman asked in a brash tone.

Pandora bowed her head. "I… uh…"

"Father," the little girl sang.

"Home."

"Friend."

"*Mother,*" the old woman said, and then sighed, a hand on her heart.

"Please, I—" Pandora begged.

"The box, she opened it."

"Not right."

"Bad, bad, bad clay," the little girl sang again.

"What do I *do*?" Pandora shouted above the clamour of noise being thrown at her. Her head was spinning and she felt sick to her stomach.

The old woman appeared close to Pandora's shoulder, seeming to reach out to her. "Don't worry, child, there's still Hope."

The young woman appeared at her back. "You don't know that."

"Hope." The little girl smiled.

"You don't know that."

"Use the box."

"She already opened the box."

"Opened the box."

"Look."

"The box."

"Hope."

"Opened it, but did not see."

"Open the box."

The voices were growing more deafening, and Pandora covered her ears. They repeated the phrases over and over until finally Pandora fell to her knees in pain and frustration.

"Stop!" she shouted at the liquid manifestations, her head swimming with their words. Instantly they dissipated, crashing into the sea as ripples in the surface radiated out from where they had stood. The silence was even more deafening than the screaming. Pandora realised she was breathing heavily, her chest moving rapidly as the panic of the situation engulfed her. Tilting her head up, she saw the sea move once more, slowly this time, as the figure of the old woman appeared.

She held a finger to her lips and smiled. "*Open* the box," she said, and in an instant, she vanished, leaving behind her the undisturbed surface of the sea.

Pandora sat there for a long while. Unwilling to move, she stared out at the abyss, watching the drops fall from the dancing fibres above. Her heart felt heavy. She had thought they would have helped her, given some advice, a path to follow, just… *something*. Instead, she felt more confused about her place in the world than ever. If the Fates had nothing helpful to tell her, then surely she was of no importance. If she was supposed to go on this journey, fight this evil, *surely* they would have known, would have had something to say. Instead she felt mocked for what she had done. Bitterly she closed her eyes and pushed herself up from the ground, and as she did the sea vanished, the threads in the sky gone. Pandora turned around to see the dim archway she had come through, a warm glow filtering through the fog that barred the exit. Sighing wearily, she marched back towards it to find Persephone.

~

Stepping through the archway, Pandora saw Persephone leaning anxiously against the wall. "Oh, you're back. How did it go?"

"I… I'm not sure. I don't—"

Persephone nodded her head solemnly. "Mmm, I thought you might say that." She rubbed a hand maternally on Pandora's back and slowly guided her back through the corridor. "Sometimes it takes a while, but you will understand eventually. When the time is right."

They reached the large door to the room they had previously left. Persephone went to open it but stopped, resting her palm on the handle for a moment, before opening the door just an inch to peer in.

"They told me to open the box," Pandora mumbled a little sheepishly.

Clearly a little distracted by what she was looking at, Persephone waved a reassuring hand at Pandora. "Well of course, dear, how do you expect to put everything back in?" Closing the door again, she turned to Pandora and smiled weakly. "I, uh, something happened while you were in there."

The familiar knot began to form in Pandora's stomach again and she narrowed her eyes at the goddess who took her hands reassuringly.

"Now I love my husband dearly, but he has never exactly been known for his kindness to others. I feel being with me may have rubbed off on him a touch."

"What do you mean?"

"Your friend, he asked my husband for something, something I thought he couldn't give."

The knot tightened and Pandora's eyes widened as she realised what Persephone was talking about. "His wife?"

She nodded, the sheepish smile not leaving her face. "Are the two of you, um…" She fidgeted with her fingers, clearly uncomfortable.

It didn't take Pandora long to realise what she was insinuating. Unable to control it, she burst out laughing with a rather inelegant snort. "Oh gods no. He's my friend, Persephone."

Relief flooded the goddess's face as she joined in the laughter. "Oh, you have no idea how much I was dreading this conversation."

Pandora was doubled over laughing; the notion of anything remotely romantic with Orpheus was too much, and it took her a moment to realise what had happened. When she did, she grabbed Persephone in excited shock. "Sorry, his wife? Hades gave him back his wife?!"

Persephone nodded, her smile now warmer. "Darling girl, even now my husband still surprises me. He has done a wonderful thing for your friend. Come, I will let them explain." With a delicate pull, Persephone opened the door of the room. Directly in front of them stood Orpheus, his face pale and his hands shaking. Pandora looked at him with concern.

"Is she there? I won't believe it until you tell me, Pandora. Is she?"

Pandora peered around her friend, unsure why he didn't look for himself. Everything in the room was as it had been before she left. Hades was sitting at the end of the table, his expression beyond boredom. The only difference being that now, a few metres behind Orpheus stood a woman. Her raven black hair fell in loose waves and she was dressed in pure white robes, with an ethereal glow, her skin ghostly and translucent. With a kind smile, she nodded slowly at Pandora.

Clutching his shaking hand, Pandora turned her eyes back to Orpheus.

"Yes," she whispered, "she's here."

With that, Orpheus let out a moan of exhaustion and relief, then sank to his knees and wept.

A Light in the Dark

Pandora watched as her friend wept. Slowly, she kneeled down beside him and held him as he sobbed. Persephone made her way to her husband and kissed him kindly on the cheek. "You've done a wonderful thing, my love."

Hades sighed nonchalantly and patted her hand. "A few years ago things might have been different. This is all your fault." He nudged her gently. "I've gone soft."

Persephone rolled her eyes and rested her cheek against his.

The room was quiet and still, everyone captivated by the presence of the ethereal woman. After a while, Orpheus' tears eventually dried, and he turned to his friend with a weak smile. "You can see her?"

Pandora turned once again to Eurydice who was still standing in patient anticipation. "Of course I can," she said, "can't you?"

Orpheus shook his head. Hades took his goblet of ambrosia from the table and sipped it. "Your friend made a very compelling argument," he said, nodding in Orpheus' direction. "I have offered him a second chance of sorts." He rose from his chair and walked over to Eurydice. "I have decided to let his wife return to the land of the living on one condition."

"Orpheus cannot look at her until you are back on the surface... in your world," Persephone explained gently.

Wiping his face, Orpheus looked at Pandora. "I must prove my trust in the gods. If I look at her before we reach the surface, she'll vanish."

Pandora frowned. "I can see her." She took her friend's hands in hers.

"You may not be able to but I can, and I'll be with you every second of the way. We'll make it back, all of us… I promise."

Orpheus' eyes brightened and he squeezed her hand in thanks. "She is everything to me," he said, tears once again threatening to fall down his cheeks.

"I know," Pandora said, her tone softening, "don't worry, she *will* make it."

Persephone broke the tender moment by squealing and clapping her hands. "Oh well, this is just a marvellous end to your stay. There's so much doom and gloom around here, it's refreshing to see such a happy ending."

"You really are quite sickening sometimes, my love." Hades teased her lightly only to be met with a clip round the ear from his wife. "I'm still in charge around here, you know," he said in a deep, threatening voice.

Pandora gritted her teeth uncomfortably at the sound but Persephone simply giggled and kissed him on the nose. "Of course you are," she said with a patronising smile.

Pandora snorted and Hades flashed her a wicked scowl before turning to his wife. "Gods dammit, woman, you are doing nothing for my reputation."

Pandora helped Orpheus to his feet, careful to keep him facing away from his wife. She dusted herself off and smiled awkwardly at her hosts. "I guess we should be making our way back then."

"Did you speak with the Fates?" Hades enquired with a weary yawn.

Pandora nodded. "They spoke of the box and said I should open it again."

"Of course they did, because that worked out so well the first time," Hades said.

The words stung, and Pandora's heart ached at the memory. "Like I said, we should be going," she murmured weakly.

They collected their belongings and prepared themselves for departure,

Eurydice standing solemnly behind them all the while.

Persephone's voice cut through the silence. "Oh, before you go," she said, skipping towards Pandora, "Hades and I have a gift for you." Holding her hand out, she rested her palm around Pandora's neck.

"What are you—"

"Shh! I'm concentrating," Persephone whispered comically.

Pandora felt something hit her chest and when Persephone removed her hand, she revealed a delicate black pendant. The surface of the stone was uncut, its natural rough form only enhancing its beauty. It was framed by a delicate golden wreath that attached to a thin gold necklace. It was so light, Pandora could barely feel it around her neck. She turned it around in her hands, tracing the rough edges of the stone.

"It's beautiful, thank you, Persephone." She smiled warmly at the goddess who then took her in a maternal embrace and moved her lips close to her ear.

"You are going to face many evils in this world." She spoke the words gently so that only Pandora could hear them. "This pendant will help guide you."

Turning to Hades, Pandora nodded in thanks for his help. He acknowledged it with a low bow of his head before gesturing towards the door. Orpheus was still staring at the door, fearful of moving. Pandora walked towards him and took his hand in hers once more. "You can do this," she encouraged, "let's get her home."

With a deep sigh, he stepped forwards and opened the door. The pair walked out into the darkness as the ethereal figure of his wife followed silently a few paces behind.

~

This time, rather than the throne room or the corridor, the doors opened out into the mouth of the cave, just behind the gates that marked the entrance to the

Underworld. As they walked forwards, the fearsome jaws opened slowly and Pandora could see Charon tending to his boat on the shore. When he saw the three of them walk through, he stopped what he was doing and smiled. Pandora felt the familiar knot in her stomach at the sight of him.

"Well, aren't you a sight for sore eyes," he called out.

Pandora smiled to herself. Orpheus nudged her for reassurance that his wife was still with them. She turned to check and nodded to her friend, hoping to ease his worry.

As they passed the gates and stepped out onto the grey beach, their path was blocked by Cerberus. The three-headed dog who had before been reasonably docile now bared his teeth, ferociously snarling, his eyes a burning blood red. Pandora bent into a crouch and reached cautiously for her sword only to be stopped by Orpheus.

"Hades warned me that this might happen. The dead aren't supposed to leave this place and Cerberus is the gatekeeper."

Pandora turned back to his wife, whose face was solemn, her eyes closed.

"What are we going to do? Orpheus? *Orpheus*."

He walked towards the beast slowly, his hands outstretched in supplication. Quietly he began to sing. He sang his story, the tale he had told back at the hall in the training school, a song that had left every grown man in the place a whimpering wreck. As he walked towards Cerberus, all three of the dog's heads followed him. While Orpheus sang, the dog began to sway appreciatively, his heads bowed and his eyes drooped, and it wasn't long before he had collapsed gently in a heap, his magnificent heads resting lightly on his paws. Tentatively Orpheus walked around him, continuing to sing gently, and beckoned behind him for the two women to follow. Pandora jogged to catch up with him, eager to make it past the terrifying creature, while Eurydice glided silently across the sand.

Walking towards Charon, they saw him scratch his head in confusion at the sight of Eurydice. "I thought there were only two of you?"

Pandora flicked the coin at him and strode boldly onto the boat. "There were, now there are three."

"Does Hades know?" His tone was serious and he frowned at the woman's presence. Orpheus clapped him on the shoulder and nodded. "Oh, well then, welcome aboard." He bowed low and waved towards the boat.

Orpheus walked straight to the bow and sat facing the water as Eurydice took Charon's hand and stepped aboard.

"I guess it's never a dull day with you two, eh?" Charon chuckled as he pushed the boat into the water and swung himself elegantly on board.

Pandora positioned herself in the middle of the boat, sitting sideways so she could keep an eye on both her companions. Orpheus bent his head down in his lap and wrapped his arms around himself while Eurydice remained standing, her gaze blank as she stared out across the water.

Charon sat down heavily opposite Pandora, a confused expression on his face. "Everything okay?" he asked in a mock whisper.

"It will be," Pandora replied, her face stony.

"Oh come on," he teased, "you mean to tell me you've just met with Hades and lived to tell the tale, not to mention saved your friend's wife from the Underworld, which by the way *has never been done before*, and that is still no cause for a smile? You should be celebrating."

"We're not out yet," Pandora replied, her face full of concern.

Sensing her worry, Charon reached towards her for a split second, as if to take her hand but decided against it and just ended up smiling awkwardly. "You'll make it, don't you worry."

Seeing the kindness in his eyes, Pandora couldn't help but break a fragile smile. He was infuriating but behind it all was decency. She felt bad for having been so cold before. "This must get very lonely," she said, her eyes scanning the boat.

Charon stared out at the tumultuous waves. "I suppose. I've never really thought about it." Something in his tone deceived him and Pandora could feel that he wasn't being entirely truthful. "I remember her." He nodded towards Eurydice, speaking in a quiet voice so as not to alert Orpheus. "She was so confused, so truly heartbroken. I'm a god with a purpose, I am the ferryman. That is who I am, that is *what* I am. I had never felt any need for anything more until I met her."

Pandora watched the ghostly woman, her robes and hair billowing in the wind. She couldn't bring herself to look at the god in front of her; no man had ever spoken to her so openly about such things.

Charon continued his story, picking tentatively at his fingers. "Meeting her, watching her heart break into a million pieces at the knowledge of her lost love, that was the first time I thought to myself that there could be something in that. Though with my work, there isn't a whole lot of time to meet anyone… I guess you could say I was jealous, as twisted as that sounds."

Pandora didn't know how to respond, but luckily she didn't have to. They had reached the shore and Charon coughed awkwardly before standing to moor the boat to the dock. Orpheus jumped off the bow like a cat and walked forwards a few paces before stopping to wait for Pandora who followed quickly behind. She held his hand as she watched Eurydice move delicately off the boat onto the sand and nodded to her friend to confirm that his wife was there.

With a sigh of relief, Orpheus called back to Charon, who was still tying up the boat. "Where do we go now?"

Charon tightened the rope he was tying and jumped onto the sand, walking towards his passengers. "Straight ahead, the cave will open out at the river Acheron. You'll be in the mountains, but it shouldn't be too far from Gliki. If you walk towards the coast, you should reach Ammoudia in less than a day. If you need a ship, that's the first place I would recommend."

Pandora shot a confused face at Orpheus. This all seemed incredibly simple compared to their journey there.

Charon noticed their concern. "Don't worry," he said, laughing, "when you're not supposed to be here, getting out is actually much easier than getting in." He shot a subtle look at Pandora. "Though once you leave, you can't come back in the same way."

Orpheus nodded encouragingly to Pandora and the two friends smiled, grateful to be near the end of this part of their journey. After so long in this dark, dreary place, Pandora was looking forward to fresh air. She went to start walking but the knot in her stomach tightened. For a moment she stood still, then, breaking away from Orpheus, she walked back towards the river, past Eurydice, who was patiently waiting, and stopped in front of Charon. "Thank you for everything," she said with a brash, slightly awkward nod.

Charon coughed, trying to hide a smile, and gestured nonchalantly towards her. "Oh, please, just doing my job, young lady. You, uh, you have a pleasant trip."

A brief smile shot across Pandora's face. As she turned to leave, she felt him reach out and grab her arm; his touch was gentle but firm, the warmth of it making the skin on her arm prickle. He held out his hand and in it lay the coin she had paid him for her journey. She held her hands up in argument but he insisted. "Please, take it. I know you have a long road ahead of you and I'm sure you have plenty to fill your time but just humour me."

Reluctantly she took the coin.

Charon shrugged. "I'd like to think I'll see you again, but without this, well, that would be a terrible day."

Pandora realised what he was saying. This was certainly no place for the living. Without the coin, the next time she'd see him would be after her death.

~

Their journey out was just as Charon had said. The way out of the cave was a long one and the ground was uneven, but it was a comparatively simple journey to what they had had to endure to enter the Underworld. Their pace was slow at first as Orpheus was hesitant to go any faster for fear of losing his beloved. Pandora took his hand and every few paces squeezed it to reassure him that she was still there, silently gliding along behind them. This soon eased his worry and he even managed to smile in earnest as they walked. It didn't take long for their surroundings to change. The dank, dark walls of the cave began to lighten, and the smell of the air became fresher. Small flowers and grasses had crept their way in and taken root in some of the cracks in the rocks.

"Can you hear that?" Pandora asked enthusiastically as the sounds of birdsong echoed through the cave.

"We must be close," Orpheus said, and his whole body began to relax at the thought of it. Just a few paces further and they saw it. The wide mouth of the cave appeared, the light of the outside world so bright it blinded them. Laughing at the sight, Orpheus let go of Pandora and sprinted ahead, plunging through the entrance into the light. He threw his arms out and basked in the warmth of the sun. Pandora began to run after him but turned back to see that Eurydice's pace had not quickened; instead, she continued to walk slowly and purposefully through the cave.

"Hang on, Orpheus," Pandora shouted, "we're coming." She walked ahead a few paces, also eager to get back to the world. When she finally reached the mouth of the cave, she looked back at Eurydice, only a few paces behind her, and stepped out into the light. As her eyes adjusted to the brilliant daylight, she covered her face and saw her friend standing only metres in front of her.

"Don't turn yet, Orpheus, she's coming."

"Okay, Pandora, tell me when," he yelled in response, almost jumping up and down in impatience.

Pandora watched as Eurydice floated elegantly out of the cave, each footstep heavy with anticipation. Her face was serene, a warm smile spreading from ear to ear as she stretched her arms out to her beloved. The first thing to pass through the mouth of the cave were her fingertips. Pandora's mouth dropped as she watched the perfect pale pink colour of her skin bloom. It travelled up her arms, across her chest, rose flushed in her cheeks and lips, and her eyes became a dark chestnut as she was slowly reborn. It was a truly magnificent sight to behold.

Pandora knew her friend would be in agony waiting and was about to call out to remind him not to look when she felt a deathly cold hand grip across her face, covering her mouth. Eyes wide, she clawed at the hand, trying to free herself. The breath she felt on her neck made her sick to her stomach as she desperately tried to break away from whoever had grabbed her. Turning her head, she caught a glimpse of the pointed features that made her heart drop to her feet. It was all too clear who it was. She tried to scream but no sound came out of her mouth. He had silenced her.

From next to her ear, a voice called out to her friend, "Orpheus, she's alive. Orpheus, look, look!" Pandora's heart dropped to her stomach as she recognised the voice as her own, stolen from her by her captor. She tried desperately to call out, to tell her friend it was Hermes, but she couldn't. She screamed silently, powerless to stop what was about to happen. The world slowed as she watched Eurydice, so close to reality, all she had to do was take one more step, that's all it was, just one more step. Hearing a sickening cackle in her ear, Hermes turned her to face Orpheus as he spun around eagerly, desperate to be reunited with his long-lost wife.

As he turned, Hermes whispered in Pandora's ear, "I win," and then vanished. The next few moments felt like an eternity. She watched as Orpheus' expression turned from elation to horror as he saw his wife stop moving, her back foot frozen in the cave, the colour having not yet reached it.

"No, NO!" he screamed, running to his wife. "What did you do, Pandora?! What did you do?!"

Orpheus took his wife in his arms and tried desperately to pull her from the cave but she couldn't move. Her eyes filled with pain at the realisation of what had happened and she gripped him in a fierce embrace. Pandora held her hands to her mouth as she watched the couple cling to each other and weep.

"Oh, my love, my darling wife. I'm here, please don't go, please. Don't leave me again."

She wiped his tears with her fingers and kissed him with devout intensity. Slowly but defiantly, the colour began to bleed out of Eurydice, leaving behind the ethereal ghostly form she had taken before. They clung to each other ferociously until the last drops of colour left her lips and she regained her spirit form.

The dead cannot live outside the Underworld and Pandora cried out in horror and grief as Eurydice's ghost was pulled roughly back into the cave, away from her husband, who fell to his knees as he felt her leave his grasp. The sound he made was barely human. Roaring in agony, he clawed at his chest as if to rip out his broken heart.

Pandora ran to him, trying desperately to explain. "Orpheus, it wasn't… Hermes, he… Orpheus, *please*." She couldn't find the words; her whole body felt like it was shutting down. Fearing that Hermes might return, Pandora knew they needed to move. She grabbed Orpheus by the arm and tried to drag him away from the cave but he was too heavy. "Orpheus, please, we need to go."

He screamed out at her and pushed her away from him but she wouldn't give up.

Locking her arms around his torso, she dragged him away from the cave. "It was Hermes, Orpheus, you have to believe me. Please believe me."

He picked himself up and shoved her again before staggering off towards the nearby treeline. Pandora took a few paces forwards before he turned back to her and screamed, "Do *NOT* follow me."

Her breathing heavy, she threw up her hands in submission and watched as her friend began to walk away again only to collapse in agony. She ran to him and fell next to him, taking him in her arms and locking them tight. He fought her with excruciating rage but eventually the grief overwhelmed him and he sobbed uncontrollably until he had no tears left to shed.

~

They sat there for a long time. Neither uttered a word – the shock had stolen their voices. The sun fell low in the sky and the light began to fade. Pandora knew they would have to find shelter soon, so after much encouragement she managed to help Orpheus to his feet and they staggered together towards the forest. It didn't take her long to set up a basic camp. The forest floor was soft with moss and the canopy thick. She lit a fire and watched as the flames crackled and sparked. Pulling from her bag some of the provisions that Persephone had given them, she tried to encourage her friend to eat but he would not. Orpheus sat limply against a nearby tree. His face was deathly pale, his eyes bloodshot and blank. It was clear to Pandora that two souls had been ripped back into the Underworld that day. It pained her greatly to see her friend in such agony. Hermes had once again destroyed someone she loved and the anger she felt in her heart was deafening.

"I was ready to kill you, you know," a small, broken voice escaped from Orpheus' lips.

Pandora turned to him and waited patiently for him to continue.

"That's what he wanted, wasn't it? He wanted me to kill you."

"I… I guess so," Pandora mumbled, picking at the earth.

"I know it wasn't you. I know you, Pandora." He smiled weakly and held an open hand out towards her.

Pain furrowing her brow, she sighed and took his hand. "Orpheus, I am *so* sorry." Her voice was hoarse and shaky. "It's still my fault. He was after me. If you hadn't been with me, it would have never happened."

Orpheus held up his hand to stop her. "Please don't, Pandora," he said. "Speculating won't change anything. I held my wife today. It may have only been for a brief moment but it is a moment I never thought I would get. *That* is because of you and I will forever be in your debt." He looked up at the canopy as he fought back the tears that threatened to spill again. "I would have waited an eternity for that moment, a moment that *you* gave me…" He wiped his eyes as his voice broke. "And by the gods, it was worth the pain."

They sat together in silence for the rest of the night, watching the fire until sleep overpowered Orpheus first and he drifted off. Pandora contemplated everything that had happened since they left Hephaestus. She had no knowledge of how much time had passed and felt uneasy as a result. Turning the necklace Persephone had given her over in her hands, she thought back to the Fates and their garbled message. She had hoped for advice on what to do next, but in reality she was no closer to understanding her path than she had been before she was dragged through the earth to Charon and his boat. A small smile escaped as she thought of him, but it was quickly gone when she remembered what the elderly fate had said to her.

"Open the box."

Persephone had dismissed the comment but Pandora wondered if there was more to it. She rummaged in her belongings until her fingers found the small wooden box. Moving closer to the now dwindling fire, she examined it intensely.

What good could possibly come from opening it again? she thought to herself, anxious of the possibilities. The Fates hadn't seemed devious. Unlike the gods, Pandora understood that they weren't fuelled by personal gain. Their sole purpose is observation and monitoring the lives of every living thing. Looking over at Orpheus, Pandora smiled at the serene expression on his face. *At least his grief doesn't fill his dreams*, she thought, trying not to think about how envious she was of this.

"What should I do, Father?" she whispered to herself. She knew he wouldn't have questioned the Fates. His trust in their divinity was absolute, but then again, he was far more trusting in them than she had ever been. She pondered her options for a long time before finally she took a deep breath and flicked open the clasp. Hands shaking, she peered into the box, though to her relief, this time nothing came out. She turned it upside down and gave it a tentative tap, but still nothing happened. Hissing in frustration, she tossed it back in with her belongings before finally falling asleep.

~

When she awoke the next day, she found herself alone. Orpheus was gone, as were all his things. Panicked, Pandora jumped to her feet and called out his name. She ran through the nearby forest desperate to find some clue as to where he'd gone but he had covered his tracks well. Not finding any sign of the direction in which he left the camp, she felt defeated and made her way back. A sudden thought stung in the back of her mind and her stomach dropped: *What if Hermes has taken him?* She quickened her pace, hoping that this was not a reality. Back at camp, she scanned the floor for clues and immediately relaxed. In the spot where he had been sleeping, he had left a small bunch of wild flowers, just like the ones he had picked for her back at the training school. She winced as she bent down to pick them up, regretting not having stretched properly, and drew in a deep breath of the woody, floral scent.

So preoccupied by the flowers, Pandora didn't even notice that the bag her belongings were in was open, and at the top of it sat the box, its lid open ever so slightly. Those flowers were all she needed to know that he was safe. He had been through unimaginable pain yesterday and it didn't surprise her that he may need some time on his own. They had parted on good terms and she was sure she would see him again.

Reluctant to acknowledge she was now alone, Pandora kept her focus on the flowers and went for a short walk. It was made even shorter as only metres away from camp, she tripped on a rock, hit her head on a nearby log and the world went black.

When she awoke, her eyes bleary from the injury, she could see something small and white sitting on her chest. As she regained focus, she realised that whatever it was, it was moving. Screaming in shock, she hit it with the back of her hand, causing it to fly through the air. She jumped to her feet, panicked and unsure of where it had gone; Pandora scanned her surroundings, her attention drawn to a rustling in the thicket only a few metres away. Steadily she stalked towards it and in a swift motion pulled apart the bushes. In front of her, a small white flame flew up from in among the leaves. It was no bigger than a pomegranate and for some reason it was floating in the air directly in front of Pandora's face. Worried that the hit to her head had done more damage than she first thought, Pandora rubbed her eyes again but the little flame remained floating in front of her. She reached out a hand towards it and with an outstretched finger, she went to touch it. However, the little flame had the same idea and a tiny little limb stretched out at the same time. Naturally this made Pandora scream. Unnaturally, the little flame screamed too.

Reunion

This is a dream, Pandora thought to herself as she walked, *it's got to be a dream*, the little flame bobbing delicately just behind her right shoulder. *Stop looking at it, Pandora, it's not real.* She stomped through the forest, all the while muttering to herself. Every so often she would turn back to check that the odd little creature was still there and every time she did, it made her jump ever so slightly.

"You're not real," she called over her shoulder, "I hit my head, this is all just a result of that. You know what" – she spun round to chastise the flame – "stop follow…" only to find that it had gone.

Looking around in confusion, Pandora assumed she had regained full cognitive control. She turned back round to carry on walking only to find herself staring face to face with the creature, causing her to yell out in surprise and irritation.

"Would you *stop* doing that," she moaned, the little creature now giggling and flitting about.

Getting that close to it, she noticed it had delicate facial features, two small eyes and a thin mouth. They arrived back at the camp site and Pandora started pacing, rubbing her temples. "So, this is really happening," she said, throwing her arms up in frustration. "How can I know? *Is* this really happening?"

The little flame shrugged.

"Can you speak?"

The flame responded with an excitable series of garbles and chirps like a small child.

Pandora rolled her eyes. "So that's a no then," she said with a sigh. "Where did you come from?"

A bright glow rippled through the flame and it babbled to itself as it flew over to Pandora's bag, sitting itself on top of the box which Pandora now realised was still open.

"I thought I closed that," Pandora said, now a little cautious. "You… you came out of there?"

The little flame nodded.

"How did you—"

The flame pointed to Pandora and mimed opening the box.

"Last night, when I opened it? You were still in there?"

The creature nodded, a small smile on its face. The little thing didn't appear to be dangerous; it looked harmless enough, almost infantile in its character. Pandora's brow furrowed as she studied the creature.

She spoke softly, "Were you in there with… you know… him?"

The little flame shivered and nodded, its gaze low.

"So, you're not on his side then?"

The flame scowled and a small growl came from its tiny mouth.

Pandora smirked, holding her hands up in a non-threatening manner. "Okay, okay. I get it. I guess we're on the same side."

The creature calmed at her words and instantly went back to the childish babbling.

Pandora couldn't understand how such a small, innocent thing could have made it in that prison for so long. She sat down on the ground in front of the box and crossed her legs.

Picking up the box, she shut the clasp tight and looked at the creature with curiosity. "How did you survive?" she asked earnestly, her voice soft.

The flame closed its eyes, screwing up its tiny face in concentration and slowly, it grew very, very small. So small that when it flew down into the weeds, Pandora couldn't see it.

She smiled sadly. "You hid for all that time?"

The flame popped back up, once more its original size, and nodded, a proud expression on its face.

"Do you have a name?" Pandora asked.

The little creature nodded and its arms waved around excitedly as it babbled frantically.

"Well, I can't understand you," Pandora said, laughing. "How am I supposed to know what it is?"

The flame paused in thought for a moment and then started flitting about. It hunched over and chattered in a croaky voice, pointing at Pandora. It then moved and started singing childishly before changing to a haughty expression and pointing at Pandora in an authoritative manner. It switched between these three impressions more and more frantically before hovering low to the ground, panting, clearly a little out of breath.

"The Fates?" Pandora guessed with a shrug.

The creature waved its arms about excitedly.

"But the Fates didn't say anything about you."

The flame rolled its eyes and held out its arms in frustration and Pandora thought back to what they had said, trying to decipher the creature's clues. *Opened it but did not see ... there's still Hope...*

"Hope," she whispered, "is your name Hope?"

The little flame chirped in excitement and flew around in spirals.

"Okay, okay, so you're called Hope." Pandora laughed before holding a hand to her chest. "I'm Pandora."

Hope flew forwards until she was just inches from Pandora's face. A tiny limb reached out to touch Pandora's nose. Although she couldn't feel it, Pandora smiled at the connection.

"It's nice to meet you, Hope."

~

Pandora knew she should try and get back to civilisation as soon as possible. She packed up her belongings and began to walk towards the coast. The walk was not a difficult one as once they had left the mountains, the terrain was predominantly flat. Pandora was pleased to have the company of Hope. Being without Orpheus, she had felt incredibly alone, but having the small flame bob along beside her made her feel a little less isolated. Although conversation wasn't exactly flowing given she struggled to understand the creature, it was evident that the little thing understood her. Pandora talked to her about everything that had happened since she opened the box. It was possible that Hope might have some idea as to what Pandora should do next.

After a few hours they rested for lunch. Pandora ate a little while the flame hovered patiently by her side. They were now getting close to the sea and Pandora could smell the familiar scent of salt in the air. It was the first time in a long while that she felt close to home. She knew her village was a lifetime away from where she was now but the smell of the sea air was comforting. It was then that Hope sprang up and flitted towards a group of nearby trees. She vanished in among the leaves and after a few moments of rustling flew out, waving her little limbs and squealing in panic.

Out of the trees shot a small owl. It was close on Hope's tail and was headed towards Pandora. Hope reached her first and hid underneath her arm as the elegant bird landed silently a few paces away. Pandora recognised the bird instantly: it was Athena's owl, the same one that had sent Polemides the message to meet with Hephaestus. She smiled and threw it a small piece of her food.

"Don't worry," she whispered to Hope, "he won't hurt you."

She heard a cross grumble come out from under her arm and smirked.

"Why are you here?" she called out to the owl.

The owl screeched in response and flew off in the direction of the coast. Pandora stood and squinted as she followed the owl with her gaze.

"That must be Ammoudia, the port that Charon told us about."

Hope mumbled incoherently before popping out and pointing towards the owl.

"Yes, we need to go that way. Athena must want to meet. That owl is hers, and if it goes that way" – she stood abruptly – "then we go that way."

Hope copied Pandora's tone in mock annoyance and Pandora snorted.

"Be nice. I really don't think he meant to scare you."

The little flame crossed her arms and snorted at the owl who playfully snapped his beak back at her.

~

It didn't take them long to reach the edge of the town. The road from the mountains was well maintained and easy to travel on. When they reached the first wave of houses, Pandora stopped and scanned her surroundings.

"Do you hear that, Hope?" she whispered.

The little flame looked around and shrugged. There was no sound, no shouting people, no livestock, not even the birds were singing.

Pandora sighed and shook her head, recognising the feeling in her stomach. "I think the Darkness got here first."

Her heart sank when she realised that her prediction was right. They walked through the ghost town in silence, the sight of the upturned carts, the rubble and destroyed homes all too much for Hope. She hid in Pandora's bag and covered her little eyes.

"Don't worry, you stay in there until I call you," Pandora comforted her.

She scanned her surroundings and realised, to her surprise, that the destruction was less severe than she had seen previously. Spotting the owl perched on the roof of a nearby building, Pandora felt anxious excitement at the thought of seeing Athena again. So much had happened since she started her journey. She was nervous that Athena would be displeased. She was no closer to finding Typhon and even if she was, she had no idea how she would defeat him. Meanwhile the Darkness he controlled was terrorising towns and villages all over the country. If it had come this far, then it must have gained some power. The owl called out and flew down to the end of the road where his mistress was standing.

Athena was in her goddess form, spear in one hand, owl now perched on the other. Pandora's breath caught at the sight and her pace slowed. A few deep breaths and some chirps of encouragement from Hope encouraged her to continue walking.

Hearing footsteps approach, Athena turned and a weary smile grew when she saw the Pandora. "Oh, my child, what a sight you are."

"Athena, I… the Darkness." Pandora looked at the tragic destruction that surrounded them. "It attacked before I could—"

The goddess held up a hand to silence her. "Don't worry, most of the villagers fled before the attack. Very few were harmed."

"How did they know?"

"It seems to be weaker than before. We were able to warn everyone, help them escape before it consumed the place. After a while it seemed to retreat, as if the attack had weakened it even further."

"Oh, well that's— Did you say we?"

"Yes, in fact, he's very excited to see you again."

Pandora's eyes brightened. "Hephaestus? Is he okay? Can I see him?"

Athena took Pandora's hands in hers. "I'm sorry, my dear, that's not who I meant."

Pandora bit her lip to hold back her emotions. "Oh, is he…"

"Hephaestus is fine, at least, we think he is. We know that he at least made it back to his workshop but since then he has refused to see any of us," she said, her voice lowered, "even me."

"I'm so sorry, Athena. It was all my fault."

"Oh, child, don't be a fool. Hephaestus was always going to protect you. He did the right thing. Besides, you were nowhere near ready to take that on by yourself. It would have killed you. You're no use to us all dead now, are you?"

Pandora's jaw tensed but she decided not to say anything. Athena didn't need to know how little she believed in her own ability. According to Athena, Pandora was their best hope. What good would it do to destroy that.

With a sudden realisation, Pandora lifted her head. "Who was it then?"

"Who was what, dear?" Athena murmured, distracted as she stroked her owl.

"Who helped you?"

"Oh!" Athena jumped. "I almost forgot." With a dazzling smile, she encouraged Pandora to turn around. Looking to the other side of the port, Pandora noticed a single ship docked. It took her a moment to realise who it was but as soon as she did, she was running towards it. The slender lines of the wood and the elegant, streamlined sales of the *Eirene* would be difficult for anyone to forget. As she got closer, she could see the men aboard the ship going about their duties.

She started shouting at the top of her voice, "Pelagios! Pelagios!"

A man appeared on the gangplank and upon seeing Pandora, he let out an almighty laugh. "By the gods. Pandora, aren't you a sight for sore eyes?"

He jumped the plank in a single stride and as Pandora collided with him, he picked her up in an enormous embrace. Of all the people she had expected to see, she had never in her wildest dreams thought that it would be him.

"I didn't realise you made it out," she said in a muffled voice as she was pressed into his chest.

Pelagios laughed again. "I told you my ship was quick, girl, and hopefully now you'll believe me."

Even though they had only met once before, Pandora felt an immense wave of emotion upon their reunion. He had been kind to her and the relief that he had survived was overwhelming. Letting go of him, she beamed brightly.

"He's been rather busy since you last saw him, you know," Athena called out from aboard the ship. Pandora tried to hide her surprise at the sudden appearance of the goddess.

"She does that a lot, doesn't she?" Pelagios whispered in amusement before beckoning towards his ship. "Please, ladies, would you join me in my quarters? We can discuss the matter further on board."

Pandora hopped up the plank with ease and the three of them descended into the hull of the ship.

Pelagios' room was large and comfortable. He spent his life on this boat and it was clear that he took pride in making it into a proper home. In the middle of the room stood a large table covered in maps and nautical instruments, as one would expect in any ship. Pandora could see drawings and notes made on several of the maps. She turned one around to examine it.

"I managed to get several people on my boat before we made our escape from Kyparissi," Pelagios explained. "After taking them to safety, I travelled to other nearby ports to see if they too had been attacked. I have been documenting my findings as I go."

Athena stepped forwards. "I met Pelagios on the eastern coast. He has been instrumental in my research."

Pelagios winked at Athena who smirked in response.

Pandora raised an eyebrow at her friends but she had more important things to ask about. "So, what have you found?"

"It appears that the Darkness is moving in specific directions," Athena explained. "When it left your village, it seemed to have split and spread out to gain more ground. The most aggressive one was what I was tracking to the east when I met Pelagios. I believe it has made its way across the sea, possibly on one of the ships that fled. Wherever it was going, it definitely had purpose."

"What does Typhon want across the Aegean?" Pandora asked.

Athena's face froze. "What did you say?" she whispered.

Pandora realised Hades must not have passed on the information yet. "Oh, uh, Hades, he told me what he thought was in the box."

"He thinks *Typhon* is behind this?"

Pandora nodded.

Athena held a hand to her head and sat down shakily. "I couldn't understand how the Darkness was being controlled, but now… It makes sense. Only a monster as powerful as him could have such control over something like that, not to mention be able to break allegiances between the gods."

"Hermes," Pandora said through gritted teeth.

Athena nodded solemnly. "I don't know what possessed him to do what he has done but Typhon has powers even I can't understand."

The three of them sat for a long time and discussed their findings. Athena was pleased to hear of Pandora's progress under Polemides' instruction. She was proud to see the woman that she had become.

When Pandora explained what had happened when the Darkness had attacked them at the village, Athena stood up and examined the maps.

"Here? At this village?" Athena asked, pointing to the map.

"Yes, that's where we were."

"Hmm, interesting."

Athena looked at Pelagios who nodded and signalled to her to explain.

"When I met Pelagios, there were survivors at the port that had been attacked. They described the same thing as you; however, instead of wolves, it was men that had attacked alongside the entity. They were half dead and shared very similar traits to the wolves you saw." She traced the map with her fingers until she landed on a small island across the Aegean.

"What are you thinking?" Pelagios enquired.

"Well, the survivors we spoke to told us they had been raided a few weeks previously by bandits. They believed they had set up camp not far from the village." Athena said.

"The wolves!" Pandora jumped up. It hadn't crossed her mind before but now the connection seemed clear. "Before I left for the town, Orpheus warned me that there had been sightings of a wolf pack in the nearby hills. We didn't come across them, but the Darkness had a pack of wolves under its command. You don't think…"

"Of course." Athena said, irritated that she hadn't thought of it sooner. "The Darkness increases its power the same way any ruler would, by swelling its ranks. It possesses creatures, dark beasts and corrupt men. The wolves, the bandits, they both inflicted harm on the people. The Darkness must have chosen them as vessels to help do its bidding. If it feeds off existing evil, then that explains why it is moving the way it is. It must have drained the immediate resources and they can't have been that powerful because it's becoming weaker."

Pelagios studied the map where Athena had pointed. "It's going to Sarpedon?"

Athena nodded. "Typhon must be searching for more powerful sources, more permanent sources."

"Yes, that's exactly what Hades thought he would do," Pandora confirmed.

"My uncle is seldom wrong about these things," Athena agreed. "By harnessing greater evils, the Darkness can grow and he can feed off of it. The more evils the Darkness can consume, the more powerful Typhon will become until…"

The room fell silent as the three of them each thought about the worst outcome.

"What do I do?" Pandora murmured, her arms crossed over her chest defensively.

"Well, Sarpedon would be a good place to start," Athena concluded. "The island is a dark place, the home of a well-known evil."

The confused expression on Pandora's face encouraged Pelagios to step forwards. "I've not been there myself, but I have heard the stories. The Gorgon Sisters, three monsters, the worst of which can turn a man to stone with a single look."

"You must reach them first," Athena continued, "and destroy the Gorgons before the Darkness finds them. Without them, Typhon will struggle to regain his power and we will have more time."

At this statement, Pandora felt a rustling in her bag and out shot a rather panicked Hope. Her little arms flailed about and she babbled nonsensically, her white flames glowing. Both Athena and Pelagios stood back in shock.

"What in Poseidon's name is that?" Pelagios shouted.

Realising her unexpected entrance, Hope immediately hid behind Pandora's shoulder, peeking out from her curls.

Athena smiled and stepped cautiously over to them. "Oh, you darling little thing. A sprite! Pandora, how on earth did you come across her?"

"She was in the box. The Fates, they told me to let her out… Sorry, she's a what?"

Athena outstretched a gentle hand and tickled Hope lightly under her arm. "A sprite. Goodness, I haven't seen one in, well, longer than you could comprehend. She looks primordial too. Oh what a wonderful creature." Athena stroked Hope affectionately before her expression turned to sadness. "My father is certainly a difficult god to understand. Why he would put such an innocent little thing in a prison with that monster I really don't know."

Hope emerged from Pandora's hair and sat coyly on Athena's palm.

"Marvellous," Pelagios exclaimed, "I've never seen anything like her."

"And you never will again. I believe she's the last of her kind." Athena cooed at the little flame who had now fallen on her side and was smiling blissfully as Athena scratched under her arm.

Pandora shrugged. "She's followed me ever since she got out. She's called Hope."

She watched as Hope glided around the room, looking at all the instruments and belongings.

"Curious little thing isn't she?" Athena smiled. "A fitting name I feel, given what she must have endured."

"Hey, don't touch that!" Pelagios followed Hope around as she played.

"Is it safe for her to come with me?" Pandora asked worriedly. "I don't want her to get hurt."

Athena smiled. "I think she's stronger than she looks. Besides, I doubt she'd leave you even if you wanted her to."

Pandora frowned. Having Hope as company had been a relief but the last thing she wanted to do was put her in danger.

"So how do I get to Sarpedon?"

Pelagios laughed heartily before gesturing around the room. "Well, I doubt you'll find a faster ship than the *Eirene*."

"Or a madder captain." Athena rolled her eyes.

Pandora shook her head. "Oh, I couldn't ask you to—"

"My dear," Pelagios said, "it would be an honour. Remember what the prophecy said? Now I'm not a gambling man any more but I'm willing to bet that the longer I'm with you, the more likely my luck will change for the better."

"Pelagios, your luck changed for the worse the day I met you."

"Oh, I'm not counting that. I'll be damned if that prophecy meant you'd bring me bad luck. Besides, it's not like it can get any worse now, is it?"

Athena cleared her throat and beckoned to her owl who was nesting on a nearby shelf. "Well, I had better be going. I should really go and visit my uncle." She took Pandora by the arm. "I have heard word of what Hermes did to your friend."

Pandora flinched at the memory.

"Orpheus is safe, you know. He just needed some time."

Pandora's heart ached at hearing his name but felt relief knowing that he was alright. "Thank you, Athena."

Turning to Pelagios, the goddess smiled. "Thank you for your help. Keep the girl safe."

"With my life, my lady," he responded with a low bow.

Athena snorted and in one elegant movement, left the cabin.

Pandora relaxed in her chair and yawned dramatically; Hope copied her as best she could.

"You'd better get some rest, young lady," Pelagios ordered gently, "I should think it's been a good while since you've had a decent night's sleep. We'll set off immediately. The journey should take us only a few days but the sooner we get started the better. I hope you don't mind but you'll be in here." He walked over to the cot and smoothed the blankets, clearly eager to make the place feel homely. "It's the most comfortable thing I can offer you."

"Oh no, I couldn't," Pandora contested but Pelagios wasn't having any of it.

"Young lady, I have spent many a night asleep on the deck of my ship.

What's a few more."

~

Despite never having spent a night on the sea, Pandora slept solidly. With Hope curled up beside her, she found the rocking of the boat comforting and for the first time, she slept a dreamless sleep.

The journey was as enjoyable as it could have been. Pandora loved her time with Pelagios. They shared stories and he showed her the various jobs aboard the ship. She was eager to help and he welcomed her questions. The crew were friendly, and she quickly felt at ease with them. They were fascinated by Hope and the presence of the two of them seemed to lift their spirits considerably.

Starting on the western coast, they journeyed around the entire south of the country before reaching the Aegean. After one particular stop at a small, friendly port, Pandora noticed a hooded figure at the bow of the ship. Whoever they were, they must have just boarded because Pandora had got to know every member of the crew already. When she asked Pelagios who the mystery guest was, he explained that he had paid good money to join them on the ship.

"A young lad, he didn't seem dangerous," Pelagios explained while Pandora raised a disbelieving eyebrow. "I can understand your caution, Pandora, but I can assure you, I am a *very* good judge of character."

"Why is he hiding under that cloak?"

Pelagios lowered his voice. "Says he escaped an attack of the Darkness but it left him disfigured. He's embarrassed and doesn't want anyone to see. He asked for passage over the Aegean to get back to his family."

"Don't you think it's a little suspicious?" she whispered.

"Well, I've told my men to watch him so if anything happens, I'll be the first to know about it. Maybe I'm going soft in my old age, but the boy looked like he needed help. Who am I to say no, especially in dark times like these."

Pandora tried to let go of her concern but that night she made sure to lock the door of the cabin when she went to sleep.

On the fifth morning of their journey, Pandora awoke to cries from the crew. Jumping out of bed, and ignoring the stinging ache of her limbs, she rushed out to the deck fearing the worst. As she stepped out into the fresh air, she realised the commotion. There was rain in the air and the now harsh sea winds whipped about them. Through the haze she saw it. Stretching out across the horizon, the dark jagged rocks sprawled mercilessly along the coast of an island.

Pelagios walked over to her and put a hand on her shoulder. "There it is, girl… Sarpedon."

THE LONELY CHILD

They couldn't have arrived at a less inviting location. The unwelcoming cliffs jutted out like knives, and fragments of rock broke away and crashed down into the depths of black water below. The rain and mist only added to Pandora's unease. This was not a place that wanted to be found.

Pelagios clapped and rubbed his hands together with sarcastic enthusiasm. "Well, this all looks brilliant… I feel perfectly happy leaving you here."

"Pelagios, I have to go," Pandora responded quietly.

He sighed and shook his head. "I know, I know. I just can't imagine how the young girl I met all that time ago can be expected to do such a thing."

Pandora smirked. "Hey, I've learned a lot over the last few months. I can handle it."

She hoped the words sounded comforting but she could tell Pelagios wasn't entirely convinced.

"We had planned to sail on to Lesbos, to take a few days on dry land," he explained. "Though I would feel happier if we waited for you." The crew had gathered close by and some were nodding in agreement.

"The weather isn't too bad, young one," an older sailor called out.

"This old girl can spend a few days here."

"We've got plenty of wine to see us through it."

The last of the comments was met with cheers from the men. Pelagios smiled warmly at Pandora.

"You see? We're not going anywhere. How long do you think it will take you?"

Pandora scanned the island. "Well, I'm guessing there aren't any other inhabitants on this forsaken rock, so chances are I should find the, um, sisters pretty soon."

"Well, if you don't return to us within three days, we'll come and find you."

"No. Please, you mustn't put your men in danger. If… If I'm not back in three days" – her stomach tensed at the thought – "well, I guess Athena bet on the wrong horse."

Pelagios put his arm around her, clearly seeing that she was fighting with her nerves. "I know you can do this. You're not the one who told me about how well you did in all your training. Now is as good a time as any to start using it."

His words, although meant to be comforting, only tightened the knot in Pandora's stomach. She nodded and tried to smile as best she could, but she could feel the anticipation building. Her nerves getting the better of her, she mumbled something about packing her things and ran below deck. Reaching her room, she slammed the door shut and slid down to the floor. Her breath was so heavy she could feel her heart in her ears. Covering her face with her hands, she tried her best to slow her breathing.

After a few moments she raised her head to see a concerned Hope hovering in front of her. The little flame babbled something that sounded like a question.

"Yes, I'm okay, don't worry," Pandora reassured her. She had got used to the creature's way of communicating and understanding her had become a little easier.

Hope babbled some more and pointed in the direction of Sarpedon.

"Yes, that's where we're going."

Hope responded with more gibberish and then she wiggled her arms around her head and hissed.

"Yes, that's where the Gorgons live."

~

Once they knew where they were headed, the crew had relished in telling stories of the Gorgons that they had heard over the years. Nearly every night, Pandora had sat with them and listened to their tales and advice.

"Half snake, half woman."

"Huge fangs."

"No, tusks."

"Now why would they have tusks?"

"They'll turn you to stone."

"Don't look at their eyes. Blood red they are."

"No, they're yellow."

"Love to lure us sailors to our deaths."

"Witches! Evil they are."

Of course, none of them had ever seen the Gorgons, but they never missed an opportunity for the dramatics. Now, sitting alone in the cabin, the three sisters began to manifest in Pandora's brain.

~

"You don't have to come with me, you know," she muttered to Hope. "You could wait here. Pelagios will look after you." Pandora was worried about Hope coming with her. This haunting island was no place for such an innocent creature. Hope scowled, flying forwards and tapping Pandora on the nose; well, at least Pandora thought she did. The little flame's touch was too light to detect so she had to rely on the visual clues.

"Did you just hit me?" Pandora scowled in mock anger.

Hope stuck her little tongue out and screwed up her eyes, causing

Pandora to laugh. As much as she wanted to stay in the cabin, she knew time was of the essence. They would have to get moving soon.

She gathered her weapons and rejoined the men on the deck. She saw they were now readying a row boat to take her to the cliffs. Walking towards the commotion, Pandora bumped into the cloaked boy. He grabbed hold of her arm.

"Oh, I'm so sorry, I—"

"Don't worry, no harm done."

She was close enough to see him and turning his face towards hers, she gasped lightly under her breath. What had once been fresh young skin was now blistered and burned. The boy's face had been damaged so severely, it seemed he only had use of one eye and one side of his lip was downturned in a pained frown.

The boy flinched as Pandora looked at him.

"I didn't mean to scare you," he said quietly.

"Oh, no," Pandora explained, her heart aching, "you didn't scare me. I just… Do you know why we're here?"

"No, I'm just trying to get home."

"Well, I'm here because of the *thing* that did that to you. I'm trying to stop it from hurting anyone else."

The boy smiled weakly. "Well, I wish you luck. Gods know we need help."

Pandora frowned slightly. Something about the boy's eyes and his grip on her arm reminded her of someone. With a polite nod, he turned his head and walked away. Pandora took a deep breath and marched over to Pelagios, ready to get going.

"I'm afraid there's no easy way to do this," Pelagios warned her as she climbed down the side of the *Eirene* into the boat. "You're going to have to scale the cliffs."

The wind had picked up and she could barely hear his voice above the commotion of the sea. Stepping into the boat, she was greeted by one of the younger sailors who grinned enthusiastically and handed her some rope.

"For the descent back down the rocks," he explained with a friendly smile.

Pandora nodded and waved back to the crew as the small row boat set off towards the island. Hope was not a fan of the rain and tucked herself up in Pandora's bag. The power of the sea was much more apparent in the small boat and Pandora could feel the swell of the waves below her as they cut through the water. A few hundred metres away from the rocks, the boy stopped rowing.

"This is as far as we can go. Are you okay to swim from here?"

"Well, doesn't look like I have a choice now, does it?" Pandora shouted above the noise of the rain.

"Good luck," the boy called as she stepped up onto the ledge.

Opening her bag, she coaxed Hope out, who seemed incredibly put out at having to hover in the rain.

"You're not going to want to be in there for this bit."

~

In a swift motion, Pandora jumped from the boat and dived into the water. She knew from the storm that the water should be cold, but she didn't feel it. Much like fire, it seemed that the cold didn't affect her in the same way it affected humans. She knew eventually the numbing pain of the low temperature would hit her, but she had time before it did. She was an inexperienced swimmer and her weapons proved a significant hinderance in the water. Nevertheless, she glided through the waves with purpose; all the while, little Hope hovered neatly on top of her head and babbled encouragingly. Pandora had enjoyed swimming in the shallows of the warm forest lakes during her childhood but had never known conditions like this. Desperately trying not to think about the icy depths below her, she set her eyes on a group of rocks and kicked ferociously. The rocks were slippery and jagged but she managed to pull herself out of the water without too much trouble. Wringing herself out slightly, she peered out to sea.

The mist had grown thicker now, and she could barely see the ship – only a dark silhouette and the dim glow of the lights made it through the fog. The rain was unrelenting and the winds whipped around the rocks with incredible force. Studying the cliffs up close, Pandora laughed. Seeing Hope's confusing expression, she pointed up to the rocks.

"From the ship this looked unscalable, but now that we're here it looks almost easy." Scanning the lower points, she spotted a good place to start and pointed to her bag where Hope eagerly settled back in. The climb was probably the most enjoyable thing Pandora had done in a long time. The weather was terrible and the situation was dangerous, but climbing was something Pandora knew she was good at. She reached the first ledge without even a hint of exhaustion. Popping open the bag, she peered in to check that Hope was still okay. The little flame had buried herself in among Pandora's belongings and was keeping herself occupied by chatting away to herself. Pandora didn't stop for long. She knew she was looking for a cave and although the island wasn't big, she didn't want to spend any longer here than necessary.

It only took a few hours for Pandora to reach the top of the cliffs. Once there, she realised that the entire island consisted of black rock. There was little vegetation and hardly any even ground. The hostility of the environment wasn't done justice by the tales she had heard: it was truly a forsaken place.

Still no sign of the cave, Pandora made for a denser grouping of trees. It was probably the only place she could set up a camp and get out of the rain. The need to eat and rest before she continued her search was very important. She turned the pendant Persephone had given her around in her hands, the coarse texture of the dense black stone mirroring the landscape.

Creating a fire in such appalling weather took some effort but eventually she got a small flame going and managed to half dry out her hair and clothes. Pelagios had packed her some bread and fish which she ate eagerly. Looking around at the desolate island, it seemed a poor place for even the Gorgons to live. She could see nothing of worth in this place. No ground to farm, no animals to hunt, no resources to scavenge. She couldn't understand why anyone would ever want to come here.

Now out of the rain, Hope was much happier and was entertaining herself, flitting around and chattering away. Pandora smiled at her new friend, glad to have company in such a dreary place. Suddenly, she heard a noise to the right of her. Turning sharply, she hushed Hope who moved to see where it had come from, but Pandora encouraged her back into the bag for safety. They heard the noise again but this time it came from the other side of the trees. It was a low, quiet, hissing sound. Pandora drew her sword from her back and her gauntlet bloomed into the feathery shield. Bending low, she dug her feet into the ground, ready for an attack. Hearing a twig break to the side of the trees, her attention was distracted and in that moment a figure jumped out of the thicket and pinned Pandora to the ground.

Dazed from the ambush, all Pandora could focus on was a pair of hauntingly beautiful green eyes, the pupils long and thin. She heard a gasp and then as quickly as she had been attacked, the figure let go and staggered back. Pandora jumped to her feet, sword poised, teeth gritted, but the monster she saw was not what she had expected. In fact, it didn't look like a monster at all. In front of her stood a young girl, just a child really as she couldn't have been more than fifteen or sixteen. She was barefoot, her pale grey skin glistened with rain and she wore a ragged brown dress. Pandora's mouth opened as she realised the noise she had heard was coming from the child's head. The girl's hair was *moving*. What she had thought were thick braids were living, writhing, black snakes. The girl's eyes widened in horror and as she opened her mouth to speak, Pandora held her breath in anticipation only to realise that the words that came out were not addressed to her.

"I know it didn't work, I'm standing here too, you know," the girl said. "I don't know, that's never happened before, has it!"

Pandora watched the girl in confusion. "Are you… Is everything okay?"

The creature laughed bitterly and began pacing up and down. "Ha! Is everything okay? Did you hear that? She wants to know if everything is okay." The girl paused and stared threateningly at Pandora again before throwing her hands up in frustration. "Don't you think I *know* everything is *not* okay."

Pandora laughed awkwardly. "I'm sorry, I'm not really sure what's going on here. Are you talking to your *hair*?"

In one motion, the snakes all lifted their heads in Pandora's direction, hissing menacingly before the young girl slumped to the floor and sulked.

"I don't understand," she said, sighing, and then raised a hand up to stroke the serpents writhing around her ear.

Pandora could see that whatever the girl had intended hadn't gone to plan. Still wary, she kept her distance but lowered herself so that she was at eye level with her.

The girl looked up at Pandora, her expression confused. "You were supposed to turn to stone… They all turn to stone." The girl hid her face in her hands and wept.

Pandora wasn't sure what to do. A part of her wanted to comfort the girl but she remained guarded until her crying had subsided.

"You're here to kill me, aren't you? They always are so just get it over with already," the child said, finishing in a whisper.

"No, well, at least I don't think so, and in all fairness, you actually tried to kill me first." Pandora shrugged, a very awkward smile on her face.

The little girl laughed weakly and wiped the tears away from her eyes.

Pandora thought it best to try and defuse the tension. Ceremoniously laying her sword down on the floor, she held her palms up as a sign of peace. "My name is Pandora, what's yours?"

"M-Medusa," the girl said with a sniff. She stared at Pandora for a long time, a curious expression on her face. "I've never spoken to a human before… and a girl too. No one ever really lasts long enough for me to talk to them. I just… I don't understand."

"Well, I'm not like most humans. I'm…" Pandora paused, trying to think of the right words. "I'm different."

Medusa snorted and pointed dramatically to her hair.

Pandora smirked. "Well, maybe not as different as you, but as far as humans go, I'm somewhat of an outcast."

"Outcast?"

"Yeah, you know, not like everyone else."

"Outcast." The girl mumbled the word again and nodded in agreement.

Pandora watched her. Her mannerisms were so childlike, she didn't appear dangerous, and certainly not evil. Surely this wasn't who she was here for.

"You don't actually want to kill anyone, do you?" Pandora said, more as a statement than a question.

Medusa wriggled uncomfortably. "I have to. My sisters, they said the humans want to kill me. That's why they… they make me turn them."

"So, if a human looks in your eyes, the human turns to stone?"

The little girl nodded and sniffed before looking around her as if to check no one was listening. "Not just humans."

She scrambled to her feet, causing Pandora to leap up instinctively, but the girl skipped over to a group of rocks nearby, coming back a few moments later with her hands closed around something. She clambered back over to Pandora eagerly, though not aggressively, and opened her hands to reveal a spider in her palm. It crawled around in her hand and she held it purposefully up to her face. It moved to face her, and Pandora watched in horror as the creature instantly turned to stone, a perfect statue, mid motion, two of its legs raised. Medusa breathed a sigh of relief and smiled defiantly.

"See, just like I told you."

"Are you just going to leave him like that?" Pandora scolded.

The girl rolled her eyes. "No, I suppose not."

She ran her hands through her hair until she found what she was looking for. A smaller snake, its scales shimmering blue, squirmed and wriggled across her fingers. Raising the spider up to the snake, it examined it briefly before opening its mouth and gently biting the leg of the statue. As quickly as she had turned it to stone, the spider came back to life and hastily ran down her arm back to its home. She giggled as she watched it scurry away.

"If you can change him back, why couldn't you—"

She stopped, the look on Medusa's face providing the answer. "Because they'd kill you as soon as you released them."

The little girl stroked her snakes lovingly, a solemn look on her face. "If I didn't turn them to stone, my sisters would kill them anyway… and probably me too."

"Are they like you?" Pandora asked, surprised at the girl's words.

"Not exactly," she said bitterly. "They're stronger than me and cruel. I don't… I don't want to hurt anyone, but they make me. They don't even know I can change them back."

Something about the way Medusa spoke of her sisters made Pandora suspect that she was less a sister to them and more a servant or plaything.

"Where are they now?" Pandora asked.

"We live in a cave not too far from here." She waved a hand vaguely behind her. "I come here when I want some time to myself. They can be exhausting, especially when they're angry – it's better if I'm not there when they're angry," she mumbled, wrapping her arms protectively around her stomach.

Pandora could see the fear in the little girl's eyes and noticed scars along both her arms and legs. She winced at the thought of being afraid of her own family.

Trying to distract Medusa, Pandora smiled. "You know, when I was your age, I used to spend a lot of time alone in the hills near my village. It's easier being an outcast when you're not around anyone."

Medusa snorted in agreement.

The two girls sat by the fire and talked. Pandora decided that Medusa posed no threat to her and soon felt relaxed in her company. She was a sweet girl and excited to have someone to talk to. She was fascinated by Hope, having been brought out from her bag after Pandora considered it safe to do so. Medusa squealed in excitement and spent a long time playing with the little flame. Living on such a barren rock, the girl was incredibly grateful to share Pandora's food. Everything they talked about excited her. She knew so little of the world and sat in awe listening to Pandora's stories. After a while, Pandora's stomach twinged. She knew she was here for another purpose and she was putting off the inevitable. Athena had made it clear that to stop the Darkness gaining power, she would have to defeat the Gorgons, but sitting here with Medusa had made Pandora question that purpose.

Medusa noticed the change in her expression. "Is something wrong?"

Pandora stared in the direction Medusa had pointed towards her home.

The little girl sighed. "You did come here to kill us, didn't you?"

Hope laughed lightly and shook her hands as if to say no but Pandora felt it best to answer honestly. "I'm sorry… Yes, I did, but I think there's another way."

"Another way to what?"

Pandora took Medusa's hand gently. The little girl flinched at the touch but didn't pull away. It hurt to think that this was probably the first friendly contact she had ever had. Pandora did her best to explain why she was there. Medusa sat in silence for a long time, contemplating what she had been told.

"So, something is coming for us? Something bad?"

Pandora nodded.

"Why?"

"It needs to feed. It is looking for creatures to feed on – dark creatures."

The little girl fidgeted uncomfortably. "And that's me?"

"No, Medusa, I don't believe you are what it's looking for."

"But why not? I'm still one of them. As pathetic as they say I am, I still… you know… hurt people."

"I know you're not what it's looking for because of this." Pandora pointed to her necklace. "This was given to me to warn me when I am close to my enemies – close to the Darkness. It's not changed, nothing about it is different around you. You're not like them."

"My sisters." Medusa clenched her jaw, her eyes dark.

Pandora nodded, unsure how the girl would take the news.

The little girl sniffed and wiped her eyes. "They hate me," she mumbled. "They're both immortal and I'm not. They think I'm nothing – nothing at all."

"You're not immortal?"

"No… They laugh at me."

"You said if you didn't hurt people, then your sisters would hurt you – is that true?"

The girl nodded. "They make me do it for fun, I'm just a slave to them. They find sailors or trade ships and attack them. Then they bring back the survivors to play with and torture. When they are bored of them, they force me to turn them to stone so they can keep them as trophies. If I refuse, they hurt me and just kill them anyway. At least if I turn them to stone, then they're not really… dead."

Medusa sighed, exhausted by the emotion that she had kept to herself for so long, and collapsed under Pandora's arm, releasing a flood of tears.

"Let me help you." Pandora stroked her arm as she spoke.

"But they're immortal. You can't—"

Pandora snorted. "Immortal doesn't always mean indestructible." Medusa lifted her head in curiosity. "If Athena sent me here to kill them, that means they can be killed. They may not die of old age, but they can certainly be killed."

"They're very strong. What if you don't win? What if they kill you? If they know I helped you, they'll…" She bit her lip and shook with fear.

"They won't kill me," Pandora said so convincingly that even she began to believe it. "One way or another, Medusa, I'm not leaving you here with those monsters. They won't hurt you any more."

"How? How will you do it?"

"I haven't worked that bit out yet but I'm sure I'll figure something out."

"Should I come?"

"No." Pandora said. "No, you stay here with Hope. She'll keep you safe."

Hope flew up into the air and growled threateningly at an imaginary enemy, breaking the sombre mood for a moment, causing the girls to laugh.

Medusa nodded and sniffed. "If you go now, they should be asleep – that'll give you an advantage."

Pandora nodded in thanks.

~

Picking her bag up, Pandora gathered her weapons and passed a few things to Medusa.

"Here's the rest of the food and water. You stay right here, I'll be back when I can."

Medusa smiled weakly and waved.

Pandora looked back at the little girl. *You don't have to be afraid any more*, she thought to herself as she set off towards the cave.

She knew the walk wouldn't take long and spent the time thinking over her plan. She moved her sword lightly in her hand, running through the drills she had learned at the school. She thought of all the things Perseus, Orpheus and Echion had taught her. All the times they had fought together, trained as brothers. All that work had come down to this moment. She couldn't fail them; she couldn't let them down.

Despite speaking to Medusa, she still had little idea of what she was going to find. A thousand scenarios ran through her head and she tried her best not to let her anxiety get the better of her. The cave wasn't difficult to spot. The landscape was bare and the low entrance to the cave was marked by a shard of jagged rock. The rain had stopped, and the air was thick with moisture. Pandora moved down through the rocks into the entrance.

The mouth of the cave was not small but manoeuvring down it silently took some time. The element of surprise was an advantage Pandora couldn't risk losing. The journey was made easier by small oil lamps fixed on either side of the walls though Pandora was surprised by how deep the cave went. She felt like she had been climbing forever. Stopping on a particularly wide rock, she took a moment to rest. She knew she couldn't stay still for too long, but her limbs were beginning to ache. Stretching her arms up in the air, she scrunched her eyes closed and yawned. When she opened them, Hope was hovering directly in front of her.

"What are you doing here?" she said, trying to calm herself from the shock.

Hope shrugged her shoulders and pointed up. Pandora looked up to see Medusa peering over one of the rocks above her.

Pandora scoffed in irritation. "What's the point of me telling you not to come if you're just going to ignore me and come anyway?"

"This place is dangerous." Medusa explained, "It's designed to be difficult to get through – without me, you'll be here for days."

"I'll be fine."

"Oh yeah? Well tell that to him."

Medusa gestured further down the cave and Pandora's mouth dropped as she looked down and saw a perfectly formed stone statue of a soldier, sword raised ready to attack.

"Okay, I see your point," she whispered back to the little girl.

"I promise as soon as I get you to their lair, I'll leave. They don't like me being there anyway."

Hope babbled a little and Pandora held a panicked finger up to her lips which caused Hope to continue babbling but in a faint whisper.

Rolling her eyes in pained frustration, Pandora rubbed her temples. "Oh, for the love of Zeus, *fine!* But, you" – she pointed to Medusa – "leave when I tell you, and you" – she glared at Hope – "stay out of the way."

"Brilliant, follow me," Medusa whispered and jumped down the rocks with practised agility. Hope chirped in excitement and zoomed after her new friend.

"Brilliant," Pandora said sarcastically before she began clambering as silently as she could after the little girl.

What the girls didn't see was a small spider, no bigger than an olive, follow them down into the cave. Its crimson body was fibrous and oil-slicked, leaving behind it a small trail of black, oozing haze.

PETRIFIED

The climb down into the Gorgons' lair was just as treacherous as Medusa had warned. Pandora soon realised that without the little girl's aid, she might not have made it in one piece. The razor-sharp rocks jutted out at unforgiving angles and the further they descended, the more sparse the lamps became until there was barely any light at all. A safe path was difficult to judge but Medusa hopped across the rocks with effortless grace. Medusa reminded Pandora so much of herself, and she smiled bitterly at the memory of her own adventures exploring her childhood world.

After what felt like an eternity, they dropped down to the lowest level of the cave and were plunged into immediate darkness. The only light now came from Hope and her delicate white glow. She flitted forwards a little to reveal the shadowy figures of enormous rocks. The entire cave floor was littered with these huge shapes that lay out in a maze in front of them, with no clear path to navigate through.

"Follow me," Medusa whispered as she slid between the shapes.

Pandora moved slowly, unable to predict where the safest path would be. She collided with one of the rocks and grabbed onto it for support.

"Hope, I need you," she called out, still clinging to the rock.

The lack of light was disorienting, and Pandora was finding it hard to move. With a quiet chirp, Hope doubled back and found her friend. Pandora was grateful for the light but immediately jumped back from the rock when she realised what it was. They weren't rocks scattered around the cave floor, rather an entire army of frozen statues. When she had fallen, Pandora had grabbed hold of the nearest statue. A man in armour, his hands raised in defence, petrified, his face a permanent mask of terror.

"Is everything okay?" Medusa called back in a low whisper.

"I've just found your sisters' friends," Pandora said, her surprise now turned to anger.

"Oh, I'm sorry, I should have warned you."

Pandora sighed. "It's okay, just a shock, that's all."

The walk through the frozen men was unnerving. Their expressions all the same, fear and horror forever in their eyes, their feet rooted to the spot for an eternity.

"We're nearly there," Medusa called. Pandora could see that the cave was widening, and the silhouettes of the furthest men were framed by a dim light that made their poses seem even more gruesome.

As Pandora reached the final wave of statues, she felt a pull on her tunic as Medusa dragged her behind one of the figures.

"What are you—"

"Shh," Medusa warned, "if I go in on my own first, I can distract them."

"But we have the upper hand, the element of surprise—"

"Yes, but you'd have to make it all the way over to them. You'll wake them before you reach them. If I distract them, I can… Oh look." She pointed to Pandora's neck.

Looking down at the necklace, Pandora saw minute fissures appear in the stone, volcanic colours of orange and red shining through.

"That tells you when the bad things are near?" Medusa asked quietly. Pandora nodded and Medusa smiled weakly, "Well, at least I know now. I'm really not like them," she said.

Pandora squeezed the little girl's hand encouragingly, and Medusa smiled before making her way down to her sisters' lair.

~

Pandora peered round the statue and marvelled at the home of the Gorgons. The narrow path they had been walking stopped abruptly and opened out onto a steep slope.

The vast cavern was well lit by an enormous brazier hanging from the ceiling that spat sparks and flames from its fiery coals. Pandora could see from the broken columns and archways that this desolate place had once been a temple. The decaying grandeur of the ruins only added to its fearful atmosphere. The floor of the cave was covered in rubble and what Pandora soon came to realise were piles of bones, both animal and human. The ruins of the temple culminated in an enormous flight of steps, littered with stone corpses, that opened out onto a wide platform near the back of the cave. On top of this platform lay the sleeping sisters.

Nothing Medusa said could have prepared Pandora for what they looked like. The two sisters were part human, part snake. Their heads and torsos were that of women, but below the waist they had serpent tails instead of legs. One Gorgon was considerably bigger than the other. Her round belly protruded unceremoniously over her acidic yellow scales. Her hair was thin and sparse and scales scattered over the bald sections of her scalp. Her face was blotchy and red, large stained fangs protruded threateningly from her open mouth, and she snored noisily as she slept. The smaller of the sisters was no less terrifying. She was impossibly thin, but from what Pandora could gather, seemed taller than her sister. Her long hair was crimson red and the scales of her tail faded from red to black. Unlike her sister, whose tail was thick and heavy, the second Gorgon's tail tapered to a fearsome point that whipped and coiled as she slept.

Pandora watched as Medusa made her way through the ruins of the cave. The girl looked so small compared to the other Gorgons and Pandora felt the anger course through her as she thought of all the cruelty Medusa had suffered in this place. Hope let out a whimper and Pandora put a finger to her lips.

"Don't worry, she'll be okay," Pandora said.

Medusa looked around her and settled on one of the frozen men a few steps further up. She crouched low, ran at the statue and with all her strength, pushed it over the edge of the stairs whereupon it fell to the ground and shattered.

The crash of stone echoed through the cave and the Gorgons woke with roars of panic. Their serpent eyes – the only thing they had in common with their little sister – flashed with rage as they scanned the ruins for the source of the sound.

"YOU!" the red Gorgon spat, her voice rattling like thunder. She slithered over to Medusa and with one taloned hand, picked her up by the throat. "How *dare* you wake us?"

The heavy sister yawned gracelessly. "What's she done now, Stheno? Petulant child she is."

Medusa squirmed and writhed in pain, but her sister didn't let go.

"What do you want, you disgusting creature?"

"I… I'm sorry, it was an accident."

"Clumsy fool." The yellow Gorgon snickered cruelly.

Squeezing her hand tight around Medusa's throat, Stheno spat in her face and threw her down the steps. Pandora clenched her teeth, and her grip around her sword tightened until her hand shook.

Medusa scrambled away from her sisters and hid behind a large rock. Looking up at Pandora, she nodded as if to reassure her she was alright.

The larger Gorgon scratched her bulging stomach and whined. "I'm hungry."

"You're always hungry, Euryale." Stheno sneered. "Medusa," she shrieked, "I believe my sister wants to hunt. Wait here while we bring back dinner."

"And tidy up your mess."

"Yes, this place is filthy. I honestly don't know why we even keep you around. We'll need it nice and clean for our food." Both sisters laughed at the joke. "I spotted a ship not too far from the coast."

"Mmm, should have a few sailors on board – I do like sailors." Euryale patted her belly menacingly.

Pandora realised they were talking about the *Eirene*. She couldn't let them leave the cave.

"*No!*" cried Medusa, standing defiantly. "No more. You can't, I... I won't let you."

The sisters grinned wickedly at each other. And together they slithered down the steps towards Medusa.

"You, the little mortal, won't let us?"

"You?"

"I-I-" Medusa stuttered as her sisters glided stealthily towards her. Now cornered, she cowered as the two enormous Gorgons peered down at her.

"*You* are nothing."

"You're mortal scum."

Their fangs glistening, dripping with spit, the Gorgons snarled and Stheno raised her hand as if to strike Medusa. The little girl hid behind her hands.

"NO!" Pandora cried, running out from her hiding place, drawing her sword from the sheath on her back as she did.

The Gorgons slithered back in shock before snarling once again as they watched Pandora slide down the bank of the cave towards her friend.

"You will not harm her," Pandora shouted.

The sisters paused, confused by the entrance of the girl, but their confusion soon turned to amusement and they began to laugh coarsely.

"My, our appetiser has come early," Stheno said, snarling, "what a stupid little human."

"Not really enough meat on her, sister," Euryale complained, looking Pandora up and down. "I say Medusa should kill her. Remind us of her worth after her insolence."

"You are quite right, sister. Medusa kill her."

The little girl smiled knowingly and ran to Pandora who pulled Medusa behind her back for protection. The Gorgons, clearly surprised by this unusual turn of events, roared in anger.

"Impossible!"

"It can't be. Medusa, you foolish worm, what is the meaning of this?"

Pandora raised her sword and her gauntlet released its brilliant fan of feathers. "I am no ordinary human."

Stheno raised herself up threateningly and grimaced. "Well, you will make a *very* ordinary meal."

She lunged forwards at Pandora who pushed Medusa out of the way before dodging the attack herself. The Gorgon hit a nearby column with such force it crumbled beneath her weight and she roared in anger.

"Get the girl," Stheno yelled at her sister, who charged at Pandora, her face contorted in a terrible grin. Euryale was slower, and Pandora dodged the attack with ease, sliding under Euryale's arm before plunging her sword deep into the Gorgon's side. Euryale screamed in agony and fell to the floor, writhing from the wound.

Stheno screamed at the sight of her sister in pain. "Wicked fool," she shrieked at Pandora.

Pandora used the moment to run up the steps away from the sisters. Sword in hand, she held it up to her ear where it extended elegantly into the magnificent spear. Taking a breath, Pandora studied her target. The large yellow-scaled sister was still writhing on the floor from the first attack but her wide belly gave Pandora an easy target. With all her force, Pandora threw her spear. The weapon flew silently before piercing Euryale deep in her stomach, making her cry out a second time; the cave rattled with the sound and rocks crumbled from the ceiling. Covering her head with her shield, Pandora dodged the debris and used the distraction to hide behind one of the columns.

Peering around the column, she could see the wounded Gorgon crawling over to the steps, her sister close behind her. With a gruesome rip, Stheno tore the spear from her sister's stomach and tossed it to the ground near the bottom of the steps where it turned back into the sword.

Pandora scanned the scene for Medusa and saw the small light from Hope's flame, hidden behind a large rock with the little girl. Pandora could feel the nervous energy rushing through her, and she tried to calm her breathing as she assessed the situation.

Stheno held her sister, fear and anger in her eyes. "Are you happy now, human?" she called out. "Have no doubt, I will make you suffer before taking your head!"

Pandora stepped out from behind the column. "Come and get me then," she shouted, an arrogance in her voice that she had not expected.

The taunt worked and Stheno howled as she slithered menacingly towards Pandora. Realising that goading her to attack probably hadn't been the best idea while unarmed, Pandora swung round the column and threw herself from the platform. She landed hard but rolled neatly across the floor before pulling out of the roll into a run towards her sword.

Stheno leaped from the platform and thrashed down the stairs but before she could attack, Pandora skidded towards the wounded sister and placed the sword against her throat.

"Stop or she dies!" Pandora shouted, causing Stheno to slink back a few steps for fear of her injured sister's life. Euryale hissed aggressively but cowered under the force of the blade.

Stheno cackled. "You won't do it. You don't have it in you, girl."

Pandora pushed the blade further until she cut through, just enough to expose a small stream of thick green blood and raised her eyebrow.

Snorting, Stheno slithered slowly closer, her tail writhing over the steps. "Kill her then. She means nothing to me."

Euryale spat at her sister and roared.

Pandora was about to raise her sword when she felt a warmth spread from the necklace. Looking down, she saw the fissures had erupted and the entire stone had been covered in a layer of molten lava, perfectly contained within the pendant.

Distracted by the necklace, she almost missed the small spider crawl across her hand, down the blade and into the Gorgon's mouth. Choking and writhing, Euryale flailed around in agony. Pandora withdrew her sword and stepped back cautiously. Stheno watched as Euryale lifted herself up, despite her injuries, and clawed at her own throat.

"Sister!" Stheno shrieked, and she hurried to her sister's side, peering in Euryale's mouth to see what had happened. Her hands desperately tearing at her own skin, Euryale let out a noise that made Pandora freeze in horror. The scream that came out of her was not made by one voice, but by many. As she screamed, a thick black smoke billowed out. Oil-slicked tendrils wormed their way out of her mouth and wrapped themselves around her body. Stheno tried to run but the vines tangled around her wrists and pulled her close, binding the sisters together. The Gorgons screamed as the smoke enveloped them in an opaque shield. Pandora could do nothing but watch in terror as the two sisters were consumed by the Darkness. Their screams, the voices of many, shook the cave and more debris littered the floor. When the vapour cleared, the monster in front of her was terrible to behold.

The Darkness had consumed them, combining the sisters with the spider that had carried it to them. They now stood as one being, their torsos gruesomely spliced with the body of a spider, their two heads roaring wildly. Their tails had been twisted together into one yellow-and-red-scaled spine that ran all the way down its back and whipped around behind it independently. The legs of the creature moved almost mechanically, each movement jarring, none of the components of the creature seeming to want to work together, and it staggered as it learned how to move. The creature turned towards Medusa and began to reel violently towards her.

"Medusa, run!" Pandora screamed as the little girl scrambled to her feet and sprinted as fast as she could away from the creature.

Hope, with fear in her eyes, flew up into the air towards Pandora and hid in her hair. The two of them watched as the monster chased the girl. She wasn't fast enough, and an enormous hand reached out and plucked her from the ground. She squirmed and wriggled but the creature had a tight grip around her. It drew her close to the terrible, twisted faces that were once her sisters.

"Let me go," she cried, desperately trying to free herself.

Two thick vines slid up the creature's neck and out towards Medusa and began to wrap themselves around her.

Thinking quickly, Pandora ran towards the monster and with an almighty swing, sliced her sword through one of its legs. The blow unbalanced the creature who stumbled sideways, losing its grip on the girl, and Medusa fell to the floor, slumped in a heap. Distracted by the wound, the monster howled. Pandora skidded over to her friend and shook her.

"Get up. Medusa get up."

Grabbing Medusa by the arm, Pandora dragged her away from the fight.

Medusa opened her eyes with a groan.

"You have to get out of here, Medusa. Get out before it takes you too."

"I can't leave you here," Medusa whimpered.

"I'll be fine," Pandora said as convincingly as she could. "You have to go. If it takes you too, I don't know if I'll be strong enough to defeat it."

With a reluctant nod, Medusa lifted herself to her feet and scurried as fast as she could back to the tunnel.

The creature noticed the movement and began to follow when it was distracted by a flash in front of its faces. It was Hope. The monster swatted at the air and shook its heads as Hope flew around, trying to confuse it.

Pandora let out a surprised laugh at her little friend's bravery. She knew what she needed to do and rummaged around in her bag until she found the box. Gripping her sword tightly in one hand and the box in the other, she ran towards the creature.

In her haste, she hadn't accounted for the tail. The monster spun around, flailing madly, and as it did, the tail lashed out, hitting Pandora with such force that she was thrown clear across the chamber and slammed into the wall of the cave. She fell to the floor in agony but drew herself back up onto her feet and ran at the monster again, opening the box and pointing it towards the gruesome creature. With a sickening laugh, the creature leaned forwards and slammed a colossal fist into the ground. The force of the hit sent a shudder through the cave and Pandora was pushed backwards by a wall of air and dust. She landed on her back again and coughed in agony. This time she wasn't ready for the landing – the impact winded her, and the box flew out of her hand and rolled way beyond her reach.

She was losing the fight. For some reason, the box hadn't worked. Time seemed to slow down to a trickle as she lay there, contemplating her defeat, her inevitable death. She had been so afraid of failure but now it seemed a gift, a burden lifted. If the box didn't work, she had no hope of conquering the

Darkness. She could feel the thunderous steps of the creature moving towards her. This was it, this was the end. Clutching her sword, she braced herself for what was to come.

A small babbling noise came from beside her. She turned her gaze to see Hope, hovering by her hand, muttering to herself.

"Hope, you need to go," she groaned breathlessly. "You can't stay here. It's… It's not safe."

Hope ignored her and continued to mumble to herself, her brow furrowed purposefully. With one tiny limb, she reached out and touched Pandora's hand which was still gripped around the sword. Pandora watched in wonder as a bright white glow wrapped itself around her weapon.

"Hope, what did you do?"

The little flame babbled excitedly and pointed at the creature before pointing at the box that lay open amid the rubble.

Although no words had been shared, Pandora understood what Hope had done. Hope hadn't just been trapped in the box by accident – she had been there for a reason. She was just as tied to the box as Pandora was. That's why she had stayed; that's why the Fates had told Pandora to find her.

With all the strength Pandora could muster, she leaned on her sword and forced herself to her feet once more. The creature, who had been moving steadily towards her, stopped and laughed cruelly. A thousand voices echoed from the mouths of the Gorgons.

"Pandora," they said, "your journey is over."

She was surprised to hear her name, but she didn't let it show.

"Ahh, it ends here, little child," the mouths said, snarling menacingly.

"No! I won't let you win."

"You have lost, Pandora, you cannot stop us. You cannot stop *him*."

Pandora raised her sword as if to attack, and the creature laughed at her determination before roaring ferociously and lunging forwards. As it pounced, Pandora spun around and threw her sword. This time, however, she did not throw it at the monster; instead, the celestial weapon flew up high and the air rang with the sound of metal hitting metal. The noise echoed around the chamber as the blade sliced cleanly through the central chain holding the hanging brazier. The giant bowl fell and crashed down with a flood of flames and burning coals, directly over the body of the beast. Pandora didn't pause to watch – she ran as fast as she could, scooping up the box as she went, sprinting around the edge of the chamber to avoid the creature's flailing limbs, jumping over the fallen columns and debris until she reached the steps. Clambering up them, she reclaimed her sword which had fallen to the platform.

Standing defiantly, she watched as the beast thrashed and howled in pain, though it wasn't long before it rose up again, its body glowing red with the heat of the coals that now covered it. Taking a deep breath, Pandora ran down the steps, jumped, pushed her foot into the dirt and slid under the belly of the monster until she came to a stop directly under it. With a scream of determination, she took her gleaming sword and sliced the belly of the spider. The wound opened with a flash of white light. Her blade now stuck deep in the creature's underside, she held the box up to the opening; the monster screamed and jerked as the souls that made up the Darkness were plunged back into the impossible prison. Its legs writhed and scraped at the ground, desperate to escape the pull of the box.

"No… *no!*" the voices screamed incoherently as they were dragged out of the creature. The vines shrivelled and thrashed in pain and the ash and fog that surrounded the body whipped up frantically in a powerful hurricane as the creature contorted and compacted in on itself, becoming smaller and smaller. Pandora yelled as the chaos around her was sucked into the box that she held, and with one last agonising scream, the Darkness was imprisoned, and the box slammed shut. Pandora gasped and as her head fell back, the world went black.

~

Pandora felt herself moving and heard a muffled voice as someone shook her.

"Pandora, Pandora, wake up!"

Opening her eyes, she regained focus to see Medusa leaning over her, her expression wrought with worry. Pandora groaned and rolled over before propping herself up. Dizzy, she collapsed again and held a hand over her eyes.

Medusa breathed a sigh of relief. "Thank the gods. You were still for so long."

"Is… is it over?" Pandora mumbled.

Medusa laughed and hugged her. "Yes, you did it, Pandora. Look—" She pointed to the necklace which was now back to its former rough black stone.

"It's gone – they're gone… and I'm free."

With the help of the little girl, Pandora slowly sat up. She felt the box in her hand and inspected it sceptically.

Hope peeked her head out from behind Medusa's shoulder and Pandora looked at her curiously.

"How did you do that?" Pandora asked. "My sword – you did something."

Pandora rubbed her temples, her head throbbing, as Hope babbled excitedly.

"That's why you stayed with me? You knew I would need you."

Hope lowered her eyes and nodded coyly before flitting back to Medusa.

"Thank you." Pandora smiled weakly. "I… We'd all be dead if it weren't for you."

Hope waved nonchalantly with an arm as if to say it was nothing.

Looking at the devastation around them, Pandora sighed. "We have to take this back to Athena." She turned the box over in her hand. "She'll know what to do." With a nod of agreement, Hope pointed to the tunnel.

Pandora staggered to her feet and stretched her arms. She had not got out unscathed. Her limbs were covered in chips and scratches, and a particularly nasty shard that had been knocked out of her leg had left a deep ravine in her thigh. She could see Medusa studying her, the girl looking apprehensive. Pandora chuckled and rolled her eyes as she traced the lines of the damage.

"I told you I was different."

Medusa smiled weakly and walked over to a nearby pile of rubble, picking up a piece of the rock as she examined the devastation of her home.

Pandora frowned. "Come with us."

"I can't."

"Why not? I can tell everyone that you're not evil, you could—"

"I could what? I can't live in the human world. I'm too… too dangerous." The little girl hung her head. "This is my home, and besides, I hated my sisters, but I like this island. It's all I know."

Pandora tried her best to convince Medusa, but she knew there was no alternative. She was right: it would be too dangerous for her to live among men, both for them and for her.

"I can come visit you." Pandora sniffed, extending her hand to her new friend.

The little girl ran to her and hugged her tightly. "I'd like that."

Saying goodbye to the girl was excruciating. She couldn't bear the thought of her being here all by herself but she knew it was the only way.

Medusa helped them navigate back out of the cave; the weather outside was still bleak but the rain had stopped, and a cool breeze whipped through the air. They walked in silence, both afraid of saying goodbye. The sun was now low in the sky. Pandora realised she must have been unconscious for most of the day. When they reached the cliffs, she was relieved to see the *Eirene* in the distance.

Medusa helped Pandora to the edge of the cliff and the two of them descended until they landed on a large bank not far from the bottom.

"If you jump here, there is a clean line to the water. There aren't any rocks below so you will be safe."

Pandora raised a doubtful eyebrow, but Medusa laughed.

"Trust me, it's much easier than the climb down."

Pandora peered over and shook her head. "Yeah, this looks like fun," she said, her voice dripping with sarcasm.

She realised that without a way of signalling to the boat, she would have to swim the entire way. Apparently Hope must have been thinking the same thing for at that moment she scrunched up her little face and held her breath. The small white flame shone brightly in the looming darkness and before long Pandora could hear responsive sounds from the ship; moments later, a boat had begun the journey to the island. Realising this was the last chance to say goodbye, Pandora took the little girl in her arms and hugged her one last time.

"Thank you for everything, Medusa."

The girl wept silently into her chest before pulling away and wiping her eyes. "Can I give you something?"

Pandora nodded with a smile and Medusa held out two small vials.

"What are these?" Pandora asked, turning the bottles over in her fingers. One contained a dark green liquid and the other a silvery white one.

"A gift to say thank you for everything you did for me today," she said softly.

Pandora looked at her in surprise.

"The silver one will help anyone who has been, um, turned."

"And the other?" she asked, though she already knew the answer.

"That one, well, I hope you don't have to use that one."

The snakes on her head twisted in the wind and tentatively, Pandora held a hand up. Two of the snakes slithered across her palm, kissing her lightly with their forked tongues.

Medusa's tears flowed as she said goodbye to her new friend.

"Go, or they'll leave you here and you'll be stuck with me." She laughed solemnly.

Pandora squeezed her hand one final time, nodded to Hope and, with a deep breath, ran to the edge of the bank and jumped. The fall into the water was not far; she plunged into the icy depths and swam swiftly to the boat. The sailor, unable to contain his surprise at her entrance, was quick to pull her on board.

As the boat rowed back to the ship, Pandora kept her eyes on the little girl. With one final wave, Medusa scampered back up the rocks to her home. Turning back to the *Eirene*, Pandora didn't see the hooded figure raise himself out of the water and begin to climb the cliffs of the island she had just left.

Only the Beginning

He tried his best to hide it but the relief Pelagios felt seeing Pandora climb aboard the *Eirene* was overwhelming. Letting out a booming laugh, he threw a blanket around her, picked her up and spun her around.

"Oh, you marvellous girl. I knew you'd make it out."

Pandora smiled weakly, emotionally and physically drained from what had happened on the island.

"Is… is it done?" Pelagios asked sheepishly.

With a nod, Pandora eased his worry and he laughed again.

Looking around at the crew, Pandora could see them whispering and murmuring to each other. She looked down at herself, remembering the damage she had endured, and self-consciously pulled the blanket tighter around her body.

Pelagios scowled at his men and they quickly began cheering and clapping. Pandora held her hand up in recognition and they dispersed, busying themselves with their work. The weather off the coast must have picked up during Pandora's time on the island. The ship had clearly taken a bit of a beating as the sailors were now picking their way through the debris.

"What happened?" Pandora asked.

Pelagios snorted. "Oh nothing, just a little damage from the storm. Shouldn't take long to repair. I'd say we should be ready to sail by the morning." Peering over at the row boat, he scratched his head. "Where's the boy?"

"What boy?"

"The boy in the cloak. He said he thought you might need help. Crazy fool jumped right into the water. I don't even know if he made it to shore. We looked for him, but the waves were too strong, I couldn't risk losing any of my men. I assumed he went to look for you."

"No, I… I didn't see anyone," Pandora mumbled, gazing back out to the island, the telltale knot forming in her stomach.

Pelagios shook his head and groaned. "Poor lad. From what he said he'd been through, it's enough to make any man jump overboard." He looked out at the water before patting her on the back. "Come, you need rest. Let me escort you back to the cabin."

Pandora wasn't given time to respond before Pelagios steered her towards his quarters.

~

Sitting her down on the bed, he went to pour her a drink.

"Is there anything I can do?" He spoke softly to her, gesturing to her wounds, no trace of revulsion in his voice. It was the first time in a long while that somebody had seen her like this and not been shocked.

"Athena warned you, didn't she?"

"Hmm?" Pelagios feigned ignorance and brought her a cup of water that she drank so eagerly, half of it spilled down her face. She wiped her mouth in embarrassment but Pelagios just stroked her hair, a kind smile on his face.

Pandora raised an eyebrow and pointed to the large gash on her leg. "She told you about me, about what I am?"

The man stood, walked over to the table and picked up a small basin and cloth. Bringing it back to the bed, he wrung the cloth out and began to wipe gently at the dust on Pandora's face.

"The goddess told me plenty of things," he said as he washed her. "She told me that you're kind, she told me you're brave and most importantly she told me that you're our greatest chance at surviving this time of darkness. That's all

I need to know."

Gesturing to the basin, Pelagios patted Pandora on the arm before walking to the door.

"I'll leave you to freshen up. There are clean robes laid out for you over there."

Pandora nodded, grateful for his care and help.

As he opened the door, he called back to her, "I'd get some sleep, girl. We'll aim to leave first thing in the morning as soon as the light is good enough. If you need anything, you know where to find me."

Pandora listened to his steps get quieter as he walked back up to the deck. She lay down on the bed and closed her eyes before startling herself and jumping to her feet. She ran over to her bag, which was now moving slightly, and threw it open, allowing Hope to fly out. The little flame gasped for air sarcastically before flitting around the room and spinning, clearly happy to be back on the ship.

"We're leaving in the morning," Pandora called to her as she washed herself. "Are you okay?"

Hope nodded eagerly and flew to the bed, nestling herself in among the sheets. Pandora laughed and rolled her eyes. She scrubbed her arms and legs until the worst of the dust and muck had gone. There was no clay on board, so Pandora was just going to have to make do as she was. Her injuries weren't too severe and luckily she still had full use of all her limbs. She wrapped a strip of cloth around the worst gash on her leg and threw on the clean clothes.

Trying to run a hand through her hair, she groaned at the state of it. She reached into her bag for the comb and her fingertips brushed the box. The touch made her feel sick. She pulled out the small container and turned it over in her hands.

"Is it really in there? It can't get back out again?" Pandora asked Hope sceptically.

The little flame nodded reassuringly and tapped the box with her tiny arm.

Pandora found her comb, wrapped up the box in some spare cloth and placed it gently back in her bag. As she hacked through the mass of knots that was her hair, Pandora snorted at the realisation that she would probably have found another round with the Gorgons easier than trying to get the comb through her matted curls. After what felt like hours, she pulled her fingers through her hair with satisfaction and wrapped it up into a bun. Now that she was clean and dressed, the tiredness Pandora had been fighting hit her like a tidal wave. Her eyes drooped and she yawned ferociously. Smiling at Hope, who had made a nest in the sheets on the bed, Pandora crawled up next to her and the second her head touched the pillow, she was asleep.

~

The next morning, Pandora awoke well rested, though a little sore. She tentatively stretched her limbs and was pleasantly surprised to find they softened easily. Tracing the cuts and dents in her skin, she tutted in mild annoyance. She poured herself a cup of water and beckoned to Hope to follow her up to the deck, the sounds of the men at work putting her at ease. The storm had passed and the sun was bright; the warmth of the morning had dried the deck and the smell of mould and rain had almost entirely dissipated. Pelagios was busy instructing his crew but stopped to wave kindly to Pandora who smiled in return.

One of the younger boys on the ship ran over to her and tossed her a chunk of bread with a cheeky laugh. Pandora walked towards the stern, jumped up onto the thick wooden ledge and ate her breakfast. She enjoyed watching Hope flit about, getting up to mischief. Hope was such a curious creature and relished the opportunity to spend time among other humans. Pandora laughed as one of the older sailors chased her around the deck.

"Hope, you're going to get thrown overboard," Pandora called out with a laugh.

"Pandora, could you keep yer sprite under control. She's causin' mischief down here."

The words were spoken in jest and with a final wave, Hope flew back over to Pandora and settled on her shoulder.

Now that the weather had settled, Pandora marvelled at how much the island had changed. What had once seemed impenetrable now looked almost inviting. In fact, Pandora thought it odd how different the place looked. She could see vegetation growing on the cliffs and the jagged shards of rock now seemed smoother. The work of thousands of years of thrashing waves appeared to have happened overnight. As she was pondering the unusual change in scenery, her train of thought was broken by Hope who was now babbling quickly and urgently, pointing at the water close to the ship. Peering over the edge of the boat, Pandora realised what Hope was pointing at.

"Help!" she screamed. "It's the boy, the boy that fell overboard. Someone help him!"

Alarm raised, the sailors worked together to drag the boy out of the water; still wrapped in his cloak, he had in his hand a tightly knotted bag.

"Come on, let me through, let me through!" Pandora pushed her way through the throng of men and watched as the boy was lowered to the deck. His head rolled to the side and the men murmured to themselves at the sight of him. With a noise of frustration, Pandora cleared them out of her way and bent down. She pressed down on the boy's chest and after a few compressions, held his nose and blew into his mouth. Repeating the process a couple of times, Pandora stared in panicked relief as the young man spluttered and coughed, spitting out a mouthful of water.

"Thank the gods," she said, sighing, as he sat up, anxiously pulling his cloak closer around himself.

Two of the sailors helped him to his feet and Pelagios moved through the crowd to see what the commotion was.

"You certainly gave us a fright, boy. We thought the worst." He clapped him on the back and the boy coughed a little more.

"I… I think I fell overboard during the storm, I really can't remember. Did I… did I jump?"

Pelagios sighed, unwilling to answer while the boy was still so disoriented. "Come on, we should get you out of those wet clothes." He tried to pull the cloak off him but the boy backed away.

"No, please, I'm fine."

"Come on, lad, you can't stay soaking wet like that."

"I said *no*." At this, the boy pulled away.

Pelagios nodded in compliance. "Okay, okay, everything is alright, lad. We're not going to hurt you."

"Where's my bag?" The boy spun around in panic, lunging for his belongings and clutching it tightly to his chest.

Pelagios shot a concerned look at Pandora who was equally worried about the boy's behaviour.

Pelagios nodded towards the bow of the boat. "If you won't let us tend to you, then go and sit over there. The sun should warm you up soon enough."

The boy gripped the edge of his cloak again and stomped across the deck. The men dispersed quickly, the drama now over, and continued to prepare the boat to leave the island's coast.

"Keep an eye on him, would you," Pelagios instructed quietly to Pandora before marching off.

"Where are we going?" she called out behind him. It was only then that she realised she didn't know what they were planning.

"We had planned to go to Lesbos but Athena wants to meet us to deal with that, uh, that thing in your… well, you know…" He gestured towards the cabin where the box remained hidden among Pandora's belongings.

"Where are we meeting her?"

"We're taking you home, young lady, to Kyparissi. She said to meet us at the temple."

Pandora's stomach tightened. She hadn't thought about ever going back there and now she felt anxious at the notion of seeing her home again, or what remained of it at least.

~

With the weather now brighter and the wind on their side, the journey to the mainland was uneventful. Pandora spent most of it above deck, admiring the power of the ship as it cut through the swirling mass of waves. The young boy remained at the bow of the boat for the entire journey. Day and night he sat, hunched over, clutching his bag close to him. Pandora didn't believe he was dangerous, but she thought his behaviour odd. It was true that he had obviously been through trauma that may well have caused his unusual demeanour, but Pandora was aware there may be more to it than that.

As soon as she saw the outline of the rolling hills that surrounded the port village she had grown up in, the memories of that fateful day came flooding back. The scars she had spent so long healing began to ache at the sight of the place.

Pelagios stood by her side and put a sympathetic hand on her shoulder.

"I know this will be difficult." He did his best to console her, but he could see from the haunted expression on her face that this would be one of the biggest challenges she had yet faced. Hope gently nudged Pandora on the cheek and did her best to chirp in a comforting manner. The closer they got, the clearer the picture of destruction became. They were entering a ghost town.

The crew stayed with the ship while Pelagios guided Pandora – Hope now firmly snuggled in her bag – down the gangplank. She did her best to appear strong, but her legs shook and she struggled to control her breathing. She let Pelagios lead her through the wreckage of her town. Keeping her gaze low, she focused on their steps to try and block out the tragedy. The light breeze whipped the dust around their feet and whistled through the leaves. That and the now distant lap of the waves upon the shore were the only things Pandora could hear.

After a while the scenery began to change. The dust road narrowed, and lush grass sprawled out at either side. Pandora noticed the first of the cypress trees. Instinctively she lifted her head and was comforted to see the road ahead of them was lit by the temple braziers. Guilt twinged in her heart as she realised she had walked past her home without even so much as a glance. It would do her no good going back there but there was a part of her that hoped if she went back, it would stand as it once had, and all of this would have just been a dream.

Her pace slowed and Pelagios stopped, concern furrowing his brow. Hope wriggled out of the bag, sensing the halted motion, and hovered up to her favourite perch on Pandora's shoulder.

"You can do this, Pandora, you've got through the worst of it," Pelagios encouraged, the tiny flame mirroring his sentiments as best she could.

"This isn't my home any more," she whispered, looking back down the road towards the town. "I have no home now."

Pelagios sighed and smiled sadly. "Well that makes two of us."

Pandora remembered the story he had told her all that time ago of the life he once had. "I'm sorry. I didn't mean—"

"Please, your wounds are fresh. Mine have had a lifetime to heal."

"How did you do it?"

"What?"

"Find a new home?"

Pelagios motioned to Pandora to continue walking, and they trudged in silence for a while as he pondered the question.

"I have come to believe that a home isn't important. You can make any place a home if you need to. It's family that matters most in this world."

"But we both—"

"We have both lost people, Pandora, it's true. Nearly everyone has lost someone dear to them. But that doesn't mean we're without family. Family doesn't just mean the one we are born into. Family are the people in your life that care for you and protect you without judgement or limitations. It can grow and change throughout the years as people come in and out of your life but that is the beauty of it."

Pandora listened intently as Pelagios spoke.

"My crew are my family, the little old woman who took me in after I lost my home is my family, you, Pandora… you are my family."

He stopped and stroked her hair lovingly.

"I never had a little girl. I always dreamed of it but I knew it was never my fate. When Tyche told me you would change my luck, I thought only of superficial meanings – money or profits. No one can ever replace your father and I wouldn't ever consider myself a respectable father figure," he said, "but I consider you my family and I protect my family with my life."

Pandora smiled weakly and without thinking flung her arms around her friend. "I can't cry, but if I could, I would now," she mumbled into his arm. "You're my family too."

The pair stood for a moment, lost in the embrace. A girl without a father, a man without a child, pulled together by fate, the presence of the other an unimaginable comfort. The moment was broken when Hope squeezed her way into the hug and cooed excitedly, causing the two of them to laugh.

"Well then," Pelagios said, sniffing, "now that's cleared up, I suppose we best go and deliver the goods to Athena. I can't imagine she would be too happy if we keep her waiting much longer."

~

Pandora smiled at the sight of the temple. Despite all the carnage that had happened, it remained stoic and beautiful in its organic construction. The light of the day was dimming, and the braziers gave off an enchanting glow as the adventurers walked up the stone steps. Taking a deep breath, Pandora prepared herself for her meeting with the goddess. She fumbled around in her bag until her hand clasped around the box, still wrapped in the cloth. It reassured her to know that the journey was nearly over. When they reached the top step, Pandora was shocked by what she saw. Athena, as predicted, was standing in front of her statue in all her glory. What she hadn't expected were the figures standing either side of her in a small circle. With a cry of surprise and excitement, Pandora ran forwards.

"Welcome, child," Athena said, her voice soft and low. She gestured around at the other people. "I believe you already know my other guests."

"I told you she wouldn't be long."

"Pretty sure I said that."

The unmistakable arguing of Castor and Pollux rang out from one side as they clambered over each other to attack Pandora with a crushing joint hug.

"For the love of Zeus, men, behave yourselves. I'm not putting my gods damn reputation on the line if you can't act like reasonable human beings, you foolish oafs," Polemides boomed, a wicked smile on his face as he stepped forwards and took his turn embracing Pandora. "Hello, little bird," he whispered in her ear before roughing her hair a little.

Behind him stood Echion, his expression warm. "I hear you've got better with that spear. I guess I'm not such a useless teacher after all," he said with a chuckle, patting her on the arm.

Pandora was overwhelmed. She turned back to Pelagios who smiled knowingly.

"You knew they were coming?" She raised an eyebrow at him.

"I'm afraid I did. Athena was very strict about keeping it quiet though so I'm not to be blamed."

Athena coughed, a mild scowl on her face.

"Not that she should be blamed either!" Pelagios quickly added, winking at the goddess.

"I'm sorry I left…" a small voice sang across the room.

Pandora turned to see Orpheus walking towards her. Her face lit up with relief at the sight of him. "By the gods, I've missed you," she said.

"Pandora, I… I just couldn't—"

"Don't. You don't need to say anything." She embraced him, and they clung to each other tightly.

For a moment, Pandora forgot they weren't the only ones in the room but a less than subtle cough from Pollux jolted her back to reality.

"Right," Athena said, clapping her hands together, "I think we'd better get to the matter at hand. Pandora managed to capture part of the Darkness on Sarpedon. An act that showed true bravery and one that I am safe to say we are all immensely proud of."

The room echoed with cheers from her friends.

"So, what now?" Pandora said.

"Well, as predicted, the Darkness was seeking out pre-existing evil in your world. It was drawn to the Gorgons both because of their reputation and their immortality. Mortal absorptions aren't enough to sustain it. For Typhon to regain his power, he needs the immortal beings."

"So, there's more of this… this thing out there?" Castor asked tentatively.

"That is correct."

"And that's why we're here?" Pollux said.

Athena nodded and motioned to the men standing around the room. "Pandora is the key to our success, but it's unfair of me to expect so much from her. If she had the support of brave warriors such as yourselves, I believe this fight would stand a greater chance of victory."

"Well count us in," the twins roared, clapping each other on the back.

Athena smiled as the jovial brothers began to wrestle. "Ah, not ones to shy away from a fight, I see."

Polemides stepped forwards and nodded. "I've left the school in good hands. Besides, someone has got to keep those two under control."

Pandora laughed as he marched over to the twins and dragged them off each other by their ears.

"I'm in too," Echion added, "if you'll have me."

Pelagios coughed before moving to Pandora's side. "You're going to need a ship. My old girl is still the fastest around," he said with a wink at Athena.

Orpheus squeezed Pandora's hand and smiled. "And I'm not going anywhere."

Hope flew out from her hiding place in Pandora's hair and circled the group, chirping lightly before settling on Pandora's shoulder. The men all looked at her, a mixture of shock and confusion on their faces.

"It's a long story." Pandora shrugged, stroking her finger against the little flame.

"Well then," Athena said, "it's decided."

Pandora was overwhelmed with gratitude. She beamed at her friends, so relieved to know that she no longer had to continue the fight alone.

Furrowing her brow, she delved into her bag and turned to the goddess. "What do I do with this?" she asked, gently pulling out the box.

"Ah, yes." Athena pressed her hands together in thought. "Well, that would be for someone else to explain." With a look to the heavens, Athena took a deep breath. "Oh, I do hate this."

With a flash of light, her body jolted up as if she had been struck by lightning. She hovered in the air, her hair flowing around her as if underwater. From her fingertips and toes a bright ethereal light beamed like rays of sunshine. When she lowered her head back down, her eyes were glowing white.

In a deep booming voice she spoke, "Pandora."

The men all took a few paces back and Pandora moved forwards gingerly until she was in front of the possessed goddess.

"I… I'm here."

"It would seem that some of my children have grown rather fond of you."

Pandora's heart stopped when she realised who was speaking. "I… You're…"

"Ha!" The voice laughed menacingly. "That never gets old."

Pandora scowled a little but held the box out in front of her.

"Ah yes, that old thing. Seems you got yourself in quite a predicament when you opened it, young lady."

"But I—" Pandora started arguing but her friends hissed at her to stay quiet. Scowl now firmly on her face, she obeyed.

"Athena tells me you intend to stop Typhon regaining his power."

"Yes," Pandora replied curtly.

"Are you up to the task? I intervened once before, but it isn't something I can do again," he said, his voice strong but with a tone of exhaustion.

Pandora nodded, her face hard with determination.

This seemed to please the father god, who then turned his attention to the box in her hands.

"The item you hold is an ancient and powerful thing. Intended to be protected by a god, I never wanted it to make its way back to the mortal world. You have my dear fool of a son to thank for that."

"There is still darkness out there," Pandora said as loud as she could without sounding aggressive, hurt by the insult to Hephaestus. "Is it safe for me to open it again?"

Athena's body moved as Zeus laughed.

"Do not worry, child. Until Typhon is back in that box, the souls that you have imprisoned do not have the power to escape. Once you have defeated the Giant, then you can deliver it to me. Do not fail this task or you… *we* will all perish."

With those final words, the light left the goddess and she floated elegantly back to the floor. Once her feet touched the ground, she filled her lungs as if she had been holding her breath and shook her limbs. "I never get used to that feeling."

The room was quiet, the men standing as statues, frozen by the entrance of Zeus. All apart from Pollux, who clapped and laughed. "Always fun when dad visits, eh?"

"Sorry, what?" Pandora snorted.

"Oh yeah, didn't you know?" Castor rolled his eyes. "We're twins but he's the special one."

"So, you're not Zeus' son but he is?"

"That would be correct… and gods does he never let me forget it."

Pandora snorted. "Is everyone a demigod or is it just you lot?"

"I'm not," Pelagios said, chuckling.

"Nor me." Polemides walked over to Pelagios and clasped his forearm in solidarity.

"Or him." Pollux jabbed Castor slyly, then pointed to Pandora. "To be fair, you were made by a god so you're not exactly *normal*," he teased.

Pandora scowled back at him before realising she had forgotten something. "I need to go to my father's house. I'm… a little worse for wear." She laughed weakly, unwrapping the cloth that hid the gash on her leg.

"Oh my." Athena marched over to her and inspected her leg. "Echion, would you be a dear? Pandora's had a long trip."

He waved in acknowledgement and with a flash of a smile, dashed down the steps towards the town.

Athena smiled at Pandora. "His father may have become a bit of a burden these days, but he did pass on his gift for running. Besides, something tells me you're not ready to go back there quite yet."

Pandora knew she was right and smiled in gratitude.

Athena lifted her head as if she heard something and walked to the centre of the room.

"Well, this has been wonderful but I must get on. Plenty of things to do. I've already spoken to Polemides and he has formulated a strategy for your next move. I will keep an eye on your movements." She marched elegantly towards the steps. "Oh, Pandora?" She beckoned to the girl to come closer. "I have word from my brother."

Pandora's stomach tightened at the thought of Hephaestus. "Is he okay?" she muttered.

Athena nodded. "He will be. He wanted me to give you these… said they might help."

Into Pandora's palm, the goddess dropped three small black pebbles, each with a distinctive white line etched across them. They were portal stones, just like the one he had used to save them back at the village. Athena winked and, with a final wave, left the temple.

~

The group of friends sat in the temple for a while. Athena had left them with food for the evening meal and they ate readily. Pandora listened to the stories of what they had been doing since she left the school. Polemides assured her that the school was in good hands and there hadn't been another incident since the fire on her first night. Pandora was relieved that Phobos hadn't returned.

It didn't take Echion long to come back with the clay and as they ate, Orpheus took Pandora to the side to tend to her wounds. His delicate hands made quick work of her cuts and the large slash on her leg healed well. He found the work fascinating.

"You truly are marvellous, you do know that?"

Pandora opened her mouth to argue but decided against it.

Orpheus waved an arm to the men now laughing over cups of wine. "Don't you see yet? You aren't different, you're *special*. Why do you think we're all here? We love you and support you. We're…"

"A family." Pandora smiled, looking over at the men.

"Exactly, I couldn't have put it better myself."

Her expression changed as she saw the men stand abruptly, hands on their weapons, before calling out into the darkness outside.

"Who goes there?"

"Show yourself!"

"What are you doing here?" Pelagios asked, sincere disbelief in his voice.

Pandora ran over to them only to see the cloaked figure of the young boy from the ship walk slowly up the steps. One hand raised as a symbol of peace, his other gripped tightly around the bag he refused to part with.

Uneasy at his arrival, Pandora stepped forwards.

The boy scanned the men around him and with a pull on the strings around his neck, he threw his cloak to the floor.

"Perseus?" Pandora whispered, her heart in her throat.

When the cloak dropped, so did the disguise it had cast over him, for now before them stood Perseus, his face tired and his eyes full of sadness.

"Pandora, I… I'm sorry I'm late."

"I didn't know you were coming," she said, a bitter tone mixed with the surprise at seeing him.

"Neither did I." He sighed. "Athena found me on the boat… She told me you were all here. I was making plans to travel back to my home, but I had to… I had to see you properly. I had to talk to you."

Pandora rubbed her temples. "You were on the boat."

Perseus held his hand up. "I can explain. My mother, she was in trouble… The king, he made me get something for him. I had to save her, Pandora."

There was so much sadness in his voice. Pandora didn't understand why his words sounded so guilty.

"You were on the boat," she said again, trying to piece together what she knew. "You fell in the water."

Perseus looked at the floor.

"You didn't fall?"

His eyes filled with tears and he tried to get his words out, but he couldn't speak.

Pandora's eyes narrowed as she looked at the bag he was carrying. It was leaking, something dripping onto the cool stone floor.

"You paid to get on the ship. You knew… you knew where we were going. What do you mean you needed to get something… What's in the bag, Perseus?"

"Pandora, I—"

"What's in the bag? Perseus, tell me, what's in the bag?!"

EPILOGUE

A hooded figure walked slowly through the rain. Covering his face from the harsh winds, he staggered towards a large opening in the mountain, the entrance lit by torches. Taking one in his hand, he made his way through the cave, the smell of ash and decay stinging his nostrils, until he reached a large dark chamber.

From within the darkness, a coarse, twisted voice rumbled, "Come forwards."

Tentatively the man walked into the darkness, holding his torch in front of him to reveal where the voice had come from. The light shone over a large circular table; carved from the rock, its surface etched with other-worldly symbols.

"Master, the girl," the man began, a tremble of fear in his words.

"Pandora," the voice hissed.

"Yes, master, she has taken the Gorgons."

"My children, stolen, imprisoned."

The man steadied himself as a rush of air flew around the room, whipping up the dust and debris.

"She must be stopped," the voice roared.

"As you wish, master."

The man lowered his hood to reveal himself. He had no hair and his skin was deathly pale; a jagged scar ran down the length of his face, through his eye.

"Phobos, do not fail me again. You have already disappointed me once… You do not want to fail me again."

Feeling a gust of wind, Phobos turned behind him to see Hermes, in human form, step out of the shadows, nodding respectfully towards the table. Turning back to where the voice had come from, Phobos watched as out from the darkness stretched a hand of sinew and muscle dripping with black oil, crimson vines and tendrils wrapped around it. The hand clenched into a fist and with a deafening boom, it slammed down onto the table.

"*Destroy* her."

THE END

The Book of Atlantis

PREVIEW

Adrift

It took a long time for Perseus to fall asleep after his unexpected arrival at the temple. His entrance had caused a considerable amount of tension. When Pandora realised Perseus's purpose on Sarpedon she lunged at him with such rage that it took the efforts of both Pollux and Castor to restrain her. It didn't matter what Perseus said, Pandora was consumed by grief and betrayal at what he had done. After the initial shock of his entrance, the others in the group knew better than to interfere and got on with preparations for their departure in the morning. Orpheus had managed to calm Pandora to some extent, but she couldn't even bring herself to look at Perseus let alone speak with him. Ashamed and exhausted, Perseus decided it would be best for him to separate himself from the others. He walked back over to the entrance of the temple and sat down against the base of one of the columns. The sky was clear that night and Perseus stared up at the stars as he waited for sleep to come.

When his eyes finally closed, his tiredness consumed him, and his dreams took him back to the unforgiving waters off the shore of Sarpedon. After jumping off the cliffs into the water, he had been caught by a wave that had slammed him back into the rocks. Barely conscious, Perseus pulled himself to the surface, kicking desperately to keep his head above the water. The waves battered him from both sides, and he spluttered as water forced its way into his lungs. Through the misty haze that cloaked the horizon, Perseus could see the dark silhouette of the Eirene. He tried desperately to swim towards it, but the waves were strong, and his clothes were heavy with water. He tightened his grip around the bag in his hand and kicked ferociously. He had come too far, risked too much to fail now.

As he pulled his way through the waves, the last words Polemides had said to him echoed in his head.

"The king has sent word." The voice was low and echoing in Perseus's memory. "He knows you're here. He says you must do what you had promised, or your mother will pay for your cowardice."

"He won't hurt her, he… he can't."

"Do you really want to wait to find out? Go Perseus, you're more than ready."

"But Pandora—"

"Pandora will understand."

"I can't just abandon her."

"Orpheus will stay with her. Your mother needs you Perseus. You are aware of what the king is asking for?"

"Yes. The Gorgon's—"

A large wave brought Perseus unceremoniously back to reality, and he continued to fight his way towards the ship. The turbulent waves near the cliffs were behind him, and he was now swimming through what seemed like endlessly black open water. Despite swimming for what felt like an eternity, Perseus still didn't feel he was getting any closer to the boat. He was desperately tired and every stroke, every kick was agony. He never lost sight of the ship and as he studied it he thought about the unexpected friend he had met aboard it. When he had first boarded the Eirene, he had never imagined that a few days later Pandora would arrive, and their paths would cross in such a way. It had pained him to keep his identity hidden from her, but he couldn't risk failure. He couldn't weigh her down with his burden when she had such a heavy one of her own.

When he had bumped into Pandora on the deck of the ship before her departure she had told him she was hunting the Darkness. He gritted his teeth as he remembered the encounter. If he had known she was there for the Gorgons he would have revealed himself to her, fought alongside her. As soon as he realised what she was truly doing he had wasted no time trying to get to her, but he was too late. By the time he had reached the cliffs she was already on her way back to the boat.

The thought of seeing Pandora again fuelled Perseus's determination and he swam with as much force as he could manage, but it wasn't enough. He was still quite a way out, still not close enough to be visible to the crew and he could feel his limbs starting to fail him. He was so exhausted, mentally and physically. Feeling defeated, and with his strength failing him, Perseus stopped swimming and just let his body float. He tied the string of the bag around his wrist so that it was secure, and let his arms outstretch. This was it, he had no fight left to give. Floating amidst the waves, Perseus felt the vast enormity of the world. It made him feel as small and unsuspecting as the day he was tossed into the sea as a baby alongside his mother. It seemed fitting that his final moments in this world would be the same as his first, adrift on an unforgiving ocean. As he closed his eyes he felt the energy leave his body. The last image he saw was the blood on his sword, the limp body of the Gorgon child in front of him, and his hand grasping the serpent hair of her severed head.

"Forgive me." he whispered as the world slipped away into darkness.